The House at Ladywell

Nicola Slade

CROOKED
CAT

First Red Line Edition, Crooked Cat, 2017

Discover us online:
www.crookedcatbooks.com

Join us on facebook:
www.facebook.com/crookedcat

Tweet a photo of yourself holding
this book to **@crookedcatbooks**
and something nice will happen.

For all the strong-minded women
in my family, past and present,
particularly Amelia, Olivia,
Jenny, Felicity and Lyra.

Acknowledgements

The House at Ladywell was inspired by the font at Mottisfont Abbey in Hampshire. I visited several other historic springs, including the Chalice Well at Glastonbury and the Wishing Well at Upwey but the Lady's Well is my own invention, as are all the characters in this novel. The Iron Age Farm at Butser Hill and the Roman villa at Rockbourne, both also in Hampshire, offered insights into life in Roman Britain, but any errors are entirely mine.

Olivia Barnes is always my first reader and her suggestions are consistently helpful; Shirley Thomas read the first draft a long time ago and always liked it; Linda Gruchy was helpful in suggesting a rearranged timeline; Jo Thomson kindly read yet another manuscript for me and Sheryl Burke's enthusiasm and comments were very welcome. My Latin is very rusty so I'm enormously grateful to Fen Crosbie who kindly took my attempt and turned it into elegant verse.

A few years ago I visited St Andrew's Church in Corbridge, Northumberland, with my friend, Gloria Shilling, and we were amazed to find the church filled with the scent of flowers although we could see no sign of them anywhere inside the church. There was probably a logical explanation but I much prefer my own, which runs through this story.

Lastly, Morley Slade never complains about being dragged across the countryside in the name of research and is always happy to help with technical stuff such as how to build a well – and even more importantly – how to get a body into, and out of, it.

About the Author

Nicola Slade lives near Winchester in Hampshire. While her three children were growing up she wrote short stories for children and for women's magazines before writing novels. Her first novel, Scuba Dancing, a romantic comedy, was published in 2005 and she now writes two traditional mystery series: Charlotte Richmond Investigates set in Victorian England and featuring a young Victorian widow. Her contemporary mystery series features Harriet Quigley, a retired headmistress and her cousin and sidekick, Canon Sam Hathaway.

Nicola enjoys painting, travelling, and anything historical – and she has been a Brown Owl and an antiques dealer!

Follow Nicola at **www.nicolaslade.com**!

The House at Ladywell

Principal Characters

Freya Gibson	Leaving the past behind
Patrick Underwood	Looking to the future
Mary Draper	Seizing the day
Sylvia Penrose	Another one seizing the day
Ann Freeman	Knows the past and the future but can't explain it
Nonie Radstone	Makes excellent coffee
Nathan Young	Can tell you about hitting doors with bicycle chains
John Fletcher	A guide at the Priory Church
Edwina Malcolm	Turned failure into success
Cathy Kingsmarsh	Knows nothing about living well
Louise Barton	Freya's closest friend
Mrs Simpson	Absolutely sure of her welcome
In the present:	*Solicitors, townspeople, babies, friends*
In the past:	*Echoes in the old house at Ladywell: the Roman girl; the Saxon housewife; the mediaeval heiress; the Tudor nun; the Stuart widow; the foreign bride; the WW1 schoolgirl*

Chapter One
'Restore the Balance'

'Hi, Freya,' Louise was calling from Yorkshire. 'I've sent you a present.'

'I know.' I was puzzled. 'I've been out all day and my neighbour just brought it round. I hope you didn't try lifting it in your condition, it weighs a ton.'

'I couldn't resist it,' she giggled. 'You might call it an upmarket garden gnome. For some reason I thought of you the minute I saw it.'

'Um, thanks – I think.'

'What are best friends for?'

I wrestled with the staples and delved into the polystyrene packing, convinced baby brain had finally caught up with her. A gnome?

'Nearly there … *Oh!*'

I uncovered my present from Louise: a life-sized hare carved in stone, poised for flight with its ears pricked for danger.

'I know what you're thinking,' she said, still laughing. 'You haven't even got a garden… but hares are supposed to be lucky and you could do with some of that.'

'You must be psychic,' I whispered as I stared at the stone creature. 'It's perfect, Lou – and you're wrong. I *do* have a garden…'

(i)
Monday, 23rd February 2015

'I'll pull in over here.' I nipped in front of a stretch limo, flashing a nervous smile to ward off any idea of road rage. To my relief the driver shook his fist but grinned and let me in.

'Okay, Patrick, got everything? Passport? Ticket? Schedule? Research material?'

'Yes'm, and clean underpants too, in case I'm run over.' My boss laughed at me as he took his case out of the boot while I reached for his in-flight bag. 'Stop fussing, Freya, I'm not ten years old.'

'Sorry,' I made a face and tucked my hand in his; he's a good friend as well as my employer. 'You'd better get a move on, Patrick, I can't park here. Enjoy California and your author talks and keep in touch. I hope all the events and talk shows go well, but of course they will. All those adoring readers!'

He stood looking down at our linked hands, his grey eyes suddenly impassive behind his glasses. When I took my hand away he put his arm round me and gave me a hug. 'It's not me I'm worried about,' he frowned. 'You're definitely going down to Hampshire while I'm away, to take another look at this old house? I wish you'd take someone with you.'

'Don't be silly,' I stared at him. 'I don't need a chaperone and you were the one who insisted I take my holiday now and use it to get to know the house. Would you rather I didn't?'

'Of course you must go,' he sounded impatient. 'You need a break, you've had no time off for months. And don't you dare do any of my work while you're there.'

I was still doubtful but he was insistent. 'All right,' I said. 'I'll be back in London before you are, call me if you need anything before the end of next week. I can't get away earlier because my friend's arriving for the weekend.'

He was still frowning. 'I know I said you must go but I still wish I was going to be around.'

'I'll be fine, Patrick.' I gave him a little push. 'You said yourself, I *have* to go. How often do you get left a house by a complete stranger? You know what they say about gift horses…'

'Be careful,' was all he said. 'Keep me posted, I worry

about you being off-grid.' He hesitated then put both arms round me. 'Let me know if there are any problems, anything at all. I'll come straight back.'

'You're not leaving for ever, Patrick,' I laughed. 'I promise I'll shout, but it's Hampshire, not the Outer Hebrides.' I checked my watch and reached up to give him a peck on the cheek but he surprised me by kissing me swiftly on the lips, before turning on his heel towards the building.

(ii)
Almost a week earlier – Wednesday, 18th February

I dashed into the office to show Patrick the letter.

'You've *what*?'

'I know, it's unbelievable, isn't it?' I was bubbling with excitement. 'Read it; hurry up.'

'Hang on, let's have a look – ""... sole beneficiary of Miss Violet Wellman deceased"' – who was she?'

'No idea,' I was practically bouncing now. 'All I know is what it says, that she's left everything to me, apart from a small legacy to a friend. I've no idea whether it's a million pounds or her entire collection of teapots.' I took out my phone. 'I was too excited to ring before I left home; I wanted to tell you first. I'll call the solicitor now.'

Patrick watched me thoughtfully as I punched in the numbers, shoving my hair – which someone once described as the colour of runny honey – behind my ear as I did so. As I listened I got more and more excited and I could hear my voice rising to a squeak.

'I'll come down straight away...' I raised an eyebrow at Patrick who shrugged and nodded. 'I'll drive, easier than fiddling about with the train. I can't stay long, I'm out this evening, but I must see it. Great, you'll have everything ready for me to sign?'

A few minutes later I put down the phone and gazed wide-eyed at Patrick.

'It's a house,' I said, dramatically. 'Ta-*daa*! Miss Violet Wellman has left me an old house in Hampshire.'

'Why did you say you'd go now?' he complained, after he'd congratulated me. 'You know I've got appointments all day otherwise I'd have gone with you.' He glanced at the time and heaved a sigh as he picked up his briefcase. 'I'd have taken you out to lunch to drown your sorrows if it turns out to be a hovel.' At the door he paused. 'Or drinks on you if it's a mansion.'

The address was 2 Ladywell House, Farm Close, Ladywell, in Ramalley, which was a small market town between Winchester and Southampton and which, now I came to think of it, sounded familiar.

'There shouldn't be any problems regarding probate.' The solicitor, Harry Makepeace, was a friendly man in his mid-thirties. 'An insurance policy covered the funeral and taxes and there's no problem if you want to take a look at the house, maybe stay a night.'

He unfolded a map and pointed. 'When the tannery closed down in the early Nineties – here – it was a body-blow to the workforce, and the brewery's recent closure took the heart out of the area. Now, though, there are embryo signs of gentrification including planning permission for some smart developments so property prices will be on the rise.' He laughed and indicated Violet Wellman's will.

'Nobody seems to know when the place was actually built,' he added. 'Miss Wellman liked her comfort so the central heating is up-to-date. It's structurally sound but very dated inside. I'm afraid it needs money spent on it.

'Mind you,' he shuffled some papers. 'I'd say the value for probate doesn't reflect the size of the property, which is considerable. The garden goes almost as far as the bed of the dried-up stream at the back, and beyond that is Puss Hill.' I opened my mouth to ask and he laughed. 'It's an old name for a hare – there have always been hares up there. It's run by a local trust and can't be built on.'

Harry Makepeace smiled at my eager interest. 'Historically, the industrial concerns, not to mention the railway sidings, meant the suburb of Ladywell was a less desirable residential area with lower house prices, hence the low valuation. Even bearing in mind the potential now the industrial plants have gone, I'm afraid you may find yourself in a quandary. When Miss Wellman died I assumed you'd eventually be able to sell but I looked into it and discovered some snags.'

He showed me an old photograph. 'There was a small filling-station on the corner,' he said. 'Opposite the pub. It went bust about six years ago and there's an on-going tussle about the site which can't be sold until it's been certified clear of contamination.'

I frowned at that. 'The underground petrol storage tanks are still there,' he continued. 'Although they were drained there's a remote possibility of seepage. The site's been grassed over but with the former owner dead and restrictions on building round here now, nothing's going to happen quickly. And that's not all...'

He explained various other covenants, saying it would be a lengthy legal process should I wish to sell. 'I thought we could get round some of these restrictions, but...' he looked regretful. 'They were drawn up around 1900 by our senior partner at the time. It's possible it could be overcome, but it wouldn't be done quickly, or cheaply.'

I was trying to take it all in. 'Can you tell me anything about her? My father's mother was Pamela Wellman before she married.'

'They were distant cousins,' he said. 'As for Miss Wellman, it's a small town.' His smile was reminiscent as he added, 'She was a midwife and over ninety, so everyone knew her. When my father drafted the will she said there were no other relatives.' He let me digest the information. 'There are certain conditions that come with the inheritance and I'll explain over coffee. It's an old will, you know. The legacy to her friend was added a few years ago and the insurance policy taken out not long after. The will was signed on 2ⁿᵈ April 1983.'

'But...but...' I stammered in confusion. 'That's the day after I was born, why would she...?'

9

The solicitor had no answer so after coffee I tucked the house keys and map into my bag, shook hands, and headed thoughtfully towards the car park. The town was attractive, old red-brick buildings mostly converted into shops, with a sprinkling of the usual high street names, along with a bakery that had a queue outside the door. Definitely worth exploring. There was also a delicatessen, as well as a couple of smart dress shops and a small department store. I stored up my impressions as I hurried along the main shopping street, Ram Alley.

As I puzzled over the name a gossipy woman halted beside the sign. 'The name's a relic of when they used to drive the sheep to market, you know.' With that nugget she nodded and went into the nearest shop while I wandered past a statue of some local bigwig in the middle of the town square.

According to the map, Violet Wellman's house was on the other side of the river, so I followed the road back over the bridge the way I had come. Instead of heading up through the cleft in the hills towards Winchester and the motorway, I turned right, My stomach was churning as I nosed the car past the station and headed west where there was a narrow ribbon of allotments along the river bank on my right. As I searched for the turning I realised the buildings in this part of town had a down-at-heel look to them. However, a large billboard displayed drawings of townhouses to be built on the old brewery site further along the river.

I nearly overshot the entrance to a cul-de-sac. 'The Fleece' pub stood on the corner and on the opposite side was a small building, its windows boarded up and weeds growing in the gutter. A forlorn board proclaimed that it was the Ladywell Beauty Salon.

I drew up at the end of the close and turned off the engine. I was shaking and my hands were wet with sweat as I climbed slowly out of the car, staring at the house Violet Wellman had left me.

A solicitor should be cautious and Mr Makepeace had

certainly fitted the profile when I'd phoned him after that first viewing.

'You're planning to move in? Well, I suppose it's no surprise. Who'd turn down a substantial property? By the way,' he added, 'I forgot to tell you. The long living-room is always known as Dickon's Room.'

'Really? Who was Dickon?'

'Nobody knows,' he sounded amused. 'It always has been; maybe you could do some research.'

There was a slight pause. 'Will you live alone in the house? Only, I sent a handyman in to check the plumbing and electrics. He didn't linger; said the house felt sad.'

'Sad?'

'Yes, sad. I forgot to mention it when we met, but the gardener who went in last week felt it too.' There was a self-conscious pause. 'I wouldn't go that far myself, but I certainly didn't fall for it the way you did, Miss Gibson.'

'Well, I *love* the house,' I insisted. 'It doesn't feel at all sad to me. One thing though, did anyone move some flowers, pot plants maybe? I could smell roses when I opened the front door.'

'Not to my knowledge,' he said. 'Mrs Draper might have done something when she looked in to give the house an airing. Didn't I mention that?' He apologised. 'The other beneficiary, Miss Wellman's friend, used to clean for her. We've been paying her a small retainer to keep an eye on the place.'

'Ah, that explains why the house feels lived-in. Did she…?' I faltered, 'Does *she* think the house is sad too?'

'Oddly enough …' I could hear the puzzled note in his voice. 'She loves the place.'

(iii)

Saturday, 22nd February

'Have you told Patrick what you're up to?' Louise, my closest friend, was on a flying visit to London before settling down to await her first baby, due in a few weeks.

11

'Sort of,' I rolled my eyes guiltily. 'He's on a book tour in the States and I did tell him I'd go down to the house while he's away, but no, I haven't actually told him my plans.' Louise looked sceptical. 'We're not in each other's pockets,' I said defensively. 'He's often away so I already work at home a lot; it's easier than trekking across town to his house. I could do something similar if I'm based in Hampshire: Friday to Monday down there, train Tuesday morning, two nights in London and back Thursday night. Patrick won't mind.'

'I'm glad you looked doubtful when you said that,' retorted Louise. 'You know perfectly well he'll be upset if you don't tell him.'

'I think it'll work, me being almost a virtual assistant,' I said slowly. 'He's been a bit odd lately, quite crabby, but when I asked if his headaches were worse, he bit my head off.'

'I'd forgotten about his time in Afghanistan,' Louise admitted. 'A head wound must have been terrifying. Maybe he's got something on his mind; working up to a new book and it's making him irritable. You said he's been all right since he left the army?'

'I suppose it could be a book,' I bit my lip but didn't let her see how worried I was. 'He'd been out for a few years before I started working for him but he still gets horrific headaches.' I wondered about that. Patrick had seemed edgy and – for a usually even-tempered man – surprisingly irritable for weeks. What if he was thinking about a new working arrangement himself? One without me? My stomach churned at the idea of having to start again; I've only just begun to feel more settled.

'What's this about, anyway? You've never mentioned a hankering to join the green wellie brigade. Apart from your time in America,' she avoided my eyes, 'you've spent your life in commuter-belt Surrey, then London. I was the one who wanted to escape to the country.'

'There are pavements and street lights,' I said mildly. 'I suppose some of it's your fault. It was never part of your plan to disappear off to North Yorkshire, all for love. It's made me stop and think, and no, Lou, I know how your mind works.' She made a face as I added, 'Don't start— I don't want a husband, but I want something that's just mine, a project perhaps. Something I can control; I do want to put down roots and Violet's house is my chance.'

She raised an eyebrow so I said, 'There are conditions attached to this legacy. I *have* to live in the house for a year, or ownership will be transferred to a charity for the elderly. After a year I can sell if I want, but there are even more complications that will arise.'

I sat quietly while Louise digested this.

'I can't refuse Violet's bequest. She wanted the house to stay in the family and she trusted me. I fell for the place on sight and I'm going to live there. I can rent out my spare room in London to help with expenses and maybe sell the flat later. At least I don't have a mortgage though I'd much rather have Dad alive and well, than have his money.'

She nodded, still concerned. 'I worry about you, Freya.'

I got up to make more tea and patted her on the shoulder. 'Me? I'm fine.'

'No you're not.' She was serious. 'You put on a brave front, you're doing it now, even to me – and yes, you're tons stronger but you're not quite right yet. It's what? Three years since you came home from America and you've just... existed.' I protested but she shook her head. 'I'm right and you know it. You're brittle and you don't have a social life, you've no hobbies apart from work and you're the only woman I know of our age who isn't on Twitter and the rest.'

'You know why I stopped using social media, Lou.' I said, stung. 'Ben didn't... and afterwards I couldn't face it. Anyway, I do have friends. I go to the theatre and out for meals and –and...'

She shook her head. 'Acquaintances, not real friends. You've lost touch with the old gang. You're almost back to the old Freya but sometimes you look fragile enough to break. I bet Patrick sees it too and that's why he's made you take time off.' Her voice trembled. 'I want you to have a life,

Freya. And running away won't help.'

I was shocked by what she said, knowing she was right, but I was touched too. 'I won't rush into anything stupid, Lou, I promise. I like my job and I don't want to lose it.'

'You like Patrick too,' Louise stated it as a fact. 'Don't make that face, I didn't mean anything by it – not really.' She hesitated. 'It's time, though, isn't it, Freya? To put the past behind you?'

She summoned up a smile. 'I don't know; maybe this is a sign – new house, new life, perhaps a new love?'

(iv)
Thursday, 5ᵗʰ March

Three weeks after that initial visit, I was consumed with doubt. Had I gone completely crazy that first day? To open the door, take one astonished look round, and decide on the spot that I was going to live there? To fall in love with a house?

Now, as I humped the last of the boxes indoors, I thought the house welcomed me.

I shook my head at my overactive imagination. First things first – get the kettle on. There'd been no conscious decision but by the time I returned to London after that first visit I had a fully-fledged plan: to move out of London and work from home. Looking back I was surprised how right it felt. Somehow I'd made this life-changing decision and here I was.

The rain had eased off on this chilly March morning and I closed the door behind me with a thankful sigh, only to be surprised all over again. There it was, the scent of flowers. Roses – my father's favourite.

'But there's nothing here.' I glanced round the panelled hall. 'Like the first day.'

There were two rooms to my right: front and back, with the lean-to kitchen beyond. On my left a long room stretched the full depth of the house. Two tiny windows either side of the front door let in some light and the hall was wide, the wooden floorboards covered with old rugs. The ceilings were surprisingly high for an old, old house and the staircase looked like oak. There wasn't a flower in sight.

(v)

Something I'd failed to mention to anyone: not to Louise, not when I was enthusing to Patrick, and certainly not to the helpful Mr Makepeace, was the letter that had been waiting for me on that first day.

Beside the front door stood a small table on which sat an old walkabout phone in a base station, and two envelopes, one large and the other letter-sized. The smaller envelope was addressed to me.

The handwriting straggled shakily across the page and the contents of the letter startled me.

'When you were born I knew you were the one. Before anything else you must go into the garden and pick some flowers. It doesn't matter what you pick: in winter look for leaves, rosemary or winter jasmine, but if it's summer pick simple flowers – a rose, a sprig of yellow broom, nothing fancy. Pick what you can and weave them into a wreath made from the rowan tree – you'll know it by the wooden bench underneath. Hang it on the hook inside the front door.

When that's done, say the words written below, making sure you're alone. My grandmother had the verse from her own grandmother and so on. I expect the words have altered over time but the spirit remains the same. Show reverence when you do these things but do this first of all. You must not delay.

You must restore the balance.'

It had been a sleety February day, with flowers few and far between but I persevered, driven by the sense of urgency in the letter. I found secateurs in the kitchen. The rosemary was easy, a great, straggling bush standing sentinel by the path, with yellow winter jasmine spread against the wall. In a

15

sheltered spot I found a clump of snowdrops and, to my delight, a primrose or two.

I had to stand on the bench to snip a couple of pliable twigs from the rowan, and back in the house I bent them into a makeshift circle and threaded in the flowers and leaves. Still under the compulsion I'd felt on reading the letter I stood on a chair to hang my creation on the waiting hook.

Saying the words Violet had written made me pause.

'It sounds like a spell,' I half-whispered, hushed by the strangeness of it all. Was Violet a witch? Wasn't this all complete nonsense? I read the words again and summoned up my rusty Latin vocabulary, almost forgotten since 'A' Level. '*Domina* means lady; something about water? And *leporum* – rabbit? No,' I corrected myself. '*Lepus* is a hare, and *benedic* – any kind of blessing can't be bad.'

There was something about the place that I couldn't explain. I felt safe and – odd as it sounds – wrapped in loving arms. The house was filled with a friendly silence and I felt comforted for the first time in ages. What harm could it do to obey Violet's last instructions when she'd given me this precious gift?

I took a deep breath and bowed my head before the ring of twigs and flowers, not in prayer but in a kind of grateful submission, as I quietly murmured the Latin words, stumbling over a rough translation in my head.

Domina aquarum
Leporumque currentium
Domina custodi nos
Locum benedic.

Lady of the waters,
Lady of the running hare,
Lady keep us,
Lady bless this place

Chapter Two

(i)

The large manila envelope from the hall table held sheets of yellowing note-paper clipped together. The writing was in faded blue ink, in a large, clear hand and it was headed, *'NOTES ON THE HISTORY OF LADYWELL FARM: Memories of the Wellman Family'* – *collated by Sarah Montagu*. It was dated November 1938. A further note stated that the author had retired from the scholastic profession and took an interest in history.

I'd Googled Ladywell, of course, but this looked like real treasure – except it wasn't. When I read it properly it was infuriatingly vague. I skimmed through it, disappointed, and went back to the beginning. What intrigued me most were the notes in what I recognised as Violet's handwriting. She clearly disagreed strongly with what the author had written.

'Ladywell, although reduced nowadays to a house in a suburb, is believed to have an illustrious history,' wrote Sarah Montagu. 'A spring of particularly pure water that was dug out over centuries to form a well, gave rise to the name, Ladywell, though other sources contend that it comes from a goddess, or Lady, who once made her home by a grove of rowan trees nearby. It is said that when she died she turned into a hare. It has often been supposed that the Lady of the well was the Virgin Mary, and the Church certainly believed this to be true, building a small chapel near the site. Wellman family lore, however, maintains that the Lady of the well dates from an earlier time but became conflated with the Christian tradition.

'The Romans arrived in Hampshire after the Claudian

invasion of 43 AD and spread out into the county. I have read in various historical sources' (maddeningly Miss Montagu failed to list these) 'that by the Fourth Century AD a substantial villa stood here, close by the river crossing.'

At the bottom of the page was a scribble by Violet Wellman. 'Nonsense, I'm afraid dear Miss M is quite wrong. The tale of a goddess, like the witches of old, probably harks back to some elderly wise woman going peacefully about her business, though it is true that Ladywell has always provided a sanctuary for hares. It is unlikely that there was a large Roman villa at Ladywell; any settlement would certainly have been nothing more than a modest sheep farm...'

'Why on earth didn't you write a proper book about Ladywell, Miss Montagu?' I dropped her notes on to the bedside table. No use complaining to the long-dead author but it was so frustrating. 'All of this – you're just teasing,' I grumbled. 'I'd love to know more about the house and family but you probably weren't told anything else yourself. I suppose it's great to have even this much.'

(ii)

He jolted awake. Oh, gods, why did I go back to sleep? The mid-morning sun warmed him even here in the shadowy safety of the gnarled bush and he groaned, reluctant to open his eyes; reluctant to admit that here was another day to tackle. His stomach gurgled and rumbled and he let out a gusty sigh. Last night he'd tried the wrinkled hawthorn berries but their bitterness made him retch, so he had drifted into a defeated, uneasy sleep. That was another thing he had to ferret out: something to eat, something to drink, somewhere to hide, and crowning all, some way of ridding himself of this terrible, gnawing fear. He forced himself to open bleary blue eyes, the lids sticky and crusted with the shameful tears of the night. An arm's length away another eye, russet gold, stared back at him.

Icy shudders ran down his spine and he closed his eyes before braving another look. It was still there: a large tawny-

furred hare lying so near he could see its flank rise and fall with the rapid beat, beat, beat of its heart. A shout from down in the valley startled them both, boy and animal, yet the hare, poised for flight, stayed there watching him with that strange calm stare.

He remembered his mother's tales – of gods and devils, of the eerie ring of stones near their home – and of shape-shifters; tales he had mocked but now suddenly plausible. The goddess Andraste took the shape of a hare and he felt foolish hope bubble up. Could it be true? Here at his side in this time of adversity? The animal rose slowly, with that curious stare still fixed upon him.

'Lady?' he murmured, ducking his head in reverence. 'Lady, look kindly on your unworthy servant. Help me…' It was a wail of anguish and the hare took flight, zigzagging down the hill, now into the shelter of a scrubby bush, now panting beside a tussock of long grass until, at the very edge of the garden below, she came to a sudden pause. He held his breath as she slipped into the lee of the wall and out of his sight. For several heartbeats he kept his eyes on the spot but the hare had vanished.

She ran towards the house, he exulted, measuring the distance. She showed me the way. He steeled himself to follow. A sign! Not every day a goddess blesses you – and foolish indeed to ignore her.

Lying on his stomach he squinted down towards the farm, wondering at the silence. When he had woken briefly at first light, the stable-yard had been all a-bustle, young lads running hither and thither as they saw to the horses before turning them out into the paddock. The house was awake too; he had spotted a gardener carrying baskets indoors. Further along the hill the shepherd was busy with his sheep.

Now the flock had vanished over the brow of the hill and the gardener and a small clutch of men and women could be glimpsed in a merry group heading towards the ford across the river. Below him, the farm, not large, but prosperous in appearance, drowsed in the sunlit silence of an autumn day when even the clanging at the forge had ceased.

The watching boy shivered despite the warmth on his bony shoulders. He could see apple trees in the orchard, other fruit too, and he thought longingly of plums swelling ripe and purple for the plucking. Before you reached the house and the river beyond, a stream trickled in a dip, and he could see what looked like a well with an overflow ditch not far from where the hare had disappeared. Was it deep enough to hide him? Dare he risk it?

Bile rose in his throat as he remembered his last full meal. Foolish money spent on a dinner too large for his shrunken belly, then stark terror when a shadow darkened the tavern door. The meat and pottage roiled in his gut as he stumbled out to the privy, his hand across his face lest the soldier at the door recognise him.

Of course there'd been no outcry, the boy sneered now at that moment of panic. I was just a drunk to him, a nuisance. He ran his tongue over dry lips. Two days, two whole days since he had wasted that ill-cooked meal. 'Unless I eat soon,' he murmured, 'I'll collapse at the feet of some bloody centurion.'

He took stock of his position, looking down at the compact main house on his right with pasture and the westward-heading river to the left. At the foot of the hill, across the stream, lay an orchard and a well, together with a small grove of rowans just before the land grew marshy. The place was deserted; chickens scratching in the yard, pigs grunting in the sty, the lowing of a cow in the meadow yonder and the smell of a tannery down river. Below him sat the farmhouse.

'I'll chance it.' He heaved himself to his feet and bent his head in reverence as he sent up a passionate plea. 'Lady, you sent me a sign. I know I'm unworthy but I beg you for your protection.'

He ran, swerving from bush to bush, crouching in the shelter of a hillock, leaping the stream by the stepping stones until he reached the overflow ditch. One despairing glance showed that the fruit had been harvested and in this tidy establishment there was not so much as a maggoty windfall lying on the grass. Gasping and panting he dropped into the dark, muddy depths of the ditch which, gods be thanked, was just deep enough to conceal him.

Once safely hidden he disconcerted himself entirely by bursting into tears.

Aula heard the intruder before she saw him. Her father and stepmother were away in Venta and the steading was taking a holiday. The shepherd was with his sheep and her grandmother had permitted everyone else to cross by the ford to visit the town, while Aula had been told to take some scraps to the pigsty. Instead of hurrying indoors to the next task, the holiday feeling had her dreaming in the shade of the thatched roof above the well until she heard someone, or something, crash into the ditch.

What should I...? Common sense told her to sound the alarm. Whoever hid in that overgrown ditch was there for no good reason. What if he should leap up and attack her? As she hesitated she heard harsh, painful gasps, wrenched from deep in his chest, and hastily muffled only to break out again. A man who wept with such abandon must need her help, she told herself. Better be safe, though.

Someone's knife lay forgotten in the shadows so she seized it and crawled back towards the ditch, conscious that she was alone, her heartbeat thundering in her ears. The haft of the knife in her hand was reassuring but even so, she began to back away; it would not hurt to fetch her grandmother's old dog from his bed. It was the desolate sobbing that made her halt and Aula's soft heart was torn. If it was a beast, she told herself, a sheep caught in the ditch or a calf maybe, I wouldn't hesitate. But this is a man...

A pair of red-rimmed blue eyes, half hidden under a tangle of dark brown hair and an untidy straggling beard to match, stared at her in horror as he crouched on all fours. Waiting for her to scream.

'Shh,' she whispered, overcome with a rush of pity as she held out her hand, palm upwards, as she would to a frightened dog. 'You're safe here.'

21

He blinked at her and suddenly his eyes rolled up, showing the whites, as he collapsed back into the ditch.

Uncertainty gripped her. Had he fainted? Was he feigning before he attacked or was this abject terror? She peered downwards and found a boy not much more than her own fifteen years. He was conscious now and breathing quietly.

'Thank the Lady,' she murmured, keeping her voice calm. 'This is an overflow ditch but the weather's been fine for the last week so you won't drown in there. It would be a different story in winter.'

A grimy hand reached up to clasp hers and their eyes met. Through a haze of exhaustion he was aware of the warmth and strength of her clasp, of the round merry face with its halo of tawny curls.

'You must go.' He spoke so quietly she had to edge closer to hear. 'I'll put you in mortal danger. Let me hide here till nightfall and I'll be gone. I won't trouble you anymore. Tell no-one you've seen me. Please?'

'What danger?' She stared at him. 'You're safe here for now, but I must know… Are you ill?' She drew back.

Their eyes met, his blue and wary, hers hazel and anxious. He took her measure and began to relax a little, and she felt absurdly pleased to be judged trustworthy. The feeling was mutual – her instinct was to trust him. He shivered, despite the heat, brushing aside his unkempt hair and took a deep breath.

'I have no fever, but what do you say to a deserter?' His voice was stronger now, full of shame and self-disgust. 'I was stationed at Isca, away in the west, but there was trouble. A visitor, an important man who…' The silence hung between them and she kept her tongue still. 'He liked – he liked boys.' It was a breath only, but she heard. 'I didn't know until he summoned me to his quarters and tried…' He hunched his shoulders. 'He ordered me to tidy his room and when I turned my back he grabbed me, tearing at my tunic, so I fought him off. I only meant to get away from him but somehow I knocked him senseless so I've been tramping the roads for weeks–; three, four, I've lost count. A month, perhaps. I don't

know if I killed him, if they're after me...' A shudder ran through his body. 'I had to get away.' He gulped. 'I stole his money and his horse.'

She frowned anxiously. 'What have you done with the horse? Not tethered outside our front gate?'

'Of course not. I sold it the next day.'

'Stay here,' she whispered, giving his hand a gentle squeeze. 'I'll fetch some food. Promise you won't try to get away while I'm gone? I can help you better than you can help yourself.'

She was gone. Could he trust her? He slumped back and tried to catch his breath, too weary to contemplate the alternative. He pulled tufts of grass and leaves over his head and hid in the dark shadow, constantly on the alert until a rustling made him freeze.

The hare crouched in the garden, half-hidden in the lee of a patch of some plant. He thought it might be Fat Hen, the seeds almost dry and ready to harvest. She was chewing but she finished her mouthful and he felt again the strangeness of her calm eye upon him. For a long moment they stared at each other, then she was gone. He felt blessed, and heaved a sigh of relief in his muddy sanctuary. Foolish and fanciful perhaps, but he felt safe.

'Grandmother? Are you alone?'

'I am.' Aula's grandmother looked up from her spindle. 'What's amiss?' She set down her work and rose painfully. 'Oh, my bones,' she grumbled. 'What is it, child? Not news from your father?'

'Oh no. As far as I know they'll be home in a week, as arranged. It's something else...'

A few words of explanation set the old woman, Flavia Petronilla, first nodding, and then frowning.

'You're sure he has no fever?'

'I'm quite sure. He's just hungry and filthy and exhausted. What are we to do? He's not much older than I am. I can't leave him to starve and if anyone gets wind...he's a deserter,

23

he could be executed. The whole house will suffer.'

Flavia Petronilla headed for the kitchen. 'First things first, take him a little bread and a scrap of that cheese. He must take it slowly, don't forget. A starving man will guzzle his food and waste it when it comes straight back up. Then, let me see...' She scratched her head. 'Filthy, you said?'

'I think it's mostly mud, it's difficult to recognise him for what he is at the moment.'

'All the better. Three or four weeks, he thinks? I suppose his hair and beard have grown?'

Aula nodded. 'I think he's telling the truth, Grandmother. He's just a frightened boy. He's... nice.'

'You could tell that in one glance?' The old woman hid a smile. 'Ah well, praise the Lady that he's had no chance to shave.' The old woman was decisive now. 'A respectable, bearded young man will be nothing like a raw recruit on the run so –' She pursed her lips. 'You're a good judge of character for your age so I'll trust your instinct though we'll be cautious nonetheless.' She rummaged in a basket. 'Here's your father's tunic that your stepmother threw out for rags.' Her voice showed her opinion of her son's new wife. 'Give him a little food and water then take him to the bath-house. When he's clean and dressed bring him here.' As Aula turned to do her grandmother's bidding, the old woman lowered her voice. 'Ask for a blessing at the well, child.'

She said no more but Aula knew what she meant as she took a jug from the shelf. At the well she drew water and after making sure she was alone, she said the words of praise and power that every woman of her family had said since time gone by. 'May the Lady bless us' she added in a whisper to the guardian of the well as she rose.

Scrubbed and neatly clad, his hunger and thirst assuaged and his beard and hair brushed and trimmed, he presented a very different picture when he bowed low to her grandmother.

'I thank you for your kindness, lady,' he said, 'though you may be put in danger if I stay.'

'Get away with you,' she scolded, but he heard the smile in her voice as she appraised him. After an unnerving wait she

nodded. 'You'll do,' she announced. 'Now, how are we to explain you?'

'I'm in your hands, madam,' he said gravely.

'You are,' she thought for a moment. 'You drank the water my granddaughter gave you?'

He nodded, surprised. 'Thank you, it was so cold and pure.'

'Good,' she said quietly. 'You will feel the benefit. Now, tell us about yourself. Make it brief, our old servant will be waking soon.'

'My name is Marcellus.' Still wary he gave no other names, no details that could be traced. 'My stepfather, who died in the spring, owned a fleet of fishing boats in Armorica...' No need to tell them it was in the far west of the province. The old woman's eyes rested on him speculatively and he hurried on. 'My own father died when I was a child and my mother two years ago. My stepbrother inherited everything and told me to leave and not return.

'I hated him anyway so the army seemed a good idea.' He shrugged, with a bitter smile. 'Not as it turned out.'

'Nonsense.' The tone was brisk but the smile was warm. 'You aren't the first good-looking lad to run foul of a bad man. You showed enterprise to get away as you did. Let me see...'

Her shrewd glance took in the way the stranger was eyeing Aula, who was inclined to blush when she met his glance.

'Did you come by those blue eyes in Armorica?' He looked startled but not, to her practised eye, deceitful.

'My mother's father came from somewhere in the far north, lady,' he said. 'He was a sailor and folk put it about that he had been a pirate, but he kept his counsel.'

'Do likewise,' she said quietly. 'How old are you, lad?'

'Eighteen in about a month. I've lost track of the days.'

'Hmm, you look more. It'll be the beard; a dark-haired man always looks older. You'd better be twenty-two, agreed? Now where are you from? Nowhere near Armorica, that's for sure.' She glanced at him. 'Ever been to Londinium?'

'I've not had that pleasure, lady.'

'Of course not, who has from these parts.' She patted his arm. 'It's debatable whether it's a pleasure or no but that's the beauty of it. You come from – let's say – just north of the city. Who can argue? If by some mischance you meet someone with knowledge of the place you simply hang your head in shame and confess that you come from a slum and have left all that behind to better yourself.'

She subjected him to another of those long, cool examinations. 'That stepfather of yours did well by you, in spite of all. At least he educated you and your accent is good.'

'I liked him well enough,' the boy admitted. 'And yes, I've been well-taught. There was an old man, too old for the fishing but good at keeping tally. He enjoyed playing schoolmaster.'

'This is a small farm,' she said. 'Not a great villa. We all work here.' She patted his arm with a kindly glance and he gave a slight bow in gratitude.

'I'll work hard for you, lady,' he promised. 'It was a strange thing,' he added. 'I slept up on your hill last night and I woke briefly at first light then fell asleep again. When I opened my eyes the second time, a hare was lying beside me in the long grass.' He frowned. 'It was strange. She took no fright but stayed with me until I was strong enough to rise, when she ran down to the garden. When your granddaughter went to find you, the hare appeared once more, for a moment, and then was gone.'

'A hare, you say?' The old woman's face was impassive though Aula stifled a gasp. 'How very curious.'

At that moment a bent figure staggered into the room. 'Oh, madam, I beg pardon, I must have dozed off for a moment.' The elderly woman peered at the newcomer.

'We have a visitor. My late sister's grandson – er, Marius Fulvius. You'll have heard me speak of her daughter who went to Londinium years since.'

(iii)

A week later it seemed as though the stranger from Armorica had been at the steading for years. Instructed to call his hostess, Aunt Flavia, he did so with a secret smile and a wink in Aula's direction.

'Here,' Flavia told the head shepherd the day after the boy's arrival. 'He's raw and he doesn't know one end of a sheep from another...'

'I do know that much,' protested the newly-named Marius.

'As I was saying,' she ignored the protest. 'He's here to learn about sheep so take him out with you and knock him into shape. He's a strong lad and a willing worker too, for all he's not had our advantages.'

'Do you like him still, your stray lamb?' There was the promise of the first frost in the air when Flavia beckoned to her granddaughter, remembering how even at the age of four the girl had staggered home with a lost lamb, the first of many rescued beasts.

'Yes.' Aula's colour rose. 'He works hard, everyone likes him and he's kind too, helping the old ones with the chores but gently so nobody's pride is hurt.' She hesitated. 'He likes to sit by the rowan grove, he says it's peaceful. Besides,' her eyes widened. 'He told me he thought he could smell flowers there but there's nothing in bloom just now.'

'Did he now?' Flavia was startled.

'Yes, though he laughed at himself for a foolish fancy. I didn't tell him that folk have always smelled flowers there, but he saw a hare too, remember?'

Flavia Petronilla stood lost in thought. Echoing down the years she heard the tale told by her own grandmother and all the grandmothers before her, of the Lady, a wise woman, born of their kin, who was buried in the rowan grove. Who could explain the scent of flowers that lingered there? Or the way she was remembered in the words they spoke at the well, in the prayers they offered up, and in the story of her flight from this life on the back of one of the hares that abounded

27

on the hillside.

'You think he's under the Lady's protection?'

The girl nodded.

'And so do I.' She was distracted by a thought. 'Remember what I told you, as my own grandmother told me? That there must always be a rowan tree here in the Lady's grove. Be sure to plant one when the time comes.' She sat up, brisk once more. 'What was I saying? Oh yes, the boy...'

Aula lowered her eyes, her colour deepening. 'I'll remember. And yes, I do like him and I don't want him handed over to the army. Besides, he makes me laugh,' she added, with a defensive smile.

'I've seen that for myself,' Flavia nodded. 'I'm fairly sure he likes you too. I've been wondering...'

She refused to elaborate but caught up with her new kinsman when he came into the garden at noon.

'Married? Of course not.' His frank laughter reassured her. 'When would I have had the time?'

An approving nod, then she lowered her voice to a whisper. 'The money you, er, liberated, from your would-be seducer? Is it all gone?'

He matched her quiet tone. 'I barely spent any of it, that's why I was so hungry when I turned up here. I'd had no chance to buy food – too many people who might be suspicious. Oh, Mithras, I should have given it to you days ago for my food and lodging. It's hidden in the – where Aula found me. I'll fetch it at once.'

'No you will not,' she seized his arm. 'Foolish boy, you're earning your keep and will do more. The money is safe enough for a day or two. No, it was a thought that occurred to me in the night; that you might have a wife over in Armorica.' She looked over her shoulder. 'And listen, my lad. I'll take a whip to your back myself if you ever again dare invoke the name of the soldiers' god in this house.'

The blow fell early the next morning.

There was a flurry of arrival in the courtyard and the women were aghast to see the master's servant. He had ridden home in advance of his master and mistress to give warning of an honoured guest who would arrive with them sometime after noon.

'Gaius Neronis Tallum,' he said when he came upon them having breakfast. 'Newly-arrived in Venta.' He looked up in surprise as the old lady's visiting nephew choked at the name, then, red-faced and spluttering, passed it off as a coughing fit. 'The poor gentleman is recovering from being attacked by thieves at Isca so the master invited him to try the healing water. He hopes you'll doctor him, mistress.'

'Of course,' Flavia rose, steely and competent. 'I'll oversee the preparations for his room myself. My great-nephew is not well today, but Aula can see to him.'

Marius shivered and at a glare from the old lady, began to cough once more, trying to sound as ill as he suddenly felt.

'You must lie down, Marius,' Aula murmured, catching her grandmother's eye. 'You're sickening for some illness. I'll bring you a healing drink.' She leaned over to touch his forehead. 'Grandmother,' she said in a clear, carrying voice. 'Marius has a fever. Can someone send word that he'll not be out on the hills today?'

She hustled him away to a small room near the kitchen. 'Here,' she hissed. 'You're safer here, it's dark and cramped and harder to make you out. Stay while I fetch bedding, then do the best you can. I'll heat some stones in the kitchen fire and put them in your bed to make you sweat.'

Her hand lingered on his arm. 'I know what my grandmother's doing. She's making sure the whole household knows you are ailing. Keeping you apart will confirm it and perhaps we can hold off this illustrious visitor.' Their eyes met, wide with anxiety. 'Whatever we give you to eat or drink, whatever medicine, whatever we tell you to do you must promise to obey without question.' Her voice quivered. 'You must trust us on this,' she whispered.

He shivered, no need for pretence this time as his belly churned with fear.

'With my life,' he said, reaching out to drop a kiss on her hand.

29

'Your sister's grandson?' The farmer's new wife, Livia Junia, had seen the illustrious visitor to the guest chamber and now she raised a haughty eyebrow as she looked at her mother-in-law. 'I was not aware that any of your kinfolk still lived, Flavia Petronilla.'

'My sister was dear to me,' was the dignified reply. 'Her daughter was a sad disappointment and ran off with a wastrel. She broke her mother's heart but her son says my niece regretted her folly and lived to be glad when her man died soon after the boy's birth. He has a real look of my father and he's a hard worker, a quick learner too... He must have picked up the fever in Londinium and I pray we can pull him through it without the rest of the household sickening.'

She straightened the robe on her shoulders and held herself haughtily erect, aware that the farmer was looking at her through thoughtful, narrowed eyes.

'I'll look in on him, Mother,' he told her. 'No, my dear,' he brushed aside his wife's outcry. 'I must greet a kinsman, a guest in my house. Have no fear, I'll take no unnecessary risks, I'm mindful of your condition. Mother?' His tone was polite but brooked no refusal. 'You'll take me to him at once, if you please.'

The cramped chamber was dark and sweltering as Acilius fumbled his way through the shadows. 'Can you not let in some light?'

'Under no circumstances,' she snapped. 'Light is the worst possible thing in cases like this and he is here so that we may contain the fever. Aula, how is your cousin?'

'He's so hot, Grandmother,' Aula rose to greet her father then bent to her task. 'He shivers and whimpers that he's cold though I've piled woollen blankets on him, a sheepskin too. I gave him the draught you advised but he can't keep anything down. I'm very fearful.'

'Let me see.' Standing just in front of the master of the house, Flavia Petronilla slipped something into the beaker her granddaughter held. 'Here we are, Marius,' she said kindly as she helped her patient to lift his head. 'Try this, my boy; one of my sovereign remedies for the fever.'

Obediently throwing in a groan or two for good measure Marius downed the drink, only to retch and vomit in earnest. Aula was there with a basin and a cool, soothing hand on his brow as the spasms racked him.

Acilius backed away but when the vomiting was over and the patient lay sweating and exhausted on his pillows, the sheep farmer approached the bedside.

'Marius Fulvius,' he said gravely. 'I am sorry to see you in this plight and I shall hope to bid you welcome more happily, very soon.'

He clapped a hand on the young man's shoulder then turned to his mother. 'I see more of a likeness to my own late brother, than to my grandfather,' he told her solemnly. 'There is a distinct family resemblance, to be sure, apart from those striking blue eyes.' He gave the boy a measuring look and nodded, saying, 'I certainly think you should shade them, Mother. As you say, too much glare could be dangerous.'

When he had left the room, Aula glanced at her grandmother.

'I had an uncle?' she enquired. 'It was my understanding that my father was an only child.'

'You heard, my girl. Do you doubt your father's word?' The reply was accompanied by a reproving stare, its severity belied by the twinkle in her eye, as Flavia Petronilla took a comb from her pocket. 'Aula's father was right to suggest we veil your eyes, lad, so we'll draw these curls across your forehead. Close your eyes at once should anyone else enter here.'

'What in Hades did you put into that drink?' Marius nodded. 'My throat's raw. I thought I was being poisoned.'

'Hush, foolish lad, of course you were poisoned,' she scolded, nodding as Aula explained.

'It was sheep's milk gone sour,' she murmured, shooting an anxious glance at the doorway. 'Mixed with mustard, a reliable emetic. Rest now. Grandmother's woman will watch you while we eat with my father and his wife and this honoured guest of theirs.'

The honoured guest was looking the worse for wear, with

31

his arm in a sling and a nose that looked newly-broken. In his mid-twenties, he was elegantly slender and dressed in clothes of a quality and style rarely seen in the countryside. He picked listlessly at the food set out before him and answered his hostess's arch remarks in a pettish voice, though he showed an interest when the young serving boy came in to remove the empty dishes.

Hah! Aula folded her lips. She felt her father's eyes on her and looked up, to be surprised into a snort of laughter as he lowered his left eyelid very slightly.

'I coughed. I beg your pardon, madam,' she answered her stepmother's reprimand with demurely lowered eyes.'

'Do you make a stay at Venta for business or pleasure, sir?' Acilius hastened to enquire.

'The former, initially,' the guest replied. 'As I mentioned earlier, I am sent as second-in-command to inspect the Imperial Weaving concern there, and charged with improving the quality of woollen materials produced. The army must be clad, after all.' He nodded acknowledgement of the polite ripple of amusement at his pleasantry. 'It is business first but in the course of doing my duty I trust I shall make acquaintances among the farmers and wool producers such as yourself, sir.'

When the meal was finished Flavia Petronilla and her demure granddaughter were horrified when their guest addressed them. 'Perhaps you had not heard, ladies, that I was subjected to a vicious attack about a month ago, just before I left Isca? I was laid up for a week and have reason to believe that the ringleader of that assault was a disaffected legionary whom I had cause to reprimand.'

Both women murmured politely as he explained. 'With this in mind I sent out messengers to the north and west, but as I was heading eastward myself, I made it my business to investigate any sighting of strange young men on the route from Isca to Venta.'

He pushed his plate away and looked at his host. 'I gather you have a visitor, a young man? Can you vouch for him?'

Acilius frowned, sitting up poker-straight, and there was a distinct chill in the atmosphere around the table. The visitor seemed aware of it and smiled thinly in apology, as he said, 'So far I have met with no success. Greatly as I regret the inconvenience to my gracious host.' He bowed to Acilius and his wife. 'I fear I must insist upon taking a look at your patient. Naturally,' he added, 'I cannot force you...'

'Certainly,' Acilius was icily polite. 'My young kinsman journeyed from quite the opposite direction but you must see for yourself.' He bowed. 'My mother and daughter will prepare him for your visit. He would not wish to receive an illustrious guest in an unkempt state, however sick he may be.'

Keeping their pace steady the women left the room in dignified silence though Aula shook with terror. Desertion was not invariably punished by death these days but uncertainty made her stomach clench. At the very least Marius would be brutally flogged and forced to rejoin the army. With his nemesis in a position of power at Venta, what chance would there be for her newly-discovered relative?

Her step faltered and she reached out blindly to the wall to steady herself.

'Aula?' Her grandmother spoke quietly. 'Courage, my child, there is some of my special herbal drink left but I worry lest that creature may need something more convincing in the way of proof.'

'I've had an idea.' Aula's eyes sparkled despite her fear. 'Listen...'

Shortly after the women's whispered conclave Acilius and his guest entered the sick room, only to halt at the foetid heat.

'What in Jupiter's name...' The younger man halted aghast in the doorway but his host propelled him forward.

'We must make sure, noble sir,' he insisted. 'My mother will tell me if we are in danger from infection.'

Flavia Petronilla glared. 'I have no time for idle chatter,' she snapped. 'Our unfortunate kinsman is approaching the crisis so make your inspection and have done. Do not touch him or lean too close,' she warned. 'This has all the signs of *a virulent disease.'*

She held a cup to her patient's lips, whereupon he obligingly gagged and vomited, his eyes closed. Aula gasped as a foul noise echoed in the quiet room and a disgusting stench arose.

'Let me see to him,' she cried, elbowing the guest out of her way. 'Grandmother,' she wailed. 'See, it is the flux.'

'Pray it is not bloody,' was the terse response. 'Out of my way, girl.'

The two horrified spectators hung back and the younger man would have made good his escape had not Acilius grasped him by the shoulder.

'Look!' Flavia Petronilla flung back the sheet. 'Blood!'

'Let me out of here.' The cry was muffled as the guest clutched his sleeve to his mouth and nose.

'Is this the man you seek?' Seeing the other man shake his head urgently, heaving and unable to speak, Acilius relented. 'We leave you in the hands of the gods, Marius Fulvius, and in my mother's hands too – where you are surely safer.'

(iv)

Next morning their distinguished visitor pronounced himself almost recovered.

'I hear that your well is said to have healing powers and I believe it, ladies,' he bowed graciously. 'The water is most refreshing, so I trust that your kinsman will soon make a full recovery.'

'As do I,' answered the elder lady serenely. 'He is weak but we shall pray. My son will have told you, sir that he hopes to continue his association with the Imperial Weaving establishment at Venta. He will increase our yield when he moves to his larger farm over the river; it is an important holding and Acilius is becoming a man of influence.' She wiped her lips on a napkin and smiled at the guest. 'This small steading here belonged to my father and my son will turn it over to Aula when she marries.

'Now,' she indicated her son. 'I suggest, sir, that while

34

Acilius pays a visit to his ailing kinsman, you might take Livia Junia for a gentle stroll in the garden, exercise being particularly beneficial in her condition.'

At a simper from them both Flavia Petronilla beckoned to her son and left the room.

'Well, Mother?' Acilius asked as they headed to the sickroom. 'You were generous with your information to our guest. It's news to me that I'm to move across the river, but...' He hunched his shoulders. 'This marriage has not brought the comfort I had hoped. Not for Aula...' he admitted as he failed to meet his mother's keen gaze. 'And not for me. It's early days, but if you think the boy worthy of my girl, perhaps you have the right of it.'

He clasped her shoulder with an affectionate smile. 'As for the lad I prefer him to our other visitor and if you trust him that's enough for me. I'll ask no questions about his background but there is one thing I insist upon knowing.'

Always a monument to dignity, his mother raised enquiring eyes.

'I can guess at how you managed the fever and the vomiting,' he said, shaking his head with a rueful smile. 'But how in the name of the Lady, did you come up with that disgusting noise and the bloody flux? For that young man is no more on his deathbed than I am.'

'It was Aula's idea,' she said as she ushered him into the room where her granddaughter sat beside the patient, shamelessly holding his hand. 'She meant to run to the privy but there were people about, so she went to the pigsty.'

Her son stared and then let out a bellow of laughter. 'The pigsty? No wonder it stank.'

Aula's eyes danced. 'I had to think quickly, Father, so I collected some of the muck and hid it in the bed in a covered pot then I took a pig's bladder from the cold store and blew it up. I slipped it in beside Marius and when you all looked away while he was being sick, he squeezed it. You know what noise a bladder makes if you let out the air.'

She smiled at the invalid. 'I barely had a few moments to explain what I wanted him to do and he managed it

35

perfectly.'

'I never want to taste that foul milk and mustard drink again,' Marius shuddered but shot a hopeful smile at his host. *'As for the rest, I did as I was told. While you all recoiled from the noise of the bladder I uncovered the pot and upended it in the bed.'*

'So it was pig shit all the time?' Acilius clapped a hand to his mouth to silence the howl of laughter that threatened. *'And the blood?'*

'Also from the pig,' his daughter grinned. *'Grandmother had it ready to make a pudding but we'll have to do without.'*

Chapter Three

The first day of my new life.

The wreath still hung on its hook and I wondered whether I ought to renew the withered flowers. If so, how often? I had no idea so I shrugged and set off to explore properly.

The panelling upstairs was painted cream and my first visit had revealed three bedrooms, all opening on to a landing as wide as the hall below.

From the front window of the long bedroom I gazed down at the short, quiet cul-de-sac. The only other house, a small red-brick cottage on my right as I looked out, was Edwardian, I thought, with freshly-repointed mortar and double-glazed sashes, a contrast to the ugly metal windows of the shabby old house that was now mine. The pub on the corner fronted onto the main road and the strange defunct beauty parlour stood to my left as I leaned out of the window to inspect my new surroundings.

As I prowled around upstairs, watery sunshine streamed in from the small arched window at the front. I'd fallen for the long, light-filled bedroom on sight, with one window at the front, and views over the garden and beyond from the back. The brass bedstead and the chest-of-drawers with one leg propped up on a book were equally rickety and there were signs that this room had once been divided. Nothing was worth keeping but looking at the traces of lily-of-the-valley on the faded curtains I thought the room must have been lovely in its heyday.

The furniture in the large front bedroom across the landing was much better: a plain double-bed in gleaming mahogany with a matching wardrobe and chest-of-drawers, the latter full of sheets and pillowcases. I could just about make out forget-me-knots on the faded wallpaper, with more blue flowers in the curtains.

I'd usually run a mile from this welter of flowery chintz but I liked it here. The bathroom bore evidence of the same taste although, as elsewhere, the sprig pattern on the walls had faded into grey. This room had been squeezed into the width of the landing at the back of the house and the small arched window matched the one over the front door. The flowery porcelain fittings looked genuinely Edwardian but luckily the chain flushed efficiently when I gave it an exploratory yank.

I loved the wide floorboards covered with rugs throughout much of the house; there were no draughts, no chill and no musty smell anywhere, so the other beneficiary, Mrs Draper, had been doing an excellent job of keeping the house alive.

Alive? What made me think that? I had reached the third bedroom, the smaller one at the back and I had the strangest feeling that the house was awake and watching me so I hesitated, seized with a sense that I should knock. Why not? I tapped and was more than half relieved to receive no answer.

This must have been Violet's room, with little purple flowers everywhere on the wallpaper and curtains, and small, intimate possessions scattered around: some well-worn books by the bed, a silver-backed set of hand mirror and brushes on the dressing-table, a matching set of violet-patterned china – pin tray, powder bowl, ring tree and candlesticks.

The room smelled fresh and clean and still with that sense that I was intruding I looked briefly in the wardrobe and drawers. Empty – Mrs Draper again, I supposed.

On the windowsill was a box, intricately patterned with inlaid wood, like one my mother called Tunbridge-ware. I lifted the lid, saw paper, letters, writing, and shut it quickly. There was plenty of time.

It was drizzling so I ran down to the car for the food I'd

packed and as I shut the boot I looked up with a thrill of ownership. According to the helpful solicitor, the central house, my house, was the oldest. It was mostly stone mixed with flint, with cute twisted chimneys on the tiled roof, which luckily seemed in good repair. The later extensions on either side looked Georgian or early Victorian, I thought, and were brick with a stone trim, a door at the side and windows up and down at the front.

The solicitor said it had once been a farmhouse sitting in its own land and it must have been lovely before it was split. It looked scruffy now but it could be fabulous, Patrick would... Hmm, yes, Patrick. I bit my lip and wondered about that uncharacteristic tetchiness. I don't think I'm being completely fair to him, I admitted. I'll get in touch in a couple of days and outline my ideas, see how he reacts.

Feeling suddenly anxious I locked the car and as I paused for another look, a middle-aged woman drove in and parked outside the red-brick cottage over the road. When she spotted me she smiled and waved as she went indoors.

(ii)

Fifteen minutes later I was unpacking in the long bedroom when I was startled by a ring at the door.

'Hello?' The pleasant-looking woman on the doorstep was the one who had waved to me. In her late forties, probably, she looked tired but a smile lightened her heavy features as she nodded in greeting.

'Hi, I'm Alison Dexter from Lamb Cottage, just across the way. I don't think there's anyone else at home so I thought I'd come and say welcome to Ladywell.'

'That's so kind.' I was touched. 'I'm Freya Gibson. Um, won't you come in?'

'I wouldn't dream of imposing on you,' Alison shook her head decisively. 'I know what it's like, I only moved in six months ago. I just wanted to say hello and to say I've made a pot of coffee if you'd like a break?'

I hesitated, there was a lot to do, but it seemed churlish to refuse. Besides, I suddenly felt the house wanted me to go. To make friends.

'Coffee would be great, thanks,' I brushed aside the moment of whimsy, smiled and picked up the key.

'What a peaceful room.' I admired the cream walls, bronze-patterned curtains and turquoise silk cushions. 'Classic.'

'Classic is what I wanted.' Alison brought in coffee. 'It's a small room, well it's a small house. Left to myself it would have been wall-to-wall beige with touches of mushroom and keynotes in écru and taupe.'

She laughed at my startled giggle. 'I have absolutely no taste, so it would have been terminally boring. I moved here after my husband and I split up and I knew the house deserved better than beige but I had no idea what to do, till someone recommended a student interior designer. I was happy to let her practise on me and she said it was useful learning to rein in her own ideas to suit a client.'

'I might need to consult her,' I confessed. 'My house is beautifully clean but it desperately needs redecorating. Even at a cursory glance I can see plenty of work ahead.'

I gave Alison a brief run-down about how I'd inherited Violet Wellman's house and she explained in turn that she was head of the Ramalley primary school.

'I've been laid low with a chest infection,' she said, heading for the kitchen to find some biscuits. 'It's a hectic term, but aren't they all? I've made things worse fretting and I could have gone in today but it would've been a struggle. Everyone told me to keep my germs to myself, so I'm taking the weekend to knock it on the head. I'm back on Monday, for the day, then off on a course all week. It's all go.'

There was a ring at the door and at the sound of cheerful greetings I began to gather up my coat.

'Oh no,' Alison came back into the room. 'Don't go, you haven't finished your coffee. That was only our chatty postman. Tell me more! I do think you're brave, setting out on an adventure like this.'

Forty minutes later I went home, assuring Alison that no, I didn't need lunch, thank you. I liked her and it was reassuring to have a good neighbour and the promise perhaps, of a new friendship. Maybe I shouldn't have told her about my vague plan but I felt a glow of pride that she thought I was brave – perhaps I was. As I took my sandwich lunch into the long living-room I was aware of a slight niggle of doubt about Patrick's reaction to my cunning plan but I dismissed it. He'd come round to it. He had to.

'You're annoyingly perky and optimistic,' Louise had said as we parted company. 'It's lovely to see the old Freya again and I really hope it works out, but promise to ring me if you feel fragile. It's a nuisance neither of us has a reliable mobile signal at present, but mind you email every day or I'll turn up on your doorstep.'

Patrick had said much the same thing about my inherent chirpiness a few months earlier when he had a hangover. 'Are you always so insufferably cheerful?'

'Pretty much,' I said smugly. 'Nothing gets done if you spend your time moping.'

'Huh. There's something in the Bible about people like you.'

'It's in Proverbs, my dad used to quote it at me. 'He that blesseth his friend with a loud voice, rising early in the morning, it shall be counted a curse to him.

There had been a period of my life when I wasn't cheerful, but that was then, and when that time ended I'd vowed never to lose my trust in the future. It had taken ages, Louise was right, but since her wedding a year earlier, we'd not seen so much of each other and I was a lot further along the road to recovery than she realised. Life had been tough and I'd been unhappy but Spring was almost here. Life was looking up.

It had been a major blow when I made enquiries, to discover that it would take another ten days to install broadband and that the mobile signal at Ladywell was unreliable.

'Find somewhere with free Wi-Fi quickly.' Louise surprised me with a text that did manage to get through. **'I'm**

41

in Ripon today, the signal's useless at home. I want daily bulletins.'

'Violet was the main objector to the phone mast on the hill,' I texted straight back, hoping she'd pick it up somewhere. 'Permission's been granted now so it should be ok soon.'

After lunch Lou rang me on the landline. 'I'm home now so I thought I'd try to catch you. What about the house? Can you afford to do it up? You said it needs new windows, lots of work.'

'It's okay,' I told her. 'Buying the flat didn't take all the money Dad left me so I've got my rainy-day fund. Anyway, the roof is sound; Violet had it repaired when the house was rewired and central heating put in, so it's watertight and comfortable for now.'

I needed to plan the potential expenses so I made more tea and went round the ground-floor making lists.

The narrow kitchen extension with a cat-flap in the backdoor was – adequate. I'd love to pull it down eventually, but the ancient fridge would have to go at once; the door-seal had perished and it wheezed painfully. I added the gas stove to my list, it looked more dangerous than the fridge, but washing machine, dishwasher – they could wait until I had a plan. Meanwhile, I could manage with my microwave and electric kettle and eat at the very small table.

Rain fell steadily all afternoon so I postponed my urge to explore outside properly; I'm not much of a gardener, though Dad always said green fingers ran in the family. There was nothing at the front, just a strip of paving the width of the whole building, and the two end houses had narrow side plots. Their land at the back was much shorter than Violet's garden which spread out behind the other two, in a distorted T shape. It was long and sloped gradually down to a wall where a narrow valley rose again towards the hills. That must be Puss Hill immediately beyond the house, I thought, staring out at the relentless grey rain sleeting down. I promised myself that I'd get up on the hills on the first dry day, and went back to unpacking and prowling round the house.

I was drawn to the long room to the left of the front door. Dickon's Room. Like the bedroom above I could see it had once been divided but the oak panelling had been patched. There was a large stone fireplace and it was the kind of room that was grand enough to call a drawing-room which must be unusual in a farmhouse.

Someone had designed and built this room with love and pride; it was definitely grand and must have made a statement at one time with that imposing fireplace and more of the wide wooden floorboards. It made a statement now and as for the window…

On that first visit I'd been halted in my tracks when I opened the door and saw the window overlooking the garden. Reaching from floor to ceiling it shouted for attention, made up of three narrow arches, obviously taken from a church and, I thought, made smaller to fit. Was it contemporary with the house? If so, this was an astonishing survival. The slim pillars that divided up the three glazed panels were covered in amazing leaves and flowers and vine tendrils, all carved into the stone and I'd gasped to see a hare, poised for flight, in one of the bottom corners.

Today, I dragged myself away from the window to trace the shape of a running hare on the stone mantelpiece, wondering who had carved it. I had a moment's panic – what the hell had I done? Maybe Lou was right and I was holding myself together; I couldn't afford to let the façade crack but… how would I cope in a strange house, in a strange town? I did some deep breathing and forced myself to relax, and to trust my instinct. When I'd opened Louise's present after that initial viewing of the house I'd been shocked by the coincidence – hares in the house and now a hare for the garden. For now, though, the newest hare could sit under the window until I found his ideal place. The hares, the house, the scent of roses – it all felt *meant* somehow and just for now I had to trust my instincts.

I made a note of the large, shabby but comfortable sofa, with its drop-ends tied up with cord. This room could look wonderful, I sighed, and in that moment I realised I'd added yet another item to my list: restore the long room to its former glory.

The Christmassy front parlour on the other side of the hall had dark-green wallpaper and crimson velvet curtains, with bookshelves either side of the fireplace. The furniture was shabby: a battered brass table, a sagging sofa and two armchairs with faded loose covers. When I thought that Violet might have slept there sometimes, it was a hike up to her bedroom, I felt a pang of regret that I would never know her.

My list was lengthening but the dining-room could wait though the 1930s dining-set would have to go. The big room, Dickon's Room – I wondered again about him – called me so I set up my laptop on a small table as a makeshift desk. At least there were plenty of sockets and I unearthed an old fan-heater to combat any chill.

I was totting it all up and making a face at all this expense, when there was another ring at the door.

A delivery driver handed me a basket planted with primroses, hyacinths and snowdrops; the card said, 'Love and happiness always'. It was signed *'Patrick'*.

I caught my breath and my eyes filled as I gently touched a primrose. I'd have to do something about Patrick. And soon.

(iii)

I'd just finished supper, when the land-line rang. Louise fussing again. I grinned, warmed by the thoughtful gesture.

'Just checking,' Louise was apologetic. 'I know you're a big girl, Freya and I've already texted and rung today. But...'

'Mother hen,' I laughed at her. 'I'm fine, a neighbour invited me for coffee and told me about the people who live either side. No sign of life yet but one's an elderly housebound lady and the other is a single woman.

'Have you got anything to sit on?' Louise persisted. 'Don't forget, I've now got loads of in-laws in the country. They all have lumpy furniture, all-over dog hair and springs sticking out.'

'Your in-laws hang out in large, draughty houses,' I protested. 'They throw another spaniel on the bed if it's cold. Most of Violet's furniture will do for firewood and I'm going shopping tomorrow anyway. I'd be checking out Pinterest for inspiration if I didn't live in a black hole. Hey! I've been so busy I forgot to tell you I also own a beauty parlour.'

I smiled at her squawk. 'I told you the solicitor says there are complications about selling the property and that includes the defunct beauty parlour. Nobody knows what it was originally; a small barn probably. Mr Makepeace is going to examine the old paperwork to see if I can get permission to let it long-term or as a holiday cottage, which would be handy if Patrick gives me the sack.'

'He won't do that,' Louise sounded cryptic. 'Have you spoken to him yet?'

'He sent some lovely flowers so I texted him, hope it gets through. I'll send him photos and you too, once I have Wi-Fi.'

I hesitated. 'Lou, he's going to Colorado at the weekend. I didn't know beforehand.'

'So? He's thirty-six; he doesn't need permission.'

'It's not that,' I faltered. 'His old army friend is at the university where Ben and I…'

'Oh, Freya,' Louise's voice was kind. 'I'd forgotten it was Colorado where… That would bring back memories. Listen, have a nice warm bath, a glass of wine – I'm quite sure you packed a bottle! Then go to bed with a good book.'

'Thanks, Mary Poppins,' I swallowed and managed a laugh. 'It did remind me but I'm fine, and yes, I'll take your medicine.'

I filled Violet's hot-water bottle while I ran a bath and, smiling over Louise's prescription, poured myself a glass of Merlot and clambered into the roll-top bath.

It was when I relaxed that the tears began. Quite without volition great, gasping sobs shook me so that I crouched in the steaming bubbles, hugging myself and rocking. I wept with complete abandon as I had never wept in the years since

45

my life fell apart. Without reservation, without inhibition, the tears poured down my cheeks while wails of desolate grief echoed round the bathroom.

When the storm abated I crawled out of the bath, clinging to the high rolled side before I tackled the task of towelling myself dry.

Blind and deaf to the outside world and to the memories that clamoured, I reeled into the long bedroom, out like a light as I hit the pillow.

In the morning I felt better than I had for years.

Chapter Four

(i)
Friday, 6ᵗʰ March

At quarter-past nine I had my first visitor of the day. A shadow showed through the glazed panel, surprisingly low down. A child? In term-time?

On the doorstep stood a small, furry brown bear. I stared. Probably not a bear? A pixie, perhaps? Bright blue eyes peered out from under a Cossack-style fur hat and a small pink nose poked over the high collar of an ancient, ankle-length mink coat. A Russian pixie?

'Morning,' chirped the small person, in excellent English with a slight Hampshire accent. 'You must be Freya. I'm Violet's friend, Mary Draper. Eight pounds an hour, two or maybe three hours a week, starting next Wednesday if that suits you. I dropped by to introduce myself on my way to the Friday market.'

I stared blankly down at her.

'Cup of tea on the go?' enquired the small person, looking hopeful.

'Of course, yes,' I stammered as I stood aside to let my furry visitor into the hall. 'Do, please come in.'

'Kitchen?' prompted the tiny one as she shed her outer covering to reveal a little old woman, even smaller than I'd thought. Without the bulk of the mink Mary Draper stood an upright four-foot-ten and vigorous with it.

I obediently made a pot of tea under my visitor's approving eye and prompted by a quizzical tilt of the head, fished out the biscuits I had brought with me. As I sat down again I gazed doubtfully at Mary who, at a guess, must be at least eighty, possibly more, yet here she was apparently intent on tackling my housework. Were there rules about the exploitation of octogenarian pixies?

'I'm quite tough, you know, dear,' Mary confounded me. 'I did Violet's cleaning after her sight began to fail and I've been looking in regularly since she went into the hospice, just to keep it up to scratch.'

Light dawned. 'The solicitor told me,' I said. 'You've kept it beautifully. It feels as though she's just popped out somewhere.'

'Did my best,' Mary nodded again. 'Violet couldn't bear to think of everything run-down and neglected.' She held up her mug for a refill and leaned back in her chair. 'Settling in, are you, dear? Violet did hope you'd keep the house. She wanted it to stay in the family and you're the last of them. She was fond of your father. My goodness, you look just like him, same colouring and that streaky-brown curly hair. Apart from the nose, that is.'

'You knew him?' I ignored the comment about my nose. It's not big or hooked or ugly, just that nobody else in the family had one like it. My mother called it aquiline. I suppose it *is* slightly beaky, but I've never had any hang-ups about it, though Ben wanted me to have a nose-job. Oh well, no point thinking about the past...

'Oh yes, your dad lived in London but always spent part of his holidays at Ladywell,' Mary said. 'Stephen was a lovely lad, never a bit of trouble. He was good-looking and all the local girls had an eye for him but he visited less and less as he grew up, which was natural.' Mary nodded. 'Violet always said you could tell a Wellman by their amber eyes.'

Amber eyes? I had no time to take this in because she smoothed her brown tweed skirt as she said, with a friendly smile, 'Harry Makepeace rang to let me know you'd arrived. He knew I was Violet's only remaining friend and he thought you'd like some company.' She ducked her head in a sudden fit of shyness. 'Only if you like, dear, I don't want to push in where I'm not wanted. I thought maybe you could do with a spot of help once a week.'

48

'It's very kind of you.' A discreet inspection showed bald patches on the mink coat so I rushed to reassure her. Maybe Mary had come to rely on the money. 'Yes,' I said. 'It would be a real help if you're sure, but your hourly rate sounds very low. I've been paying a lot more in London.'

'London!' Mary snorted. 'More fool you, dear. No, we'll start like I said. I planned to clean for your neighbour, you know, Sylvia Penrose, but that high-and-mighty housekeeper of hers insisted on hiring a cleaning company. Sylvia's a widow, same as me; we were at school together and we get on fine. These days I just pop in for a cup of tea for the company and a chat, and I'm going to help her with...' She let the sentence hang there and took another biscuit.

I was intrigued and tried to find out more about Mrs Penrose but Mary just looked mysterious.

'Sylvia married a Londoner and lived abroad,' she said, getting to her feet. 'I stayed home and married Bill and never regretted it, though it's been lonely these last years. Sylvia persuaded her husband to buy the house as an investment but he liked the ex-pat life so it wasn't till he died, a year ago, that she came home. Now she's at the mercy of his grasping niece.'

I opened my mouth and she added, 'After Sylvia's money, though I doubt she'll get it. Now, I must get on to the market. It's a ten-minute walk at your age but I came by bus. There'll be one along in a few minutes.'

She arrayed herself in the coat. 'Snug as a bug in this, a freebie from the hospice shop a while back. They couldn't sell them, you see, though it's on its last legs now.'

I wondered whether anyone had ever thrown eggs at the moth-eaten mink but it seemed unlikely. Mary was so proud of her bargain and surely not even the most rabid zealot could argue that the fur would look better on a live animal? Any mink looking like that would be torn to pieces by its fellows as a dangerously sick deviant.

'I talk to it, you know, dear?'

I blinked and she twinkled at me. 'I miss my old cat, you see, and I don't want another at my time of life. The mink is

49

the best I can manage.' She straightened her hat. 'Do you like cats, dear? Or dogs?'

'I've never had a pet. I'd quite like one, though,' I said. 'A cat, perhaps.'

'That's nice, dear,' Mary nodded approvingly as she glanced at the fading wreath over the door.

'I see you found the rowan tree,' she commented. 'Violet got agitated when I visited her in the hospice, you know. Said she'd forgotten to leave a note to tell you to replace it when it dies. There must always be a rowan tree at Ladywell, she said.'

She refused to elaborate so I let it go, promising to plant another tree when the time came. A glance outside at the depressing grey sky decided me. 'I'll give you a lift and you can show me the shops,' I told her, picking up my bag and keys. 'It's no trouble. I've no idea how much I'll be buying and I don't want to get caught in a downpour.'

(ii)

'Spirit is telling me all about you!' The stranger tightened her grip on my unwilling hand. 'Spirit knows all about your sadness in the past.'

One minute I was crossing the town square in the company of a little old lady who had just signed on as my employee and possibly substitute grandmother, next minute I was mesmerized, a rabbit in the pale, damp glare of a stranger's eyes, tethered by the pale, damp clutch of a stranger's hand.

Mary Draper started forward to the rescue and was halted by a peremptory wave from the unoccupied hand.

'Spirit knows, and Spirit is telling you that your mother will be with you soon.'

'You're sick!' I wrenched my hand away, recoiling in distaste. 'My mother died years ago.'

'No, dear,' insisted the unwelcome seer, breathing heavily through her mouth. A tiny dribble of saliva appeared at the corner and I stared in disgust. 'You're wrong. Your mother is still in this world. The one who passed into Spirit wasn't your mother.'

With that she turned abruptly on her heel and headed off towards the small department store.

'There!' said the woman who had been at her side, proud as a hen with a newly-hatched duckling. 'Such a privilege. She's the guest speaker at the Old Chapel, eight o'clock the day after tomorrow and for the next three Sundays. She never usually gives private messages.'

Seeing her quarry disappear she set off in pursuit, calling back over her shoulder. 'She's never wrong, you know. I'll see you soon, Mrs Draper.'

'Not if I see you coming,' snapped Mary angrily. 'Freya, I'm put out about that. I don't know that woman but I do know Diane Govern. She's difficult at the best of times but this must be a new craze.'

I was shaking and I felt sick and panicky. Even without the insane claims it's not a good feeling to have a complete stranger dribble at you.

Mary pursed her lips. 'Come on, we'll go to Nonie's just across the square.'

The warmth of the café and the smell of coffee brought me out of my state of shock.

'Two coffees, please, Nonie and two toasted tea-cakes.' Mary greeted the thin, sixty-something woman.

'My treat, dear.' Brisk but kind, she brushed aside my protest. 'Your blood-sugar needs a boost after that carry-on. Oh, you haven't been introduced. Nonie, this is Freya Gibson, Violet's young cousin. Freya, this is Nonie Radstone.'

'That's Anona – it means 'harvest' and I was born at harvest time – call me Nonie,' the café owner began, looking at me through steamed-up glasses. She caught Mary's eye for a moment before disappearing into the kitchen while I joined Mary in the window. The coffee was excellent and I tucked into a tea-cake that dripped butter.

'I'm sorry, dear,' Mary sipped her coffee. 'Diane Govern suffers badly from foot-in-mouth disease and her friend is obviously from the same mould.'

I nodded blankly, struggling to damp down my own bewilderment, while Mary explained briefly. 'Diane's a big noise in a local group that rents the redundant chapel over the road. The other members are harmless enough but that one has a poisonous tongue. I'm surprised they've taken up with clairvoyance, they've fallen out with most of the local churches, including the spiritualists. Still, Diane leads the others by the nose and I think she's taken over since their pastor left.'

I drank my coffee and remembered to download my emails using the café's Wi-Fi, though I was pretty much on auto-pilot.

'Why would that woman say such a thing?' I could hear my voice rising in sharp distress and I managed to calm down as Mary cast an anxious glance round the café which was temporarily empty. At the counter, Nonie Radstone looked up and I saw Mary glance over at her, before she patted my hand.

'My mother...' I stumbled over the words. 'She had pancreatic cancer five years ago. My mother is dead.'

Chapter Five

(i)

From:fmgibson@ladywell.me.com

'It was surreal, Lou. I'm using the free Wi-Fi in the Library. Dropped Mary off at her flat, but it really shook me up. Might check out the museum next-door, then home. If it stops raining after lunch I'll tackle some weeding. Btw do you like my new email address? How's that for commitment to the new me?'

The museum was just a few rooms beside the library but I was unsettled and not ready to be on my own. The woman at the desk smiled and handed me a leaflet then went back to her computer while I wandered round, reading the display boards. Ramalley's prosperity had begun with sheep farming and from that had come the tannery, the wool trade, and the cheese market. In Roman times there'd even been an Imperial fulling mill in Winchester – and the high quality local wool ended up on the backs of Roman nobles.

I moved on from pre-history until a display of Roman pots caught my eye. I remembered Violet's note denying there had been an important villa at Ladywell; judging by the lack of anything more interesting, she was right.

One thing that did stop me in my tracks was a large glass-topped wooden box containing a skeleton, laid out as it had been discovered. The skull was tucked between the leg bones, separate from the rest of the body. I'm not squeamish but these bones looked sinister somehow.

'Gruesome, isn't it?' The museum guide was beside me. 'They discovered him when they were digging the foundations for a petrol station. It's at a cross-roads and it's believed this poor devil died on the gibbet there.'

I looked blank. 'What's going on with the skull? That's unusual, isn't it?'

'Not really,' she leaned against a table, happy to talk. 'You can see from the card it's a late Saxon burial, probably around 950AD, give or take a few decades. It's the only one of its kind ever found in Ramalley though decapitated skeletons have turned up in Winchester and to the east of the county.'

She leaned forward. 'You can't make it out from here but there are cut marks on the vertebrae and his hands were tied behind him.' She shook her head. 'Makes you shiver, doesn't it? The Saxons usually buried their dead reverently, laid east to west, flat on the back, arms at the side, but this chap seems to have been thrown in anyhow apart from the deliberate placing of his head. Why?' She shrugged. 'The most likely explanation is that he was a monk who broke his vows.'

I read the information sheet. 'It says he was a young man, late teens or early twenties. Maybe he discovered celibacy wasn't all it was cracked up to be. It seems a drastic punishment, who could blame him? We'll never know who shopped him.'

(ii)

I saw the monk again last night, sneaking round here. That fellow, singing his psalms and making believe to be so holy. Holy? Not him, he don't have a holy bone in his body, God punish him.

Mistress is right taken in and Prior over in the town too, but they'm incomers both. Proper fools they be, blinded by a face so fair, not a pock on him, not like most Christian folk. Old mistress now, she'd have sent him packing, but Master likes a quiet life and lets his wife rule the roost like his old mother and grandmother. Mistress keeps a good house, mind – a fine hand at baking and the healing arts – but indoors he do what he's told or rue the day.

'For shame, Wat.' Master cuffed me on the head when

Mistress snapped at him as I stood there sullen and silent. 'Brother Aelfric asked how you did, you great lummox. Answer him.'

I said nothing, nary a word. Speak, when I knew his purpose in coming here? It was weeks since the day I carried my big stick to keep young Mistress Osburga safe as she strolled round the market in town, chattering so kindly to me, nodding to this one and that, her gold-brown eyes shining.

Then there he stood, at the miller's stall while the Prior asked after the miller's family. We had business there so Mistress Osburga, she waited politely till the Prior stopped talking – and a time that was, since Father Prior likes the sound of his own voice. She stood there, peaceful-like, and I saw her lift her eyes and notice the young monk.

Young monk, I say. Young man is what she saw, the monk she saw too late. He was handsome and his eyes lit up as he smiled at her and I saw her downfall in her face. He took her hand in greeting and exclaimed aloud, and I knew 'twas because Mistress kept her busy with the spinning. The grease from the fleeces kept those little hands soft. He held her hand a shade too long and I kept watch on them at the market in the following weeks, so quiet, so proper, so innocent in their dealings.

Innocent!

Aye, so now I hung my head and coughed, while Mistress scolded and Master, goaded by her frowns, set about apologising for me.

'Alack, Brother Aelfric,' he said all bluff and hearty, the way he talks to priest and Prior. 'No use expecting poor Wat to know his manners, not when he's all mazed. He turned up here nine years ago fit to die, but my old grandmother she kept him alive like any lost lamb.'

Master lowered his voice and whispered in the young man's ear. 'Pity it was, truth be told, but there, she healed him as best she could and he keeps to the dogs, poor wight. He does his best for them, weak as he is and getting weaker. I beg you to forgive him.'

'Of course,' said the monk, full of Christian charity as he

tried to take my hand. 'I'm sorry for you, Wat, poor fellow. What happened, Master Oswin? To place such troubles on this poor man?'

Master explains, just as if I didn't stand there with my mouth open to speak.

'Poor soul,' says he, patting me on the shoulder with a hand like a great ham. 'Michaelmas time, it was. He never spoke for many a day but we heard all about it; a stampede of frightened cattle in the market, they said, and poor Wat trapped underneath. Left for dead, he was, but someone picked him up and brought him to my old granny. God in his mercy let him live, poor lad, though sorely twisted where his hip was smashed.'

Oh Lord, I prayed. If it be your will, strike Master dumb, for I knew he was going to tell it all, even the thing that yet has me wake in sweating nightmares, weeping for my loss and shame. Oh Lord, will you not, just for once, be on my side?

Useless to pray to a Lord who'd ignored my pleas these nine years so I had to listen while Master again lowered his voice to a booming whisper. 'Wat was trampled by the beasts, to be sure, Brother, and his hip damaged, but so were his – er – his vitals. He was nought but a lad of twelve then and he's a lad of twelve still in some ways. Even down to his voice.'

There, he'd told it. My shame for all to hear, not just that monk, but her too, Mistress Osburga. I lifted my head and through the tangle of my hair I saw pity spring to her eyes before her father gave me a push.

'Well, lad, after all, no man can blame you for a surly fit now and again, though you should take some honey and horehound for that cough,' he said kindly.

I slept fitfully that night, tossing and turning so even the dogs set to grumbling and the old hound bitch tried to give me a nip with her toothless jaws. I pulled the torn sheepskin round my shoulders but 'twas no use so I gave up on sleep and crept out to the garden where the moon was high and the scent of spring all around. The air lay gentle on my poor chest that

56

was right sore from coughing so I curled up in some long grass by the old wall that divided the orchard from the holy well. I thought I might catch an hour or so of sleep until I heard a rustling across from under the rowans in the grove. I saw shadows and knew the monk was there with her. Their whispers floated on the still air.

A laugh, so low and gentle I scarce believed I'd heard it.

'Must you go?' Her voice, for his ear, sweeter than I'd ever heard, ever dreamed.

'I hate to leave you, my love.' His voice cracked. 'These last weeks have shown me heaven here on earth.'

Rage rose in my breast, rage and grief. My eyes bulged and tears fell all unnoticed as I writhed in a torment greater than any before. He was here. He had enticed her from the safety of her father's hearth, the safety of my constant worship, the safety of her mother's watchful eye, and brought her here to lie in his arms like any whore from Ramalley town.

I lay there and listened with a sword in my heart while they whispered and kissed the more, with urgent murmurs and the rustle of clothing, gasps and moans, and her little cries of pleasure, while he choked back a shout of triumph.

I heard it all as I lay there pretending 'twas I who held her. I whose name she moaned and I who took her, little though my poor broken body could do. I loved her but as I lay spent with the anguish of it, trying not to cough though the sound of my groans was stifled by their own cries, my heart turned to a splinter of ice as it came to me that this was not their first coupling. Weeks, he'd said, so they had met like this more than once. It was a bitter truth, that she was his and never could be mine.

(iii)

Next morning I mucked out the dogs and horses as usual while I plotted, that coldness in my heart sharpening my thoughts. Fortune favoured me at noon when Master summoned me.

57

'Here, Wat,' said he. 'Get you across to the Priory with this cheese and a pot of honey for Father Prior. He's partial to our making and – 'tis wise to keep him sweet, eh?'

He gave me a nod and a boisterous clap on my shoulder as he waved me off. I think he was surprised when I gave him a smile of sorts, and a dip of my head, but he laughed again as I left. Scuttling crabwise along the river I spotted two hares leaping in the stubble field so I stopped and threw a stone at them. I hate hares with their easy grace and though men say 'tis bad luck to harm them here at Ladywell, I was glad when I hit one.

Luck was with me that day at the Priory. The gatekeeper knew me and nodded me through. Father Prior himself chanced to be strolling in the sunshine as I limped towards the cloister.

'Ho, there,' he called out. 'You come from Lady's Well, do you not? The cripple who attends Mistress Osburga?'

'Aye, my lord.' I fell to one knee and bowed my head, struggling with my cough before I could give him the message. 'Master sends you a cheese and their finest honey, with his humble duty.'

Father Prior was pleased to raise me to my feet as he admired his gifts. 'You should ask your mistress for some of her excellent honey for that cough,' he said, all graciousness. 'Pray send my gratitude to your master and your mistress,' he added, looking fierce as I knelt again. 'What is it now?'

'I saw something, my lord, and my conscience troubles me sore.'

'Well? Get on with it, man.'

'The young monk, Brother Aelfric,' I told him, making my voice all a-quiver with fear which in truth was no difficult task. 'I saw him last night over at Ladywell, my lord. In the garden where he'd no right to be.'

The Prior's brow darkened. 'Go on…'

'I can't hardly bear to tell you, my lord, but he had our young mistress with him.' I trembled again, and made my speech falter, then I had to turn aside, coughing. He put a hand under my chin and forced me to look up.

58

'Well?'

'The monk, my lord, he had his way with her.' There, I'd told it, the tale that would break him.

'You are sure of this?' His voice was harsh and dry and his words dropped into the silence. 'You cannot be mistaken?'

'No, Lord.'

'Perhaps she flaunted herself? Taunted him with womanly wiles?' He sounded hopeful and I hurried to smash down his hopes.

'Oh no, Lord, 'twas the monk forced the young mistress. I heard her cry out and would have gone to her but I was afeared, me being as I am and the monk so strong and tall.'

'Of course, of course,' he murmured. I made so bold as to rise then but he took no offence, just stared across the cloister garth with a bleak, forbidding frown.

'He befouled the Lady's well, Father Prior. I heard him draw a bucket and wash in the holy water after his wickedness. The little mistress had run away from him, gasping and weeping but I dared not let her know I'd witnessed her shame.' I hid a smile as I hung my head, piling sin upon sin, then I had a sudden thought. 'I beg of you, Father Prior, don't let Master know it was me told you this and don't let on that it was Mistress Osburga he ravished. She's innocent, I know, and they are good to me, a poor useless wretch. I would not have told you but I feared for my soul. Tell them it was some drab from the town.'

I saw contempt as well as pity in his hooded eyes. 'You need have no fear,' he said abruptly. 'No man shall know that yours was the voice that told of this sacrilege.'

Matters moved fast after that, no surprise to me. The Prior was a stern and righteous man and this was on his own doorstep. I wish I'd been present when Brother Aelfric was called to account. Prior must have been like an avenging angel, so tall and lean and afire with rage, those dark eyes burning in his noble face, but I saw naught of it and almost before the tale reached Ladywell, the young monk was taken.

'Dear Lord above,' Master shook his head in pious wonder

when the news was brought to him. 'I thought him better than that, a right and true young monk. Ah well, 'tis a lesson to us all not to be deceived by a handsome face. Eh, wife?'

'Indeed, husband.' The mistress pretended to be interested in naught but the embroidery she did so well, but there was an anxious look upon her comely face as she glanced round for her daughter. I was cleaning out the hearth and when she caught my eye she jerked her head slightly towards the door, we two in sudden complicity.

I slid out of the house, stopping to cough again and again, then I limped down the garden. I knew she would have run like a frightened hare to her special place where even in winter folk say you can smell flowers.

'Who... oh, 'tis you, Wat.' I heard relief mingled with her sobs as she lay broken at the centre of the rowan grove. 'Oh, Wat, I shall die. What will they do to him? What will become of me? Father and mother will never forgive me.'

I comforted her as best I could but we both knew nothing could save the monk, not with the Prior's pride so shamed and hurt. He had kept his word and made no mention of his informant's name but all knew Aelfric had been his favourite and gloried in it, so there were monks aplenty to be glad at his undoing. I helped her indoors into her mother's care then hid myself away to gloat with the dogs on his downfall.

Had I known what would befall me a few scant weeks later I believe I should have fallen down with my wits all awry. First, though, came the trial and the young mistress moving through the days like a soul gone astray, so pale she was, and her eyes red and sore from weeping. The trial was rushed through, no doubt by Father Prior's command, and the outcome no surprise to any man. Death by hanging, followed by beheading to mark his shame; his head stuck above the town gate for all to know what would befall any monk who broke his sacred oath.

When the sun rose on the hanging day Mistress gave out that Osburga was sick of a fever and taken to her bed. Master, older and greyer by ten years, looked like a man going to his own grave when he took me aside with many a glance to make sure none could hear.

'Wat,' he said, solemn and fierce at the same time. 'I place you in charge of the household, keep my women safe this day, all able-bodied souls being at their work.' He shook his head and turned to the gate. 'A bad business,' he said. 'A terrible, bad business. He was a good lad at heart, I'm sure, and nobly born 'tis said, but dear Lord, the injury he has done to me and mine. I'm headed for the crossroad, Wat, to see him despatched and maybe say a prayer for him. Mind you keep them safe while I'm gone.'

Indoors the mistress was all a-bustle, her face sad but purposeful, and when I looked in the door, she beckoned.

'How is your cough, Wat? I hear you all the time – cough, cough, cough, cough – enough to break a rib in that poor chest of yours. Do you cough up blood, poor soul?' She pursed her lips when I bent my head in meek admission. 'Here,' she said, with a kind of shivering sigh, her face full of pity. 'I brewed up some honey and a few herbs; do you take it, sip by sip, whenever you feel a coughing fit coming on. 'Twill give you ease and comfort so make sure you come to me for more when this is gone.'

I was surprised but pleased at her care, when she had never taken to me before, thinking – as I knew without need to ask – that I was ugly and a blight on the house, and that the sight of me could curdle cream. I knew too, without knowing how it came to me, that she blamed me, just by being there, for the babies she lost.

Perhaps the horror that was unfolding at the edge of town had softened her.

(iv)

Master said naught when he returned late that day, not a word to me, not a word to any save his wife, and that in private. A day went by, and another, a whole week of days and then I was summoned to the house. I cleaned myself as best I could and went indoors, to find Master seated in his carved chair with Mistress and their daughter beside him.

61

Osburga looked right peaky, her eyes stained and sore with the weeping, her merry laughter silenced. She turned her head away from my gaze and stared at the floor while her father cleared his throat till Mistress gave him a nudge.

'There is something we need to ask of you, Wat,' he began, shifting uneasily in his chair. 'First I must make sure of your loyalty to me and to my family.'

'I would die for you, Master,' I said, and meant it. They mended me as best they could and treated me kindly when other masters would have left me to die. I wondered what was in his mind and saw that Mistress was watching me all the while, that cool, considering look on her face once more.

'Good man, good man,' he nodded. 'We stand by our own, Wat, as you know, and if you help us in this matter you'll never regret it.'

'What matter, Master?' I ventured and saw Osburga's shoulders convulse as she sobbed, while her mother looked fierce.

'The matter of the late monk,' he said, with a crack in his voice. 'It seems he did badly by Mistress Osburga and left her for dead...'

She raised her head to deny this, but he broke in on her. 'Well, well, no sense in talking, the lad has paid for his sin but there is another trouble come upon us.' He glanced hopefully at his wife but she sat there, her eyes demurely lowered.

'The thing is, Wat,' he lowered his voice. 'Mistress Osburga has need of a husband and that right soon, there must be no delay. Will you serve your master in this matter and be joined in lawful wedlock with my daughter?'

I tried to speak but the cough overcame me and I had to sink to the floor. In the darkest watches of the night such a thing had never occurred to me. I could scarce believe it.

'Well, lad?' He was jovial now the secret was out. 'What say you? Our daughter's shame must never be told, but you're a good and loyal servant and we believe you are the man to trust in this matter. You shall not lose by it, upon my oath.'

I spent the next days in a state of bewilderment. Master arranged for the wedding to take place quietly at the Priory with Father Prior himself performing the ceremony. I was taken indoors and washed and trimmed and dressed in a tunic finer than I had ever worn and Mistress was warmer in her manner and smiled at me now and then, stiffly to be sure, but with none of that awkwardness, looking away rather than face me.

When the time came to cross the river to the Priory I set off in fine spirits, conscious that the folk at the farm were agape with astonishment at my luck. There were murmurs, to be sure, that there was some secret afoot, but they spoke kindly. One or two of the men even knowing that I was not whole, clapped me on the shoulder and made bawdy jokes when there was no danger Master might hear.

Not if I were to be torn in twain would I confess to them what Master had said. 'Though you sleep within the house, Wat, Mistress Osburga will sleep alone. We'll preserve the look of the thing but this is a marriage in name only, you hear me?'

I nodded. In truth my chest was so painful and my cough so exhausting, I had no room for lustful thoughts – or means to act upon them anyway. It was enough to know I could be of service to my young mistress and her kin and I swore to be faithful unto death.

'This is the man?' Father Prior gave me a cold glance as I scuttled along in the family's wake. 'I hope you will not betray the trust your master puts in you – er – Wat?'

'Wat Wellman, my lord,' I answered, aglow with pride for Master had told me himself that this should be my name henceforth, as I was to become one of the family.

The ceremony was short and private and in less time than I thought possible I found myself married and back at the house for a small feast to mark the occasion.

'Have you some more of that syrup, Mistress?' I asked in a quiet moment as dusk approached. 'My cough was sorely troublesome last night and has been so all day and if I'm to sleep within doors I fear to disturb the household. Your

medicine soothes my chest so well, 'tis like magic.'

'No magic, Wat,' she said, not meeting my eyes. 'Just herbs and honey – and – I've added poppy juice – warranted to take away all your troubles.' She reached for a small flask. 'Here, Wat, take this when you lie down on your bed.' She looked sorrowful for a moment then straightened her shoulders. 'May God grant you rest this night and ever after.'

(v)

As I left the museum I felt sorry for the poor young monk, if that's what he was, but at least the museum volunteer's story had taken my mind off the strange psychic woman. Feeling calmer I dropped into the nearest pub for soup and a roll.

At home, an hour later, the landline rang. Louise.

'Are you okay?' The warm, anxious voice comforted me, pushing aside the confusion and loneliness. 'Why not shut the time warp for a week or two and come to us?'

'I'll be fine,' I felt better at once. 'I've got just over a week's holiday left and I'm going to explore the town, but thanks anyway. I'm not upset anymore, it was just weird.'

'I was always a bit nervous around your mum,' Lou said tentatively. 'She was such a perfectionist I was terrified I'd spill something and make a mess. Your dad was a love, though.'

'He was, wasn't he? Though he'd do anything for a quiet life and I used to wish he'd... Oh well. As for Mum, she had impossibly high standards,' I said ruefully.

It had been a strange day and I was exhausted, what with the close encounter with a psychic and the hours spent weeding in the afternoon. I'd poked in the vegetable patch and surveyed the bramble-covered rockery at the bottom of the garden, but it looked uninviting so that was a project for another day.

After supper I wandered into Dickon's Room, with a glass of wine. Patrick's flowers were in the place of honour on the great mantelpiece with its strange carving of a running hare.

What to do? It was still early and if I went to bed I'd only lie awake, tossing and turning, but I had no urge to start anything new. That was when I remembered the wooden box in Violet's bedroom. If any clue to my astonishing legacy existed it must be there.

'Better get it over with.' As I bent to smell Patrick's flowers and leaned my head against the cool stone of the mantelpiece I had an overwhelming urge to call him.

Better not. There was that yawning gap between us lately where before, there had been friendship and laughter. Did he...? I reached up and stroked the stone hare that ran its endless race – and forced myself to look at a future without Patrick.

Feeling sick, I shook my head and made reluctantly for the stairs. Once more I had that strange impulse that I should apologise to Violet for intruding on her privacy but the feeling in the house reassured me.

The top papers in the box turned out to be a bundle of Christmas and birthday cards so I set them aside. The next thing I took out was a copy of my own birth certificate. The full one.

What on earth?

My hands shook as I smoothed out the creases and scanned it, wide-eyed. My place of birth was down as 2 Farm Close, Ramalley, Hampshire.

I only ever remembered seeing the short certificate, probably last time I applied for a passport, which – of course – was at the flat so I couldn't check. No wonder Ramalley had sounded familiar. Mum had told me I was born in Hampshire but she didn't go into detail.

I felt humbled. Violet had left me her house because I was born here.

I ran downstairs for another glass of wine before checking the other contents of the box. The solicitor had offered to store the deeds of the house but here were some fascinating newspaper cuttings clipped together. The top one, dated 1960, had a headline: 'Retirement of Miss Dorothy Wellman, popular Headmistress of Ramalley Primary School', showing a woman surrounded by small children. I laid it aside, wondering who she was. The surname suggested a relative.

I left the letters unread for now and picked up another birth certificate. Violet Wellman, born 18th January 1919, registered by her mother Dorothy – so that's who she was. The space was left blank where the father's name should have been. Something else to think about but for the present... My eyes were drawn to a folded piece of paper at the bottom of the box.

I felt strangely reluctant to pick it up. It might just be a misplaced shopping list but on the other hand...

I unfolded the paper and found a handwritten account of an agreement between Violet Wellman, Marion Gibson and Stephen Michael Gibson in early September 1982. I read it slowly, trying to take in the significance of the bald phrases.

An arrangement had been made between Violet and the two Gibsons, my parents, namely that, as soon as possible, Violet would procure a woman who would agree to bear a child for them; a child that Stephen would father.

At this point, I gasped aloud, my hand clapped to my mouth.

The next paragraph stated, just as impersonally, that Violet would look for two or three candidates to allow for failure. The reward for a successful pregnancy would be five thousand pounds to be paid through Violet. If a woman failed to become pregnant or was not needed after she had agreed, she would receive five hundred pounds.

Squeezed in at the bottom of the page was a note: a healthy female child had been born on Friday, the first of April 1983, my birthday, but that the mother refused to accept the five thousand pounds. There was no mention of how many lesser sums, if any, had been paid out.

Freya Marion, weighing 6lb 1oz, was delivered at 4.30 in the afternoon by Violet, and the birth of a female child born to Marion and Stephen Gibson was registered the following day.

Chapter Six

(i)
Saturday, 7ᵗʰ March

Despite the shock and feeling of loss, because it was a kind of bereavement to know that Mum wasn't my mother, I slept soundly, untroubled by dreams of decapitated corpses or psychic voices. I woke with a start on Saturday morning. Patrick had been standing by the mantelpiece downstairs, staring at the running hare in the carving. In my dream he turned to me and smiled, his eyes alight with amusement, and something else I couldn't read. 'Freya,' he said, holding out his hand to me… Then I woke up.

I was confused. I'd been Patrick's PA for more than two years, just as his books hit the best-seller lists and offers started to roll in. Although adventure stories aren't my favourite form of fiction I appreciate the skill that goes into his fast-paced military action thrillers; his writing is good and the plots have huge numbers of fans on the edge of their seats.

Shy and business-like at first, our working relationship soon developed into a close friendship that suited me fine, but lately I'd caught Patrick looking at me with an unreadable expression. Then there was that unexpected kiss at the airport. What did that mean? And how to reconcile that with my sense that he had retreated into himself?

'You lock things away in boxes inside your head,' Louise observed once. 'While I run around like a headless chicken you just get on with things,' she'd added. 'It's an admirable way to behave but I sometimes wonder if you ought to let rip once in a while, Freya. You're so organised and controlled I worry you'll snap one of these days.'

She was right. I *am* organised and tidy and always one step ahead, it's the way I function. I sighed as I ate tea and toast, making yet more lists, but however much I was in denial I knew there were things beyond my control and that was unsettling to someone like me. There were two of Louise's 'boxes' that I'd have to open soon; the one with Patrick inside and now the other one, into which I'd thrust last night's disturbing discovery. I braced myself. I'd need time to take this in and make my peace with it – but not today.

The sun was struggling through the clouds so I ran upstairs and leaned out of the back window. The house was on a slight rise and the land sloped down past the boundary wall. Beyond rose Puss Hill, dotted with sheep and lambs, but with no sign of a mad March hare anywhere.

Time to explore, so I tucked all the unanswered questions back in their boxes. Like Scarlett O'Hara, I'd think about that tomorrow.

Parking was not allowed directly in front of the house but there was plenty of hard-standing on either side of the road. There was no vehicle access to my garden at present but I hoped it might be possible to organise something. The garden was mostly lawn and thanks to the gardener sent in by the helpful solicitor there was nothing major to be tackled apart from the wilderness at the far end, though it must have been too much for Cousin Violet for ages. I recognised the rowan tree and immediately behind the house were the flagstones I'd weeded the day before, surrounded by crocuses and primroses, daffodils and violets, some already flowering.

Yesterday I'd thought Sleeping Beauty's impenetrable hedge of thorns at the bottom of the garden looked uninviting and even in this morning's sunshine I approached it warily. It still didn't appeal. I gave it a reluctant poke with a stick and hit rubble. Could it be the ruins of a privy? I made a face at the idea of hiking all the way down the garden on a snowy night.

The sunshine was warm for the middle of March and I wandered round, notepad in hand as I made yet another list, this time noting the condition of the fences and trying to identify some of the plants. More money, I sighed but I wasn't worried. Apart from my time in America I've always been an optimist and I could feel something almost like happiness beginning to bubble up inside.

Violet had given me this chance and I wasn't going to mess it up. Should I go back to the library and email Patrick with an outline of my ideas? No, I was supposed to be on holiday. I chewed at my bottom lip and wondered. He was disciplined and patient by nature and it seemed unlikely that he'd sack me on the spot – the idea sent a chill through me and I gave myself a shake, suddenly thoughtful.

'You like Patrick,' Louise had said and she was right. I let myself acknowledge it. I *did* like him, and in spite of my niggling anxiety over his current abstraction – could it just be over a new book? – I remembered the message of love with his flowers. This wasn't the right time to open that particular box I told myself sternly, but for some reason I felt surprisingly cheerful anyway.

Patrick would soon be back in England and I'd deal then with whatever was – maybe – happening between us but there was something even more pressing. Two things really, though they might be connected. I'd thought the psychic woman mad when she claimed my mother was alive; it made no sense at the time, but now? Violet's note mentioned the woman or women she planned to recruit for this baby caper. Could it be true? It was hard to see how or why anyone would invent it but how to find out? Mary Draper might know, but would she tell?

(ii)

I'd been so shaken the previous day that I'd forgotten half the things I wanted, so after lunch I decided to walk over the bridge and explore; a ten or fifteen minute walk, according to Mary. The sun was out and if I followed the sound of church

69

bells I should end up at the Priory. I window-shopped in Paradise Row, one of several narrow alleys, and was attracted by a poster in the window of a shop selling crystals and dragons. It advertised the forthcoming appearance of well-known psychic, Ann Freeman, whose pale eyes stared out from the photograph.

I made a note of the time and walked on but when I arrived at the Priory I was foiled in my attempt to explore inside because half-a-dozen sparkly bridesmaids with fairy wings spilled out of a stretched limo so I headed instead towards the department store across the Square. The owner of the café by the market, Nonie somebody, was wiping down tables in the sunshine and gave me a friendly wave. It seemed odd that in only a couple of days I was already on nodding and waving terms with three women: Alison, Mary and Nonie at the café.

All right, they were all older than I was, but that was rather nice, comforting somehow. There'd be younger friends in the future.

I enjoyed pottering so I set aside all the things that were on my mind: a box for this weird stuff about my mother; a box for Patrick; a box for what I needed to do in the house. Bracewell's, the small department store, had a good coffee shop and a large section for carpets, curtains and upholstery fabrics. I would check them out later on.

Back home I had a sudden urge to climb over the garden wall and scramble up Puss Hill. The view from the top was amazing. The town spread out below and the river meandered westward until it joined up with the River Test. Although the sun was still shining the wind whistled through a gnarled clump of hawthorn bushes and with a last look along the hills behind me, I beat a retreat.

I spent a lazy evening listening to Violet's old radio and prowling about the house making plans until I went to bed. The lack of Wi-Fi and 3G made me realise how much I relied on my smart phone and iPad but just for now I was beginning to enjoy the novelty of being offline even though I usually answer emails, texts and messages as they arrive. The one thing I did miss was the constant dialogue with Patrick, wherever he happened to be, asking about this, complaining about that. I knew he'd never dream of interrupting my holiday so I was using this hiatus to consider my feelings for him. And his for me...

I couldn't sleep so I picked up the family history Violet had left me. I was tantalised by the snippets Miss Montagu dropped into her narrative and promptly abandoned unexplained, but having read her notes several times now, I knew I was lucky to have this much knowledge of the place. Resigned, I turned to the next page. Her writing style was dull and I was sleepy by the time I reached her views on whether Ladywell had been affected by the Black Death in the middle of the fourteenth century.

'There is reason to believe a small chapel was built at Ladywell in the late twelfth century to manage the steady traffic of pilgrims to try the healing waters. *See my attached note.*' (It wasn't, of course. Attached, I mean. It had probably been lost for decades.) 'It is likely that this was founded by the renowned Bishop of Winchester, Henry of Blois, grandson of the Conqueror and brother of King Stephen. This chapel may have been an offshoot of the Knights Hospitallers from the nearby Precentory of Bedesleigh. Although records reveal that the plague swept through the town and the Priory, there is no evidence that Ladywell, safely across the river from the source of the illness, suffered. The dwellers at the farm must have thanked Providence for their safe delivery.'

Miss Montagu speculated that the purity of the water in the well might have contributed to their immunity from the Black Death and I suppose she could have been right. My last hazy thought was that if you drank clean water and washed in it occasionally, it must surely have increased your chance of survival. Still, I supposed the family *must* have escaped the plague since here I was, apparently, the last of the line.

I slept soundly for a third night in a row, though my dreams were too fleeting to recall, and I woke on Sunday morning with a new sense of purpose.

I had no idea how things would work out but I was more

and more certain I was in the right place, that this old house at Ladywell was where I was meant to be.

(iii)

Philippa shuddered awake as a shaft of pale spring sunlight slanted across her face. The room dipped and swayed, the slightest movement painful, every bone, every muscle aching. When she dragged herself upright she found herself in a tangle of soiled linen in Mistress Isabel's own bed in the upper chamber.

A faint mewing startled her. Beside her lay Isabel herself, all skin-and-bones, tell-tale swellings at her neck. Shallow breaths scarcely lifted the bony chest and a dribble of dark blood gathered and fell from the ashen lips.

Philippa drew back in horror, staring at the ravaged body of her young mistress.

Plague? Here? She held her breath and listened. The house was always alive; chatter around the fire; folk great and small to see the master; monks and an occasional pilgrim to the holy well. The family: Mistress Isabel and her parents, the Master and the Mistress, the hub of the whole place.

Not a sound. Nothing but the rapid, fluttering gasps of the girl beside her.

Her head began to clear and Philippa remembered fevered dreams, pain and sickness, constant wailing.

Sweet Jesu! Did I take the sickness too? She searched and recoiled from the foul stickiness of a burst bubo under her arm. She stank of vomit and pus, as vile as the disgusting smells from the overflowing piss pot, and she gagged. Days, she must have been shut away in here. How could that be? Who else was here? She raised her head again. The farmhouse lay way from the main roads, protected by the remnant of the great royal forest to the west. But never so quiet, never so still.

Master Godwin and his lady, silent behind the screen. What of them?

'Did they all flee when the nightmare began? Leaving us helpless?'

The silence pressed down on her and she shuddered. 'I remember screams,' she frowned. 'And my head, like to split asunder, but...are we two the only living souls?'

Her voice echoed in the silence and suddenly she was full of practical thoughts: something to wear, something to eat. A foot to the ground had her sprawling on the floor, feeble as a baby.

The stench in the room was overpowering but she hauled herself up staggering like an old woman. Isabel won't grudge me a gown to cover my nakedness, she thought. It was Isabel, dearest friend and closest ally at the Manor, who had insisted Philippa be trained as her waiting woman.

Master Godwin's wife insisted on being addressed as the Lady Hilda though her husband was a mere farmer and, what was even less acceptable to her high notions, also a merchant dealing in wool, though she liked his money. Neither could deny their delicate only child.

'I trust you will serve your mistress well,' was the lady's icy comment to the living reminder of her husband's solitary lapse in all their years of marriage. It was a nagging sore to the Mistress, a malignant providence that caused the true daughter to be frail and the bastard upstart, the changeling, to bounce with good health and vitality. That the girl's grandmother had been a by-blow of an earlier master of the farm was a double shame, swallowed with haughty dignity.

Philippa braced herself to peer behind the screen that separated Isabel from her parents but her father and his wife were beyond mortal help, as was the serving maid huddled on the floor. Sick with fear, Philippa clutched at the bedpost for support. Surely that was the Lady Hilda's best pewter jug on the windowsill? She gulped down great mouthfuls of water before going back to Isabel to dip a cloth into the jug to squeeze water on to the cracked lips. Praise be, the fever had broken, but Isabel lay still, her eyelids bruised and purple. Philippa dabbed with the wet cloth again and tidied the straggle of light brown hair.

'I'm going downstairs, sweeting,' she whispered to the unconscious girl. *'I won't be long'.*

Her shift was soiled beyond wearing, so she took a cloth from the coffer under the window and wiped herself as clean as she might before dressing in a linen shift. Did it belong to Isabel or her mother? No matter, Isabel grudged her sister nothing and the lady would complain no more. Next was a robe of fine wool, woven and dyed russet only last year by her own hands, then with her hair braided tidily under a kerchief she was ready for whatever awaited her.

(iv)

She swallowed a sob and ventured down the narrow stair. There were no other bodies; the entire household must have fled to the village, those who had not died. She threw wide the great door and a bracing wind made her shiver but would cast out the stench of death. What next? Food... In a crock she found half a loaf turning mouldy.

'They say the sickness can take days,' she seized a knife and scraped away the powdery blue crust, then softened the bread in a beaker of ale. It tasted stale but she sucked at it until a movement near the cold hearth near scared her out of her wits. Master Godwin's favourite dog rolled his eyes at Philippa, but nuzzled her hand, seeking comfort.

'I wish you could talk, old friend,' she said, fondling the soft ears, glad of the company. *'How many days has it been? Isabel complained of a headache, and the Lady Hilda retired to her chamber, also clutching her head. Was that the start of the fever?'*

Master Godwin, a genial man, had seemed unusually irritable. She struggled to remember. The Precentor...

'Yes, the Precentor was here. Father said it was an honour.' She pictured the tall old man taking farewell of her father and crossing the meadow to the chapel beside the well. Something else... *'I took the pitcher,'* she faltered. *'I followed at a respectful distance and as I drew the water I said the words.'*

74

The words and the water; the words you always said when you drew the water, in health or in sickness. Had she known there was danger? The words, passed down from mother to daughter, aunt to niece, known only to the women. No more surprising that the sun had risen than that she should say the words of power; but when? Yesterday? Earlier?

It was hopeless, there was a veil drawn across her memory, but there was that pitcher. The Lady Hilda's pride and joy was not on its usual shelf but in the upper chamber where Philippa was certainly not welcome.

I must have carried it, she guessed; did it save my life? Everyone knows the water at Ladywell has virtue.

She found a bone for the dog and scraped mould off a hard lump of cheese, sniffing at some smoked ham, then put it with some of the bread into a small basket. There was more ale in a flagon too so she headed back towards the staircase, pausing with a groan and a hand in her aching back.

'Help, please help! Is someone there?'

Horror! Her knees gave way and she sank onto the bottom stair, holding firm to her basket lest its meagre contents spill. Again, a weak cry from the family parlour, the one place she had not yet explored. She hauled herself up, trembling as she followed the cry. The parlour door was open...

'Who...Who is there?' Philippa crossed herself, 'Lady, guide me, Lady keep me safe.' Conventional words but her prayer was to a different Lady – the one who watched over the holy well.

An arm waved feebly in the air for an instant.

Gathering her wits Philippa seized her basket, hitched up her skirt, and stumbled into the room. What she took to be a bundle of draperies resolved itself into a young man, half-dressed and huddled for warmth in a tapestry, Lady Hilda's pride and joy torn from the wall. He blinked at her.

'What... what happened? Where is my... where is everyone?'

She poured ale and held the beaker to his lips. 'Here, take a sip. You'll feel stronger if you can take a bite too.'

He clutched modestly at the tapestry and sipped at the ale while she fed him some moistened bread, like a baby bird. Morsels of cheese followed in quick succession.

'I never remember being so hungry,' he croaked, looking affronted at the bubble of hysterical laughter that escaped her.

'We must both have taken the plague, but none so badly,' she stammered, sobering. 'Here...' She took a brisk look and found the telltale signs in his armpit where the swelling had burst. She ignored his blushing protest and spoke as though to a child.

'You need something to wear,' she patted his shoulder. 'We have to...we must discover who... what is left.'

The forlorn body of another young man lay nearby amid scattered belongings. She picked up a shirt, a good woollen tunic and hose.

'Here,' she found a cloth. 'Clean yourself first. I think... there were two of you?' He nodded wearily as she struggled to remember. A young knight, Sir Robert le Ridet, and his attendant squire, the two young men. They brought no servants but had they had brought the plague? She counted the days. No, that was wrong; Isabel took sick the night they arrived so the plague was here already.

He hesitated, staring first at the tunic in her hand and then, through eyes suddenly filled with tears, at his companion. His lips tightened and he knelt clumsily beside the body, his head bowed in prayer.

Philippa sank to a bench, grateful for a moment's respite, not able yet to face her own loss, nor yet to give way to desolation. To keep at bay the storm of tears that threatened to engulf her she rose, steadier on her feet now, and prowled about the room while the young man struggled to compose himself.

'Come now' she ordered. 'Dress yourself. A tapestry is not knightly attire.'

After a prayer that broke on a sob, he whispered, 'I can scarce think straight.'

Her voice grated, harsh and bitter. 'They are dead and we are living. All we can do is survive'.

She picked restlessly at a loose thread on her sleeve and braced herself to put the past behind her: a precious jewel to be taken out and savoured when she felt safe. 'Dress yourself, the sun may shine outside but the month is March and none so warm you can risk your death of cold.'

'No... you're right,' he said slowly, with another despairing glance at his dead companion as he reached out for the clothes.

'I'll be above stairs.' The memory of Isabel smote her conscience.

'Dear God, sweeting,' she cried at the chamber door. 'Forgive me. Here's food and water. We'll have you well in no time.'

Her words echoed in the chamber where wan sunlight struggled through the narrow window and cruelly illuminated the gaunt, blue-tinged features of the girl in the bed. Isabel lived but barely, every breath a struggle.

The stench in the room was overwhelming so Philippa dragged the fouled bedding behind the screen, though the piss pot and its contents went out of the window. She moistened the cracked lips again, tempting her with stale bread dipped in the water from the well. 'Lady,' she whispered. 'Help her, help us.' And she murmured again the words of the Lady's prayer, over and over.

Water dribbled over Isabel's chin and Philippa cast around in dread. 'Some oil,' she gasped and ran to the inner room. 'Your mother's precious perfumed oil will help you, dear one.' She dabbed it on the blue-veined temples: nothing, not a flutter only the faintest breath that scarce disturbed the air.

Shivering from fear and cold alike, she remembered her words to the young man downstairs: we must survive, she had said. To seize this second chance of life she must be warm so she clad herself in Lady Hilda's finest surcote, adding her father's handsome cloak for extra warmth.

'How thin I have grown, how pale.' She stared at her reflection in the Mistress's hand-glass and saw Isabel, her own face as fine-drawn as her sister's.

There was a tentative knock and the young man tiptoed in, haggard but handsome in the blue tunic.

'Mistress Isabel?' he whispered nervously.

'Here.' She handed him the bowl while she sponged the other girl, chiding him when he blushed and looked aside as she opened her sister's shift to check the angry swelling there.

'Sweet Jesu! Must I do all? 'Tis no time for modesty, I'm not asking you to wash her, just hold the bowl and mind you don't drop it. The well is too far and I'm none so steady on my feet yet.'

'I...beg pardon, mistress,' he stammered. 'I am not used to young ladies. You must be fond of her; your waiting woman and your half-sister, is she not? I believe your father mentioned her.'

She frowned at him absently, only half attending. Her waiting woman? Before she could correct him the girl in the bed gave a last gasping sigh and was gone.

Philippa drew a painful breath and held back her tears as she covered her sister's face, brusquely refusing any help. They went downstairs and she set him to sweep the floor.

'I'll fetch more water,' she said. 'No, I know the way. Thank you,' she added wearily.

At the well she said the words that were as natural to her as breathing then gulped down great draughts of the healing water until the tears finally flowed. Back at the house the young man was no longer alone. There was a newly-kindled fire in the hearth and an elderly woman, haggard and anxious, stood at his side. Almost faint with relief Philippa steadily held her gaze until the old woman held out her arms.

'Mistress – Isabel, my dear, dear lamb.' She folded the wary girl in her trembling arms. 'This young gentleman told me all, but oh, to find you safe and well when your poor father and his lady are...' She closed her eyes and shivered. 'I found my...granddaughter...'

'Oh, Cicely.' It was a shudder of relief. She hugged the old woman even more closely. 'You're alive, I scarcely dared

hope.' She turned to the young knight with a tremulous smile and tears on her cheeks. 'This is Cicely, my – my nurse. My half-sister was her...' She paused and took a deep breath, spurred on by an encouraging squeeze from Cicely. 'Philippa was her granddaughter.'

The old woman met her eyes in a long, level gaze. After a few moments she gave a decided nod and patted the slim shoulder.

'I could not rise from my bed,' she shook her head. 'The sickness spread through the steading and I hungered for news of you – of all here in the house. There are folk fit to tend the beasts now so they've been fed at last, and none dead of neglect, praise the Lady. There's work enough to do,' she added, kind but brisk. 'This young gentleman is heaven-sent to help us. Take a bite, young sir, we have sad and heavy work before us this day, then do you seek the holy brothers at the chapel yonder.' She picked up her basket. 'Here is fresh-baked bread, some cheese too. I'll warrant you are ready for it and Phi – Mistress Isabel has brought water from the well. It will not help the dead if we starve.'

Philippa diligently followed her grandmother's commands and with the help of some hardy souls who trailed up from the village, the dead were laid out in the garden and a fire lit to burn the fouled mattresses and linens. None of them had strength to dig a grave today but a murmur of voices announced a party coming from the chapel.

'I am Father Mark, the Sub-Prior, and here is Brother Peter.' The taller man made the introductions. ' Father Prior sent us from town to enquire after all here but there is no-one still living at the chapel, not even the Precentor. It is a great joy to find you safe, Mistress Isabel, though I grieve for the loss of your honoured parents.' He looked grave and added, 'The sickness struck with deadly speed and only now, after days of it, are we counting the cost. Even the Priory has but nineteen souls still living. Nowhere is untouched and half the townsfolk dead.'

They had brought with them four lay brothers who were set to work at a safe distance from the house where the western hills met the lower meadows and Father Mark conducted a hasty funeral with the suddenly distraught Philippa as chief mourner. Despite the present turmoil in her mind she wept as her father and Isabel were buried in the communal grave.

At length all was done. The young man, who had been an invaluable help once he began to regain his strength and set aside his sorrow, fidgeted on the bench beside the long table as Father Mark considered what was to be done. The old nurse, Cicely, stood quietly to one side as befitted her station, but Philippa was conscious of her comforting presence. Not a word had passed between them that could not have been heard by any man, but the bargain was sealed and safe and Philippa had her grandmother's blessing on what she planned.

Master Godwin had been eager to secure this impoverished and landless knight as a bridegroom for his daughter, the last of his line. He hoped to establish an heir and found a dynasty though not every potential husband of rank would care to overcome the joint drawbacks of a sickly bride and a father-in-law of yeoman stock. Money, though, could open most doors and smoothe away most difficulties, and Master Godwin's coffers were temptingly full and the farm exceedingly prosperous.

Philippa's head was filled with memories of those she had buried. The servants from the farm had been all but wiped out though the village, a handful of cottages, had fared better. Was it only luck, or had the water she always drank from the Lady's well played a part in her survival? Master Godwin had scorned the old tradition of the healing properties and preferred to sup on ale, while his lady haughtily drank her wine.

She looked sidelong at the priest and made up her mind.

'Father Mark, I believe Sir Robert le Ridet was in correspondence with my father about a marriage.' She chose her words with care. 'My mind is a maze and I know not how far the arrangements had progressed before I took ill, but I am the last of the family now. There is none other to inherit.'

There, she had said nothing but the exact truth and she had staked her claim. Philippa held her breath as she raised her eyes to stare at the young knight.

He cleared his throat nervously as they all looked to him.

'Do you have the documents, young sir?' Father Mark spoke with compassion for the young man's grief.

'It... everything was ready,' he managed to croak, looking at the priest in surprise. 'The marriage was to be held the next day but Mistress Isabel was the first to sicken.'

He bowed towards her and to the priest, and rummaged in his belongings.

'Here are the papers, Father, all signed by both parties, the Precentor also.'

Philippa glanced under her lashes at the young man.

Father Mark, decisive as befitted a man with his eye on the position of his ailing and enfeebled Prior, was aware of the advantage in having a tenant personally beholden to him.

'My children,' his smile was benevolent. 'I believe the best course of action in these sad circumstances is to allow matters to proceed as Master Godwin himself planned, and the Precentor sanctioned. A period of mourning should follow, of course, but the proprieties should be weighed against a steading left without a guiding hand at such a time. I am confident that Father Prior will approve.'

'I do not fear hard work, Father,' urged the young visitor. 'I can be of real use here and I have no ties. Let me learn to manage the steading for Mistress Isabel.'

The priest nodded, approving but impatient. 'That, young sir, is precisely what is in my mind. It may be that the chapel will no longer be separate from the Priory but that is not for us to decide.' He paused thoughtfully, rubbing his chin, while Philippa recalled her father's jovial laughter at the rivalry between the Precentor and the Prior who coveted the thriving trade in relics and miracles at the small chapel. Could the Precentor's death be a blessing in disguise for herself and her holding?

She blinked away tears as she recalled her father that last night, nodding politely at the honoured guest's witticisms,

81

while he winked at his beloved natural daughter standing so demurely behind her lady.

'The land must be worked,' said Father Mark. 'The beasts tended also and I propose to leave the lay brothers with you for now, to work the farm. After all, Master Godwin held this land under the Priory and you are thus, my dear child, under our guardianship. Rather than appoint another tenant I suggest you lay aside your grief and I will marry you and young Sir Robert here, at once.'

Philippa's head jerked up at that and she gazed round-eyed at the young man across the long oak table. He too raised his head in astonishment, jolted out of his grief by some shock that she failed to understand.

'But... but I'm not... It's a mistake. I mean...' His voice tailed away and he looked as though he had been struck a telling blow. As Philippa stared at him the curtain lifted a little and she had a blinding flash of revelation. Their eyes met and he flinched under her startled scrutiny as he stammered again. 'I can't... it wouldn't be...'

'Well, lad?' The kindly priest's patience was wearing thin. 'Not married already I take it?' He chuckled at his own jest. 'Come, come, I make due allowance for your sorrow and sickness, but time is pressing.'

They stared at each other, the boy trembling and confused but with a sudden calculation in his eyes and the girl, startlingly aware of his situation because of that brief moment of returning memory; sure too, that her own secret was unassailable. Only her grandmother knew and they were linked by blood, by affection and by expediency. Cicely would never give away the secret, so Philippa made up her mind. She took a deep breath and smiled wanly.

'As you wish, Father Mark,' she bowed her head.

She heard a long, shuddering sigh from her bridegroom, but not until they stood before the priest and were made man and wife, did she dare steal another glance at him.

May God forgive me, she prayed, *and I'm sure He will; after all, He helps those who help themselves. If nobody is left, the place will revert to the Priory and my father would rather have razed it to the ground with his own hands. This way Ladywell is safe.*

Her memory, though still fragmented after the fever, was coming back and that one clear image stood out.

She could picture Sir Robert le Ridet and his squire seated at table before her world changed forever. Sir Robert telling her father that no, he had no living relatives and would be glad, a landless knight, to settle in this quiet backwater and become a farmer after spending much of his life abroad.

She heard again her father's exclamation as he examined the young man's shield with its picture of a running hare while Sir Robert explained that the name 'Le Ridet' came from an ancient word for a hare.

'Dear Lord,' Master Godwin had spluttered. 'A hare, is it? 'Tis a match made in heaven for we have hares aplenty hereabouts.'

Sir Robert, with his sallow, pock-marked face and lank dark hair – and his attendant, with that thick thatch of light-brown Saxon hair and bright hazel eyes.

Taking note of her new husband's sturdy strength and the returning glow of health, his ruddy, fair colouring and the sudden spark of adventure that lit his face, Philippa thought of her beloved half-sister and of her father, Master Godwin, whose greatest anxiety had been that his line should continue and his holdings prosper.

'I feel no guilt,' she cried silently. 'This is the only way. I pledge myself to maintain my father's house and land as he would wish, and I pray for the Lady's blessing.'

She took a deep breath and held out her hand, with a smile that held a secret.

'Welcome, husband,' she cried. 'Welcome to your new home at Ladywell.'

Chapter Seven

(i)

Sunday, 8ᵗʰ March

Just after twelve I opened the door to Alison Dexter from Lamb Cottage over the road.

'Fancy lunch at the pub? The neighbours quite often drop in on a Sunday,' she explained. 'If anyone's there you'll get the introductions over.'

'The Fleece' was an unremarkable Edwardian building, warm and cheerful, with an open fire and a scatter of customers propping up the bar. Two women and a burly, white-haired man hailed Alison and made room for us.

'Hi, Alison.' That was the slender brunette in smart leather trousers. 'It's my shout today, what'll you have? And…' She smiled in my direction.

'Gin-and-tonic, thanks, Edwina,' Alison nodded. 'You too, Freya? I expect you've guessed this is our new neighbour, Freya Gibson, from number two. Freya, meet Edwina Malcolm who lives the other side of the pub on the main road, just round the corner.'

I smiled my thanks to Edwina as the second woman came forward, her hand outstretched.

'I'm Cathy Kingsmarsh,' she said. 'I live next door, at number three.' She and Edwina might be about the same age, I thought; somewhere between fifty and sixty, though Edwina looked younger, with her smart outfit and expensive grooming. Cathy was actually better-looking, with an attractive but fleeting smile, but her default setting seemed to be downcast. I wondered how well any of them had known my cousin Violet.

'And Edwina's friend, Graham Whitcombe,' Alison added.

We moved to a table near the fire and amid the chatter over lunch I was conscious that Edwina and Cathy were watching me. Well, of course they would, I told myself impatiently. Get a grip. I'm an incomer; they're bound to be interested.

'Did you all know Violet Wellman?' My words fell into a sudden hush as Cathy and Edwina broke off their conversation and stared at me. I felt as though I'd said something embarrassing. 'I just wondered about her,' I explained. 'I didn't know her at all, you see, so I thought perhaps…'

'I was born in number three,' Cathy said. 'Miss Wellman actually delivered me and apart from a few years when I worked in Brighton I've lived next door to her all my life.'

'I'd never even heard of her,' I said, 'but I gather she was well-known as a midwife. I half-expected to find hundreds of baby photos around the house, but I haven't found any yet.'

'She did have lots,' Cathy nodded. 'Every shelf and table was covered, but when her sight started to go she burnt all the photos and gave the frames to the hospice shop. She said she'd be irritated if she couldn't see to dust them all and she had her memories anyway.'

'That's right,' Edwina chimed in. 'Practically everyone in Ramalley over the age of about thirty-five was delivered by Miss Wellman. Our photos were there, Cathy's and mine.'

Alison sat beside me.

'What do you do for a living, Freya?' she enquired and their heads swivelled round.

'Me? I work for Patrick Underwood, the novelist. I'm his PA and researcher.' There was a stir of interest, particularly from Cathy who perked up immediately and clasped her hands together.

'Patrick Underwood?' she breathed in awe. 'Oh, he's one of my all-time favourite authors, his books are marvellous. I saw him in that documentary and he was so good-looking and funny.'

Edwina rolled her eyes. 'What a stroke of luck, Cathy.'

She looked across the table at me. 'It's quite an honour,' she gave a light laugh. 'Patrick's not far behind Elvis as far as Cathy's concerned and she's got all his books. Fancy you working for him, Freya.'

'What's he like?' Alison put in. 'He comes across as quiet and charming but tough in interviews. Is he really like that?'

'He's all those things,' I agreed. 'He did two tours of duty in Afghanistan and was wounded and decorated though he likes that kept quiet, so yes, he's pretty tough. He's quiet too, until he knows people really well.'

'He's ex-SAS, isn't he?' The man with Edwina broke into the conversation for the first time.

'He's certainly had some adventures,' I said. 'It's all good for the books and he has friends still serving. They keep him up-to-date when it comes to research.'

'Why did he leave the army anyway?' That was Cathy. 'He was due for promotion to major. Didn't he want to go on up the ladder?'

'He was left with a problem in one eye,' I explained, keeping it brief. 'Although he recovered well, laser surgery wasn't an option unfortunately and he felt it wasn't good enough for the job in hand. He could have gone on to Staff College and further promotion but that wasn't for him so he left and went into a City job.'

It was no business of mine to speculate about Patrick and the SAS and I kept quiet about the one time Patrick had let me briefly into his private hell.

'I was bloody good at my job but I couldn't do it properly if I wasn't at the top of my game,' he'd told me quietly, his face impassive. 'Staff College didn't appeal so I went into the City.' His face had creased in a cynical grin. 'That was even more of a battlefield.'

I knew what he was talking about. His previous PA gave me a brief but very confidential run-down during the handover before she retired.

'The City job was fine,' she sniffed. 'His heart wasn't in it but he did well and it took his mind off not being in the Army any more, but then a colleague got her claws into him and pushed and nagged him to go higher and higher.' She shook her head. 'All he really wanted to do was write thrillers and settle down with a family. He'd actually done rough drafts of the first three books, in his spare time while he was still in the army, though he'd never sent them to an agent. Marriage and babies had no place on *her* agenda and when he started writing the fourth book she made her choice and dropped him in favour of the chairman of the board.'

She held my gaze as she fired her parting shot. 'He thinks his heart's broken,' she smiled fondly. 'It's not, of course, but I'd be grateful if you'd treat him gently till he's over it. Look after him for me, he's a good lad.'

'He stayed on in the City,' I told Cathy. 'When his first book went into a bidding war and was such a huge success, he decided to risk writing full-time. The rest is history.'

'You *are* lucky to know him so well,' she sighed. 'Is there any chance he'll come to Ramalley? It would be wonderful to meet him and maybe get him to sign all my books.'

I wondered if they'd think me rude if I got up and left after lunch but luckily Alison glanced at her watch and squawked, 'Heavens, I must get back. I've missed a week and I'm off on that course on Tuesday, there's a ton of work to catch up with before tomorrow. Coming, Freya?'

It was the signal for the group to break up and there was a general movement towards the door. Edwina and her man turned right while Alison and I waited for Cathy to finish fussing with her coat.

(ii)

I spent another afternoon weeding and hoped I wasn't pulling up anything rare or endangered. Harry Makepeace, my friendly solicitor, had been right. It was a sizeable property when you looked at the extent of the garden and there was the funny little beauty parlour too. When the legal stuff was sorted I'd need to see if I could let the place. My initial inspection had revealed an open space downstairs, divided at the back into a tiny kitchen, with a loo and one room upstairs. It looked snug enough so perhaps I could get away with painting it throughout and cut down on expense.

I sat on the wall at the bottom of the garden with a mug of tea in my hand and admired the shadows of the clouds on the hillside. I couldn't hear any traffic, just the birds singing and the rustle of grass as it rippled in the light breeze.

Suddenly a brown head was raised just across the dried-up stream and a bright amber eye stared straight at me.

I held my breath and the hare emerged warily from the long grass, still watching me, and we stayed there, woman and animal, alone and silent. With a skip and a flirt of its long legs the hare leaped away up the hill, leaving me breathless and enchanted. A hare – a 'puss' – on Puss Hill.

Something else I remembered from my last discussion with the solicitor: 'There are legends about the hares of Ladywell,' he told me. 'Nothing specific, only that any man who hunts or kills a hare in the area will get his just deserts. There's certainly a clause in the deeds of your house that prohibits you from hunting or killing a hare.'

Soaking in a hot bath to soothe the stiffness after several hours' weeding I realised I'd spent a whole day without worrying about the past – or the future and furthermore had enjoyed lunch with a group of complete strangers. Real progress. Louise would say my self-esteem was clearly on the up and up!

I dithered about the Evening of Clairvoyance at the redundant chapel. Should I go? Would I regret it if I did? Would I regret it more if I didn't?

In the end, buoyed by that unexpected burst of confidence, I drove over the bridge into the centre of town. I was sceptical but the whole thing was so peculiar I felt I had to go. The red-brick building was open and I could see a few people heading that way. Common-sense told me to turn round and go straight back to Ladywell, but common-sense took a back seat. Something, someone – Violet? – insisted I should hear what, if anything, that strange woman had to say.

I felt a bit sick but there was no denying she'd been right. Not once I'd found that memo in Violet's box, so I took a deep breath and went in. If I sat near the back I could slip away if I hated it. A board carried the poster with the unflattering photograph and proclaimed that Ann Freeman was an internationally acclaimed clairvoyant, so I handed over the entry fee.

(iii)

Tonight's entertainment was evidently popular in Ramalley because the hall was more than half full, with seating for about fifty people.

Bustling here, there, and everywhere was the woman who had been with the psychic in the market, Diane something, so I kept out of her way in case she dragged me into the limelight as someone singled out by the star of the show. I bought a coffee and sidled to a seat near the back. I'd wondered what to wear but jeans, boots and a jumper under a warm jacket looked pretty standard among the audience.

There were more women than men by about ten to one and I was intrigued to see that they failed to fit any particular category, with quite a few young women as well as elderly ones, and several obvious mother-and-daughter pairs. A small neat woman in navy slipped into the seat beside me with a smile.

'She's very good, you know,' she confided. 'Have you heard her before?'

'No, I've never been to anything like this,' I volunteered, almost scalding my tongue as I sipped the boiling coffee. 'I've no idea what to expect.'

'Oh, you'll enjoy it, dear,' said my neighbour settling herself comfortably. 'Some people don't like it, you know; they think it's wrong. I find it uplifting though I've never had a message myself. And who's to say the messages don't come from the angels?'

I liked her idea and decided to go with the flow. Suddenly there was a ripple of excitement and Diane Whatshername –

Govern, that was it – strode importantly to the lectern and called for silence. Ann Freeman stood quietly and I studied her with interest. Better turned out than the other day, she was obviously in her working outfit, a high-collared blue blouse under a grey suit.

'Friends,' intoned Diane Govern, with unction. 'We are fortunate to have Ann with us, for the first time in Ramalley. Those who have heard her speak in Southampton will know that Ann is a gifted messenger who brings comfort and enlightenment to lonely and despairing souls.'

Ann Freeman waited for silence. She seemed more impressive in this setting than when she had grabbed my hand and forced herself on me and I began to relax. I had no expectation of a message but I'd at least hear her out. She gave a neat little speech of thanks and welcome, then cast a sweeping look round the hall.

'I'm with a lady over there,' she pointed to her left. 'One, two, six rows back. Yes, that's right, the lady in a green coat.'

The woman in question wore a look of mingled delight and apprehension.

'I have a gentleman here,' Ann informed her chattily. 'All I need from you is your voice to help me channel, as a bridge if you like. Say yes or no, but don't give me any clues He's giving me the name George. No, he says it's Gordon. Does that mean anything to you, dear?'

'Yes.' It was a frightened little voice.

Ann Freeman smiled encouragingly and continued. 'He's telling me he passed over with chest pains, a heart attack.'

'Yes,' agreed the woman in green, her hand fluttering to her mouth.

'It was very sudden,' said Ann with a solicitous frown. 'He'd never had a day's illness in his life, had he, dear?'

'No.' Tears trickled down the listener's cheeks.

'Now don't be upset,' soothed the medium. 'He wants you to know that he hardly suffered, just a brief pain, and then peace, but he's worried about you. You're to see the doctor at once, he's telling me; some problem with your knee. Is that right?'

'Yes,' she choked.

'There you are then,' Ann smiled with satisfaction. 'Our loved ones are just the blink of an eye away and they keep a loving watch all the time.'

I tried to hang on to my cynicism but I was impressed in spite of myself as Ann went round the hall with similar messages, though there were a couple of unexpectedly light-hearted moments.

'I've a message from Victor,' Ann announced and a middle-aged woman raised her hand.

'He says did you ever find his teeth?' To her credit Ann kept a straight face as the other woman goggled at her.

'No, we never did,' she said. 'It was embarrassing. We had to bury him without his dentures.'

'Well,' Ann told her solemnly. 'He wants me to tell you he absent-mindedly put them in an old treacle tin in his shed.'

'Fat lot of use that is,' snorted the bereaved daughter. 'We chucked his rubbish in a skip and sold the house.'

Most of the messages seemed trivial, about lost keys rather than lost teeth, and I was getting restive but there was a distraction. When I heard movement I glanced over my shoulder to the row behind. An elderly man was calmly rearranging three vacant chairs and as I watched he laid himself down across them. To my fascinated horror he took a small bottle out of his pocket and proceeded to put drops in his eyes, apparently oblivious to the stir this caused.

Ann Freeman halted in her progress round the hall and stared down at him.

'Aha,' she said, her pale face creasing with an unexpected glimpse of humour. 'My psychic senses tell me you've recently had trouble with your eyes.'

'My word,' he said earnestly, 'that's clever of you. I had my cataract done on Tuesday.'

Ann caught my eye though she clearly didn't recognise me and we waited, but he was quite serious. She shook her head with a faint smile in my direction and continued her demonstration.

One woman was exhorted to stop her feud with her sister

as it was causing pain to their late mother. Another heard she would soon be flying to New York, that it would not be a pleasure trip and that she knew why. One glance at the woman's scowl and clenched fists confirmed Ann was spot on. I was dying to know what it was about.

That moment of shared amusement banished all thought of escape and as the stories unfolded I forgot my own problems. After an hour Ann was slowing down and Diane Govern attracted her attention. She nodded wearily.

'Just one more,' she agreed, taking off her thick-lensed glasses and rubbing her eyes. She put them back on and looked benevolently at her audience.

'The young lady over there,' she indicated. 'That's right, dear.'

Oh God, she was pointing at me. I felt shaky, knowing I must look just like the other people chosen during the evening, excited but scared.

'I can't make this out,' Ann was struggling. 'I have your mother, but she *isn't* your mother. Does that make any sense?'

Mum – Marion, it *had* to be her.

'Yes,' I whispered through dry lips.

'She wants me to tell you that she loved you from the day you were born and that everything was done in love.'

Ann paused and tilted her head as she looked in my direction.

'Yes.' I could only manage a thread of a voice.

'I don't understand what she's trying to tell you,' Ann sounded puzzled. 'Something about an old man wearing a funny hat. And a necklace, I think. I'm sorry it's muddled, dear, it happens when I'm tired. All I can say is that you were conceived in love, you were born in love and you'll have love for the rest of your life. It's waiting for you just around the corner if you'll only open your eyes.'

With this, Ann Freeman smiled at the gathering and sat down heavily, slumping wearily into her chair. Diane called for thanks and appreciation of Ann's efforts and ended with a concluding prayer.

I sat through the closing proceedings without noticing anything. The woman in the next seat touched my arm tentatively as the hall began to empty. She'd been thrilled when Ann's attention fell on me, and sat open-mouthed as the confused message emerged, as though she felt a vicarious satisfaction at being so close to the action.

'Excuse me,' she whispered as I chewed over Ann's words. 'It's time to go, dear, they're shutting up shop.'

'What? Oh yes, I'm sorry.'

I snapped to attention and gathered up my bag and jacket, smiling politely as I made my escape. She clearly hoped to winkle out the story behind those cryptic remarks, but the last thing I wanted was to mull over the evening's events with a complete stranger. Come to think of it, I wouldn't even want to discuss this with a close friend. I couldn't, anyway, because Louise was visiting her in-laws who had even worse mobile phone reception and very dodgy broadband.

I suddenly realised I was starving. It was getting on for ten, and the rock cakes on sale had looked as though they lived up to their name, but now I could smell something enticing. I followed my nose to the fish-and-chip shop and was driving over the bridge when my phone bleeped.

'Plans changed, arrive LHR from Denver Monday morning. Talk soon. Patrick. X'

Chapter Eight

(i)

Monday, 9ᵗʰ February

I cursed the hold-up on the M3. What if I missed Patrick? He'd texted his flight details but I still had no idea what made me suddenly grab my keys and drive to Heathrow. It was just that when I woke before six, I knew I had to go. He wasn't expecting me; it was routine to let me know of any change in his plans, but the more I thought about it as I drove up the motorway, the more it made sense. I'd put aside my recent panicky doubts and pick him up, stopping for lunch on the way back to his flat, and then tell him about my cunning plan. What could go wrong?

I dashed into Arrivals and stared at the passengers meeting and greeting. No sign of Patrick, unless – wait a moment – there he was. An oddly disconsolate figure slumped on a chair, bags beside him, eyes closed and his glasses in his top pocket.

'Patrick?'

'Wha…? Oh, thank Christ it's you, Freya. I feel bloody awful.'

He looked it. His skin had a grey tinge to it and his usually bright grey eyes were red-rimmed and exhausted. His dark brown hair stuck to his forehead and he looked gaunt and haggard.

'What on earth… Is it your head, Patrick?' His legacy from Afghanistan, the head wound, had left him subject to crippling headaches. 'Did this start before you left Denver?'

He made an effort to sit up, groaning as he did so.

'Um, yes – no. It does ache, my head, but it's not that. It

was food poisoning before I left LA.' He paused and frowned. 'Must have been the fish. I wasn't right on the plane but I held it together till I got to Denver. I felt bloody awful by then so I grabbed a cab to the nearest airport hotel, which is where it all made a bid for freedom. I think I got rid of everything I've eaten in my entire life but at least I managed to collapse in private, thank God.'

'Oh, poor you,' I felt my heart flutter and I did sympathise but at least he'd managed a faint smile. I wondered what to do with him. It would be cruel to drop him home alone so I made the only possible decision.

'Come on,' I heaved him to his feet and propelled him towards the door. 'Are you okay to walk? Good, I'll bring your bags. It's not far.'

He wobbled a little and accepted the hand I gave him as we walked towards the multi-storey. Luckily I'd parked quite near so we toddled slowly to the car and I deposited him in the passenger seat while I raced off to the pay machine. God only knew how this was going to work out but I shelved the problem for the time being and suddenly came across a small, shuffling man in a blue boiler-suit, carrying a bucket. I never found out where he was going or why he needed a bucket, but it was a godsend. Not only that, it contained a paper towel roll that gave me an idea.

'Excuse me,' I accosted him hopefully. 'Can I buy your bucket? And the paper towels? I'll give you – twenty quid,' I added, when I checked my purse.

'No worries, love,' he said cheerfully as he took the twenty pound note, solemnly handed over the bucket, then legged it. I wondered what story, if any, he would concoct to explain the conspicuous absence of bucket.

Patrick was as I had left him, leaning back, eyes closed and looking dreadful, so I strapped him in, secretly alarmed at this childlike obedience. Patrick, by inclination and training, never did anything without first weighing up the pros and cons.

I slid into the driver's seat and put the bucket on his lap, with the contraband roll of paper in it.

It was raining by the time I pulled out of the car-park, saying, 'We're off; don't be sick on the paper towels.' I hesitated. 'This is no time for delicacy, Patrick, sorry. Are you just throwing up or are you erupting at both ends? I might need to plan for sudden stops en route.'

He opened his eyes at that and slid me a pained look.

'I'm not doing *anything* now,' he said, with dignity. 'I holed up in the hotel until it all calmed down and I could face a shower, then I organised my flight home. Don't worry, my bowels, as far as I dare state positively, are all right for the time being. I'm probably bunged up for life anyway. I've been popping Lomotil like Smarties, all across the Atlantic.'

He winced at my hard-hearted giggle and closed his eyes again, with a failing hand to his brow. Relief and a sudden glow of happiness filled me as he looked over at me with a faint grin before leaning back against the headrest. If Patrick was up to playing the drama queen he was feeling better. He was certainly pleased to see me and his colour had improved too.

Before I drove down the slip-road to join the motorway he was fast asleep which was all to the good, explanations could wait. My mind raced ahead. He'd have the front bedroom, of course; it would only take a few minutes to make up the bed. By some mercy the rain dwindled away to a slight drizzle by the time we drove down the hill towards Ramalley. The journey had been uneventful and Patrick slept the whole time, not stirring until I stopped outside Violet's house. My house.

'Wha...? Where...?'

'Everything's fine, Patrick,' I soothed. 'You'll feel much better in the warm.'

He let me lead him upstairs without protest.

'Go to the bathroom then you can sleep.' He hesitated. 'Off you go,' I said, giving him a gentle push in the right direction.

I ran downstairs to fetch the bucket in case of emergency and on my return found him sitting heavily on the edge of the bed. He looked exhausted by all this effort, getting upstairs, going to the bathroom, and he turned a bewildered face towards me.

He had me worried now and I knelt to take off his shoes. There was no trace of the frowning aloofness of recent weeks and I'd never seen him like this, meek and submissive, without a shred of his usual decision and competence. I got him out of his trousers and shirt too. I soon had him tucked up in bed with a hot-water bottle to put on his stomach to ease the soreness and found his prescription painkillers in his sponge bag.

He'd admitted to a headache so I made sure he took a pill.

'I'll leave the door open,' I said quietly as I pulled the curtains across. 'Give me a shout if you need anything, but try to sleep.'

He was almost off but he reached out as I straightened the fleecy blanket. He took my hand and held it to his cheek as he snuggled down like a trustful child and I caught my breath, immeasurably touched. It was so unlike the tough, self-contained Patrick I thought I knew. I gazed down at the suddenly young, vulnerable face on the pillow, with a clutch at my heart.

This would never do, I gently disengaged my hand. Helping him upstairs and into bed had disconcerted me because I was suddenly conscious that this was a man. How long had it been since Ben…? Ages since I really looked at a man. Supporting Patrick's long, lean body, brought home to me all that was lacking in my life.

I had no idea what to do about it.

(ii)

Luckily I wasn't called upon to do anything at that moment, not about my love life or lack thereof, and not about explaining the proposed changes to my way of living. I checked on Patrick every hour or so but he was dead to the world so I left him to it; sleep would do him more good than anything else. Leaving a note on the kitchen table I drove over to the supermarket in town and picked up bland food that ought not to upset an already disturbed stomach. The clouds parted after lunch so I put in several hours in the garden until only the bramble patch was left and I was staring at it unenthusiastically when Cathy from next-door called over the fence and handed me a cake. I liked her but didn't dare let on that Patrick was asleep upstairs. She'd certainly want to meet her idol and he was in no state to face a stranger. As it was, she hung around, chatting randomly about this and that, all the time darting glances at me when she thought I wasn't looking. Did she know about the baby plan? It made sense that Violet might have recruited her neighbour.

When she finally stopped talking I had a bath, made an omelette and spent a quiet evening reading and listening to the radio until at ten o'clock I heard him stumble along the landing.

I raced upstairs as he emerged from the bathroom looking better but still exhausted and half-asleep so I gave him another of his strong painkillers and tucked him up in bed again. An hour later I looked in on my way to bed and put a bottle of water beside him, with a glass and a couple of biscuits.

I straightened the bedclothes and it happened again, that sudden clutch at my heart; something physical as though I'd been grabbed and shaken. He'd caught the sun in California and his skin had a healthy glow, no longer tinged with that grey exhaustion. His breathing sounded less hurried too. I felt another pang when I spotted silver in the dark stubble but he still wore the vulnerable-child look that had so moved me earlier.

I swallowed and tip-toed out of the room feeling startled and expecting to lie awake all night, tossing and turning while I digested this new revelation, the way my feelings for Patrick had crept up and ambushed me. Alone in the dark I admitted that I'd loved Patrick all along, but did he feel the same? I'd been racked by anxiety for the last few weeks as he retreated into himself and, always an easy prey for self-doubt, I'd come to the conclusion that he wanted to break up our working relationship. Now, I didn't know. He'd turned to me when he was ill and miserable, so what did that mean? I dropped off straight away and slept through till half-past five, surprised that I hadn't tossed and turned all night.

Sleep eluded me so I dipped into Miss Montagu's notes which were as dull as ever. I hoped her classes had been livelier when she was teaching because her writing was seriously stodgy. The Roman villa had been large; the Black Death stayed the other side of the river; the builder of the house was unknown but must have been important and wealthy... (*'Unlikely'* was Violet's pithy comment). Under the Stuarts the farmers were even richer and more important. *'I believe we can discount a rumour that there was a witch in the family,'* pronounced Miss Montagu. *'The Wellman women were greatly respected in the town, regular churchgoers who would never have indulged in unnatural practices.'*

Frustrated yet again by her sparse remarks I abandoned Miss Montagu and got dressed because the house was chilly. Patrick was snoring gently, but seemed better. Rather than disturb him I tiptoed out and went downstairs, where I made a cup of tea and wandered into Dickon's Room, switching on the fan heater to warm myself up.

As always the window drew me and I peered out into the garden where the sky was beginning to show pale silvery streaks beyond the hill. My hand caressed the carved flowers and leaves and traced the delicate stone tendrils and buds while I marvelled again at the skill of that long ago craftsman. I stroked the hare that was poised for danger in the corner of the stonework and leaned my head against the slender pillar. Who had built this house? Who had loved this place so dearly?

(iii)

'You're home, then, Kat?' The farmer raised his head from his tankard and gave the newcomer a jaundiced look. *'Not caught a husband yet?'*

'Is that what you hoped, Pa?' She looked down her long nose, so like his own, her light-brown eyes flashing. *'You*

should have thought of that before you sent me away. There was a sad lack of husbands on offer at that damned convent.'

As he drained the last drop of ale, Katherine's eyes softened and she clapped him on the shoulder. 'I was sorry to hear about Joan and the bull, Pa. You'd have thought she'd have more sense than to walk across the field when he was in a fine old temper and she in the family way.'

'Ah well,' he reached up to squeeze her hand. 'The truth is, Kat, she was in a fine old temper herself, so I doubt she thought twice about what she was doing when she up and stormed out of the house.' He sighed gustily. 'I can't be bothered with a new young woman in the house. I thought 'twould be easy to get a son but first your mother, God rest her sainted soul...' He crossed himself, looking sentimental. 'She did her best but all she rose to was a clutch of sickly girls, and you m'dear, the only one to survive.'

'Yes, Pa,' her tone was caustic. 'Wasn't that fortunate for you, what with your next two wives dying so inconveniently? At least you're not left on your own.'

She spotted an anxious face peering round the door and beckoned to the serving girl.

'I'm starved, is there aught to eat? Bread and cheese? And some of the master's ale, if you please.'

'Poor old Pa,' she murmured as ate. 'You had bad luck, didn't you? Who expected Bess to die in childbirth and the baby with her? And Joan was another buxom wench even if she did have that funny cast to her eye.'

Struck suddenly by the same thought their eyes met. He said it first.

'You think that's where she went wrong, poor wench? A'cos of her squinty eye she thought the bull was running away?'

'Could be.' She straightened up and primmed her mouth, guilty at her misplaced mirth, but rejoicing inwardly to be home and laughing with her father. 'Poor soul, it's not right to laugh but I reckon you're right to give up on another wife. Folks won't want to risk their daughters on you. They'll say you're a Jonah.'

Dickon Wellman nodded sagely. 'Aye, and breaking in a new wife takes up a deal of my time and to no avail.'

'Better not say things like that when you bump into Joan's family,' she reminded him with a twinkle. 'I'm to stay at home now, am I? No more attempts to get me off your hands?'

'Ah now, 'twas never for that reason, Kat, as you well know.' He cracked a faint smile. 'It was more than my life was worth to have you and Bess together in the house you'd managed since you were a little moppet while your Ma ailed. The convent was a good enough plan then. We'd heard rumours about His Grace the King and his quarrels with the clergy but who'd have guessed it would go the way it has.' He pushed himself up from the table to reveal broad thighs and a large belly. 'A few years and a clever girl like you might have risen to Mother Superior, not thrown out with all the rest when some jumped-up clerk bought the place.'

'So I might have done,' she nodded, calling the little wench to make up a bed. 'The convent was a shambles. Mother Superior spent her days playing with her little dog and riding out on the hills with her confessor, and the rest of the sisters had no notion of lifting a finger when the cat was away.'

She glowered in reminiscent disgust. 'I wanted to take charge of the housekeeping and accounts. I'd have had it all straight in no time, but Mother Superior took against me. She said if so be I was keen on bookwork I could take myself off to the scriptorium and help with the illuminations to the missal they planned to present to the bishop. Tcha!' she snorted indignantly. 'Bookwork, when there were rats running free in the granary, a prodigious waste of food in the kitchens, and four legs in some of the beds almost every night. And in the highest of all, though that was best ignored.'

She went to the door and her gaze swept fondly across the land, from high on the hills down towards the river. 'I've missed it so much, nigh on five years wasted when I could have been here.' She heaved a sigh then skewered him with a frown. 'What's been going on here, Pa? The house is falling *about your ears, the thatch is rotten, there's a tree growing out of the chimney and half the windows boarded up. 'Tis hardly fit for the pigs to live in, let alone you and me. What's to become of us here at the farm – and the holy well and the chapel too?'*

'Ah, that...' It struck her that he looked sheepish. 'I was going to tell you about that. The fellow acting for the King's Commissioner rode by a couple of months past. Did you hear they sold off the priory church over yonder to the townsfolk of Ramalley? They had a legal right to buy, it seems, because they'd been using part of it for services. He said he'd come to take a look over here.'

'And?'

'Seems nobody gave a thought to the chapel so it was never included in the sale. The long and the short of it is that I offered to buy it all, the chapel, the well, the land and this house too. There being nobody else interested and he wishful to get it off his hands, we shook on it.'

'But that's good news, Pa, great news.' She hugged him then shuffled back as they both looked slightly abashed at such exuberant affection. 'What are your plans? First thing, we must put the house to rights. What about the monks at the chapel here? There can't have been many left by the end.'

'Ah...' He looked at his feet. 'I can't turn out those old fellows, can I? Brother Dominic sits by the fire all a-tremble, Brother Anselm's near-blind, and Brother Rohan don't know Michaelmas from Monday. 'Tis all one to him.'

She narrowed her eyes and he shrugged. 'It would be hard on the old fellows if I threw out the two young'uns that do all the work of the place.'

Next morning Katherine dragged her father out to survey the farm.

'Nonsense,' she scolded. 'Stop all that mumbling and grumbling, Pa, you're not forty-five yet. What would Mother say if she saw you making such hard work of a little stroll? You haven't told me why you let the house get so bad, but I can see why – you're too fat, Pa, that's the trouble. It's more than time I came back to sort things out here. To think we

have His Grace's lusty antics to thank for my release from bondage. Ah well,' she sighed as she steered him towards the river. 'Mother was right. She said just before she died, seven years since, that no good would come of his goings-on with that Bullen whore and right she was. Look what became of the wench, dead on a scaffold these three years gone.'

'Hold hard, girl,' Dickon Wellman wheezed along in his daughter's train but when he reached a gnarled rowan tree he put out a hand to support himself. 'Funny thing,' he said, staring up at the greening boughs and picturing the froth of snowy blossom to come in May. 'My old grandfather told me there's always been a rowan tree here. Once there was a great grove of them all round, but this one stands strong yet and when it's old, another must be planted. Dire bad luck, he said, were the tree not renewed. You remember that, Kat, if it happens in your time.'

'You know I will, Pa,' she nodded as she gazed at the sheltered spot and sniffed the air. 'I could have sworn I smelled lavender just now, Mother's favourite, but there's none growing nearby. Still, it's sheltered and peaceful here.' She followed him as he made his way to a fallen tree trunk and they sat in companionable silence, enjoying the unexpected March sunshine.

'You still haven't told me why you let the house get so bad,' she said. 'Or what you mean to do with the chapel, Pa.'

'I'll pull it down,' he said. 'The well-house too. I've a mind to build a fine new house with the stones, right here. What do you reckon?'

'A house?' She sat up straight and stared about her, then stood up to examine the ground. 'I like that idea,' her eyes shone. 'But can we afford it, Pa?'

'Never you mind.' He looked smug and tapped the side of his nose then, as she frowned, he smirked. 'The thing is, Kat, the King's man was no farmer. He was some fat old lawyer from Winchester with no more idea of the value of this land than one of our sheep, so when I put in a paltry offer he didn't have the wits to ask for more. I couldn't believe it when he said the place was mine. I expected to haggle but no, he

handed it over like a lamb. That means there's money and to spare, though that's our secret, mind. No need to spread that news abroad. Then, if you please, he said he'd throw in those odd fields that belonged to the Priory, the ones adjoining our land and the hill pasture along with it. Even the monks' sheep that grazed up there. Silly old fool. Nobody wanted it, he said. The townsfolk were only interested in the Priory church and the smallholdings and granges were being sold off piecemeal.'

The complacent smile faded from his large ruddy face as he put a careless arm round her shoulders.

'The farm is in good shape but as to the house, I know I've let the place go.' His face fell. 'Right sorry I am but I've had this idea in mind since we first heard that Master Cromwell and His Grace had their sights on the monks and their wealth. If the great houses were to go I reckoned there'd be no hope for a tiddy place like the one here, so I set my mind to it that I'd buy the land and the chapel and build, like I say.

'And say what you will, Kat,' he rumbled. 'You're past nineteen and a husband you must have, despite your fine talk, and well you know it. I shan't rest easy if I die and leave you unwed. These are troubled times and a woman with a tidy bit of land will need a man's protection.'

(iv)

The day after her father announced his plans Katherine made her way to the chapel to assess potential building materials and to greet the old men she had loved since childhood.

'Well, Brother Anselm,' she said after the first cries of welcome had abated and she was sitting between him and Brother Dominic whose shoulders trembled constantly, thin and frail under her gentle embrace. Old Brother Rohan paid no heed to the conversation and sang tunelessly in his corner to the fat tabby cat curled up snugly on his knees. 'What think you of Pa's notion to build a new house?'

'A fine idea,' two of the old men chorused, the one head

nodding more than ever while the other's sightless eyes closed in contemplation of glories he would never see. 'Your father is a hardworking man and a kind one. He deserves a house suited to his station in life.'

'He's naught but a yeoman farmer.' Her response was dry. 'He'll need to make sure this new house isn't too grand or we'll attract notice from the wrong quarter. Think of the tales they tell about the cardinal's palace at Hampton. His Grace thought it fit for a king – and took it.' She looked at their anxious, wrinkled faces and sighed. 'Have no fear. I doubt His Grace will covet Pa's house, nor any of the local gentry, either. Thank the Lord we're out of the way here at Ladywell so let's pray most of the traffic stays across the river.'

'Amen to that,' quavered Brother Dominic, adding hopefully, 'Master Dickon did promise he would never put us out of house and home and glad we were to hear that, for what would become of the three of us else? The young lads can find work on the farm and in building this house of yours, but there's precious little we can do but pray.'

'Prayers are always welcome, brother,' she assured him. 'Don't disturb yourselves, Pa and I will be glad of your company wherever we live. I do wish though that I had someone to help design this house. Pa leaves it to me and I'm unhandy at such a task.'

'You need Brother Ambrosius,' they chorused. 'He was away in France when the King's commissioner turned up at the Priory and turfed the brothers out and by the time he returned the place was sold, so he moved over here to give us a hand. In a fine taking about it, he was, he'd been to London to see what he could find out, but it was no use.

'He's away to Winchester now to see if he can wheedle some money out of the bishop for our needs. He's a fine strong fellow and used to oversee our little infirmary once a week till we had word to disband. He said that was nonsense. There's precious few visit the holy well nowadays, but those few will still come expecting help. Ambrosius said it was only right the church should pay, do they answer to Pope or King Harry. But there, Master Dickon will see all's right.'

'Aye,' the blind monk chuckled. 'In a rare temper Ambrosius have been about it so he downed tools last week and hared straight off to give the bishop a piece of his mind.'

'That he did,' the quavering voice joined in. 'He'd seen the Priory over yonder as a stepping stone and had an eye to preferment. The old Prior was getting on and Brother Ambrosius saw himself in charge. 'Twas a rare disappointment to him.'

'Ambrosius should get married.' Brother Rohan looked up, startling them with one of his increasingly rare moments of clarity. 'He's a fine upstanding young fellow and needs a rich wife, better for him than a priory, any day.' As they turned to stare in astonishment the old man broke into a fit of wheezing laughter. 'Aye, a wife is what we all need, my brothers. I have a mind to find one for myself to see what I've been a-missing all these years.'

Katherine's hands were full which left her no time to fume about her father's hint regarding a husband, or to pine for the convent, not that such a thought entered her head.

'You're enjoying yourself, aren't you, mistress?' Moll, the younger of the two female servants observed shyly, as they walked over to the chapel one morning soon after Katherine's arrival. 'All this bustle?'

There were no other young women at the farm and no near neighbours so they had perforce become friendly and Katherine, bubbling with excitement at having a house to design and build and oversee, appreciated the girl's interest. Dickon Wellman, having announced his decision, seemed to have shot his bolt and spent most of his time at the chapel, drinking ale with the old brothers, or inspecting his new wool-sheds. Besides, it was lambing time and the shepherds worked off their feet, so he helped where they were overstretched and was glad to leave all matters domestic in his daughter's capable hands.

'You do as you please,' he told her. 'I've no time to spare and no hand at fripperies and such, but what I will do is dig the old well deeper and strengthen it. As to the house, there's

106

that pair of great old oaks that came down in the storm five years since and I've been keeping the timber.' He blew his nose loudly, looking sentimental. 'Had it in mind to build a house for a long time, Kat, but when Joan died, the heart went out of me. No sense building a house with no son to follow me but Old Harry goes a-wenching and here you are, home again.

'As for this fine new house,' he patted her on the back and laughed as she buckled slightly at the knees. 'That's women's business. All I ask are high ceilings for I'm a large fellow, and a fine big room with a handsome fireplace to sit beside on a winter's night. With that, and a fine bedchamber above it, I can die in grand comfort when the time comes!'

'It's all very well Pa saying that,' Katherine grumbled. 'I can see what he means and I know what I'd like myself, but I've no way to tell if it will come out right.'

'Brother Ambrosius should be back from Winchester soon,' Moll suggested. 'He might give you a helping hand.'

'More like to hinder.' Katherine rubbed a hand across her eyes. 'We can try, though from what the old fellows said, he'll be a deal too eager to take charge and I'm not standing for that.'

'D'you suppose Brother Rohan has found himself a bride yet, mistress?' giggled Moll. 'For my grandmother has a mind to drop by and look him over. 'Tis two years since my granddad died and she says she misses a man to cook for.'

Katherine joined in the laughter. 'Could she cope with him drifting off into fairyland? Mind you, it's not such a foolish notion, Moll,' she added looking thoughtful. 'I reckon Pa would pay her to look after all the old men if she decides against marriage. They'd be cared for which would be a weight off my mind. Pa's too.'

As they approached the chapel and the monks' living quarters Katherine was surprised to hear the sound of an axe, accompanied by a cheerful baritone. The two young women tiptoed round the corner and halted in surprise.

A half-naked young giant swung the axe in time to his song as he split a tree trunk into logs. At Katherine's

107

involuntary gasp he looked up and lost his rhythm.

'For the love of God, woman,' he shouted as he flung down his axe. 'I nearly chopped my own bloody leg off. Have you no more sense than to distract a man when he's at work?'

'Don't you dare speak to me like that,' she snapped, trying to steady her breathing. The axe had landed perilously close to his leg. 'I have a perfect right to walk where I please, and you should take more care. There's no Infirmarian to see to you now.'

'Not true.' His mouth twisted in a smile and she blinked at the change in his tanned face. The black eyes narrowed into amused slits and his face creased, revealing through the dark stubble a pair of dimples any maiden would covet. 'I could look after myself though I'd have to issue instructions about cauterising the stump and keeping it clean.' He hitched his habit back up over his shoulders and gave her a sweeping bow. 'Brother Ambrosius,' he said with another smile. 'Lately Infirmarian of this place. Do I address our landlord's daughter?'

'I thought you'd gone to Winchester.' Katherine stammered as she nodded.

'I've come back,' he glowered. 'My trip achieved precious little, nor did I expect it. The bishop is away and the archdeacon washed his hands like Pontius Pilate when it came to a tiny place like this. I gave him a piece of my mind and left him bleating.'

She smiled at that. 'What will you do?'

'I thought I might help build your father's grand house,' he said cheerfully. 'I hear you need a man of vision, someone who can tell the masons what needs to be done. That I can do. I have a turn for such work and would have made it my profession had other things not intervened.' Again there was that shadow as he scowled. 'I thought my heart would break if I could not draw, but disappointments are sent to try us and it's harder to die of a broken heart than a boy might think. Still, here I am, without a job and at your service, Mistress Katherine. Let me help you in this.'

She was touched and intrigued. 'I'd be grateful indeed,

Brother Ambrosius,' she nodded. 'Pa, my father, will only repeat that he wants these two important rooms, one above the other, and he cares naught for the rest of the house, leaving it all in my hands.'

'Better call me Hugh,' he nodded. 'With my tonsure gone and a new beard,' he rubbed his chin and grinned ruefully as it rasped, 'Brother Ambrosius may safely be left behind. Hugh Beauchamp must take his place, though truth to tell I might have to work on that as well for the Beauchamps hold no high place in King Henry's heart. Let me stack these logs and I'll join you indoors.'

(v)

Within a week Hugh and Katherine had hammered out a plan with Dickon's approval and Hugh spent much of one whole day pacing the proposed site and surveying the ground. He looked round as Katherine approached with a jug of ale and two horn beakers.

'Stand here with me at the front door,' he pointed at the ground in front of him. 'I've laid out sticks to show the rough pattern of the rooms. Your father tells me time and again that the house must look modest as befits a simple farmer.' They both laughed and Hugh explained. 'I propose to have a plain roof and the front of the house will be simple, set with a door in the middle, and windows beside. From front to back runs a passage and to the left of the door is the long, handsome room your father craves. On the right lie more rooms for family and servants, the kitchen quarters out at the back. What say you? Here, walk with me and I'll show you.'

He took her hand with a courtly grace and an impish smile as he led her through the doorway. 'Here is Dickon's room,' he explained. 'Better start thinking of furniture and fripperies or your father will be disappointed. You do know this house is really for you?'

'Yes,' she admitted. 'Our family has been here many a year and he's set on keeping it that way. King Harry's wenching has done us a favour. Now, show me some more of *this invisible house.'*

'I like it,' she giggled, at the end of the tour, tickled by the absurdity of Hugh's imaginary building. 'What is above?'

'The stair in the hall, here,' he indicated a row of sticks. 'Your father's bedchamber exactly above his handsome parlour with a smaller fireplace echoing the grand one below. A wide landing above the hall, then more rooms to match the lower floor.' He squinted into the sunshine and grunted. 'There's enough dressed stone over yonder, I reckon, to build this fine house, what with the stone from the derelict well-house too, so long as we mix it with flint. 'Pity they skimped on the monks' quarters or there'd be stone enough for all, but there, better keep it simple and not draw unwelcome attention. The holy well can have a simple frame to hold the winch and this house shall be mostly stone at the front and back, with the kitchen and the rest flint with a rubble infill. As to a cellar,' he said thoughtfully, 'we're between the river and the well here and though this spot is on a goodly rise we'd better see what turns up when we start digging.'

He surveyed the land towards the river. 'I'll let you into a secret, Mistress Kat,' he grinned at her, black eyes sparkling. 'I went over to the Priory yesterday, marched in as bold as you please and demanded to see the maps that show the way the river has changed course over the centuries. They'll be useful to us so I brought them back. From our point of view this has been an excellent thing. Where it silted up in times past, has turned into good, solid farmland so better safe than sorry but I believe we're in no real danger.' He looked thoughtful again. 'When the house is finished we could reclaim more land from the river bend and shore up the bank.'

'You've been exceeding busy,' she said. 'We'll be moving in on Friday at this rate.'

He smiled at that, a mischievous twinkle in his eyes. 'I brought something else back with me. You'll remember the chapel here has those little old arched windows? They're not big so we'll set them one at the front and one at the back on

110

the upper floor to let in light, and there are two little ones hardly bigger than arrow slits that can sit either side of the door.'

'Before you pull their home down around the old men,' Kat laughed, 'we should move them into our house. Their quarters adjoin the chapel, after all.

'I like your ideas, Hugh, but what else did you bring back?'

He shot her a conspiratorial grin. 'Hush, this is our secret. I heard the new vicar was rebuilding parts of the Wolsey Chapel and prudently forgetting it was renamed in gratitude to the old Cardinal when he presented the Priory with a chalice. I had a quiet word with the masons' foreman over there. I set his wife's broken arm last year and he's grateful, so he set his men to load one of the unwanted windows on to our cart and offered to come over soon himself and rebuild the window here. The glass broke and the stone frame is cracked but that we can make good. As I drove out of the gate I passed the vicar so I gave him a respectful salute and hid the window safe in Dickon's barn.'

'For shame,' she teased. 'You're no better than a thieving magpie! Where do you think to put it a great tall thing like that in our house?'

'Have no fear,' Hugh's eyes were merry. 'Don't forget, the windows in the chapel are smaller than in the church but if it proves too tall, why, the masons and I will make it fit, or make the walls higher downstairs. As for where – the window will be out of sight. The front of your father's house shall be as modest as he asks, with nothing to make any king or lordling envious, but the back – ah, the back,' he looked smug. 'The back of the house will be glorious – and secret!'

Katherine giggled then held her breath as a hare sped along the edge of the field.

'Did Pa tell you,' she asked as they sat drinking their ale. 'He wants a hare carved on the mantelpiece in his lordly room.'

'He did,' Hugh squinted but the hare had gone. 'He told me folks round here set great store by hares.'

'We do,' she was suddenly serious. 'Great store. It's said that any man who kills a hare on our land will live to rue the day.'

Dickon Wellman approved the plans and the former monk's change of occupation.

'They said you were a clever fellow,' he nodded, with a knowing smile at his daughter. 'See, Kat? Just what you're looking for, I warrant.' He let out a bellow of laughter as Katherine's lips closed in a tight, angry line so he turned to the younger man. 'I've given it some thought,' he said slowly, 'this question of your name. Hugh has a good ring to it but Beauchamp – now that's a name that spells trouble to me. Am I right?'

Hugh hesitated. 'My father was of noble stock, I'll say no more,' he admitted. 'As a boy of fifteen, he alone of his father and brothers survived the battle at Bosworth.' His dark-browed face lit up in a wry grin. 'He fought on what I would call the right side but many a more prudent man these days would say was very much the wrong one.'

He looked up as Dickon Wellman made to speak. 'Sir?'

'I say plain,' declared Dickon, thumping the table with his fist. 'If your father fought for King Richard then he fought on the right side and I care not who hears me. Or at least,' there was a twinkle in his eyes. 'I do care, but you know what I mean.'

He fell silent for a moment, reflective and sober. 'I'll tell you something I never told before,' he said solemnly. 'No need to swear you to secrecy, you'll not betray me.' He settled his bulk comfortably and Katherine listened intently while Hugh's face creased in a frown. 'My old great-aunt told me this tale when I was a young lad. Said I should know, as the only child living.

'My grandfather, Ned Wellman, was the younger son and back in King Richard's day he upped and said he was off to fight for the king. Naught his parents could do and besides, he was in the right of it, they thought. Many folk hereabouts felt the same, though to see the Blue Boar Inn nowadays *you'd never know it. Aunt Margery told me the landlord over there near toppled off his ladder in his haste to paint over his inn sign and cover up the white boar that was the king's own emblem. Still, that's beside the point...*

'No word of how Ned fared reached the farm but they heard about the battle, and the king's death at the usurper's hands. Eight months after Bosworth Field Ned Wellman reappeared, lean and angry, with money in his purse. He had a lanky boy in tow who would be thirteen come August, he said. His stepson, they asked? He gave no explanation then or later so they put it about that the boy was his wife's lad, she having died. After a while they were hard put, my old aunt said, to remember aught different.

'What about the battle, they asked in whispers when he arrived. Had he been there? No, Ned told them, he had not fought at Bosworth but rode North the day before on the King's urgent business, and so bleak was his face none dared question him. He stayed tight-lipped about whether that business had prospered and he maintained a forbidding silence about the boy. One snippet he did let slip was that there had been an elder boy, ever an ailing lad, who sickened there in the North and died, and that the younger lad, Dick, almost followed him from the same fever. He'd regained his strength but for some reason he lost his voice and had never spoken since.'

Katherine poured more ale for her father and the former monk who sat there intent. The farmer nodded his thanks and went on with his tale.

'Aunt Margery said people cast sideways glances at the boy. Dumb, was he? Simple more like, they said, but the family spoke out stoutly in his defence. 'Twas clear the lad understood every word, and did any task they set him. Right good at reading he was, writing and reckoning too. When his brother died screaming of a bellyache, Ned took on the farm, and soon the boy was the grandson the old folks had always wanted. He grew up strong and healthy, with his blue eyes and fair hair and the great height that I get from him myself.

'See here, Hugh, and you too, Kat, I say again this must

be secret.' His face was solemn now. 'My mother was the daughter of a Wellman cousin whose family moved long ago to Salisbury, and came here on a visit. Their marriage was a happy one but I never heard my father speak but the once and that on his deathbed when he was still a young man. He reached for my hand at the last and gripped it hard as he said something I've never forgot. A slow, rusty kind of whisper he had. "Dickon," said he. "When I die, go you and pluck a sprig of the green broom and pin it to my hat. Let me be buried with the flower of my family proudly worn."

'Well, I'll tell you! My thoughts whirled in my head for I knew, as all men did in those days, what family it was that took their name from the planta genista, the green broom. It seemed like madness but he rallied to groan his last word, "Bosworth was our ending, my son." That was all and he died an hour later but I remembered my old aunt's tale and I did as he asked.'

Hugh cleared his throat, sounding loud in the silence that followed Dickon's rumbling speech. 'I... I believe I take your meaning, Master Wellman,' he said quietly and glanced at Katherine who was staring in awed silence.

'I am honoured by your confidence and you may trust me, as I in turn will trust you,' said Hugh to his two companions. 'My father's first wife and sons died when the fever swept through London so my mother was the second wife and I the child of my father's later years. Father had friends on high but no money and from an early age I had a turn for drawing so I hoped to make my way in London; travel abroad mayhap, work with masons and learn to draw up plans for houses. When I was fourteen father fell foul of the King's Grace, with naught but a few words out of place.'

An unexpected smile brought out Hugh's dimples as he added, 'Mind you, the words out of place happened to be, "Henry Tudor has no claim to the throne of England" spoken out fierce and loud at Westminster, so you can see the King's point. Father never did have any common sense.'

He shrugged. 'My father was taken off by a fever in the Tower and before my mother breathed her last soon after, she *begged me to take myself out of the King's way and join the Order.' There was a pause and Katherine and her father watched his face twist in another of those wry smiles. 'I lay no claim to piety but it served its purpose and after fourteen years I had hopes of becoming Sub-Prior, but for the King's wenching.'*

'Aye,' Dickon Wellman nodded sagely. 'See here, lad, I reckon we understand each other so I suggest you take my name, there being no kinsman close enough to claim it. You carry on building my house and then help me with the farm. What say you?'

'Never mind what he says,' Katherine burst out. 'What of me, Pa? Am I invisible? Have I no say in this?'

'Fool girl,' he stumbled to his feet, his cold anger more terrifying than the usual bluster. 'I told you before, Kat, you're a woman with no brother, no uncle, and when I die you'll be a woman alone and that's not safe, not nowadays. Not safe. You'll obey me in this or I'll beat you, you stubborn wench. I will have it so, for I see the hand of God. Here are you needing a husband and Hugh needing a home so I'll see the pair of you wed before I die.'

(vi)

The weather helped. The third dry summer in a row this one was exceptional, and while Hugh and Dickon kept an eye on the levels in the well and dug out waterholes against drought, everyone on the farm and in the village set to with a will when they could spare the time, to prepare the ground and dig the foundations. The master's new house was an object of wonder and soon enough the masons made such good progress that some of the stone walls were up to head height. To the delight of the old monks, Hugh designed a small alms building close by for them to live out their lives in comfort.

One twilight evening Hugh beckoned Katherine to follow him.

'Have you dug out the footings for the alms house?' she asked as they reached the building site.

He shook his head. 'Dickon says this spot is where the old rowan grove once stood,' he said. 'I've found something. See here…'

Scraps of rotten fabric surrounded a bundle of brittle yellow bones laid as though asleep and Hugh bent his head in prayer.

'What shall we do?' whispered Katherine, aware of a faint scent – of lavender, she thought.

'It's a woman,' he said quietly. 'She's been here a long time so we'll not disturb her. Stay with me while I cover her again. The monks' cottage shall be on the other side of Dickon's house.'

She stared at the bones then crossed herself. 'Hugh, I think – we must plant more rowan trees close by. I feel it – here.' She touched her heart.

A week or two later Hugh heard her calling. Looking up he saw her flushed and panting in the unfinished doorway 'There's trouble. Pa's heard that a new King's man is due to arrive any day to oversee the transfer of the Priory church into the town's ownership. They say he's one of Master Cromwell's men and right zealous on the King's behalf, according to Pa's crony. He's pledged to root out any who are not whole-hearted for the King.'

She jiggled impatiently as he took it in. 'I know we've not spoken of Pa's plan and I was angry when he proposed it, but now…' She stumbled over the words. 'I believe it is the only way to keep you safe.'

He opened his mouth. 'No, let me finish,' she said, scarlet but determined. 'If this man is full of zeal he'll have lists of names and may come here seeking Brother Ambrosius or worse, Hugh Beauchamp, son of a man who was loyal to the house of York. Let him find Master Dickon Wellman, a farmer who bought the priory lands fair and square from the King's appointed commissioner, and who is now building a fine, but not too fine, house with the aid of his daughter and her upstanding husband, a distant kinsman.'

Their eyes met briefly and they both looked awkwardly at

the ground. 'I see,' he said slowly. 'You may be right, Mistress Kat, but it must be done swiftly.'

'Pa reminded me that old Brother Rohan was once ordained a priest though most, including the old man himself, have forgotten,' she was blushing. 'He sometimes married the pilgrims at the well so Pa reckons Rohan must marry us at once. Pa's friends in town will make sure it stands. He orders us to get home without delay and change into our good clothes.'

'Mistress Kat,' he said gently. 'I know this is hasty and you should be courted, but I'll make you a good husband. This I promise.'

She blushed again and risked a shy glance at him.

The black eyes twinkled as he took her hand. 'We'd better hurry,' he said, chuckling. 'We must catch old Rohan while he's making sense, lest he marry your father to the donkey by mistake.'

'Lord save us, what a day!' Dickon Wellman dominated his half-built room, with the space on the wall where his fine mantel would stand and where the Priory window would look out to the hills at the back of the house. Before that happened Hugh's mason friend would carve the hares Dickon had ordered, one on the mantel and another on the window frame. As for the bones buried under the house, Hugh and Katherine never spoke of them again.

At mid-morning, the farmer had marched his daughter, her new husband, and the old monks to inspect the new house, and here he stood, arms akimbo, feet wide apart. Although he had no idea of it, he looked remarkably akin to the King's Grace himself: a great height with the breadth running to fat, small shrewd blue eyes looking keenly out of a ruddy face, a sandy fringe of beard to match what remained of his greying hair.

'Here we are at last, my daughter and my son. Welcome to the family, Hugh. I'm proud to call you a Wellman at last. I trust you find yourselves well and truly wed this fine sunny morn?'

117

The bridegroom grinned as he nodded and glanced fondly outside where his wife was administering strong drink to old Rohan who sat on a log with his friends and who was still, a day after the wedding, almost overcome by his brief return to old glories.

'Well and truly wed, Dickon, so you can stop nudging me. When are we to expect this zealous King's man?'

'Aye, well,' Dickon Wellman's eyes almost disappeared as his face creased with mirth. 'Did I not tell you? Dear me, I must have clean forgot what with all the jollity of the wedding feast. Word came after noon yesterday that 'twas all a mistake and the new man was bound for Andover from Winchester with no plans to come here and interfere with innocent folk.' He gave his son-in-law a sly grin. 'Mark you, I saw no point in putting off the wedding.'

Chapter Nine

(i)

Tuesday, 10th *March – early morning*

There was no sound from Patrick's room so I washed my hair
in the bath. This reminded me about getting a shower
installed and I made yet another note, then it was back
downstairs for more tea and some toast and to dry my hair. I
laid a second place because he'd be hungry whenever he
surfaced. It was past seven-thirty, so he'd been solidly asleep
since ten o'clock last night, and for hours before that. I was
pretty sure he hadn't stirred in the night because I'd have
heard the clanking of ancient plumbing.

There was no news from Louise which was unusual and I
wished I could update her about Patrick. Better to phone her
when I actually had something to talk about and anyway, her
in-laws' farm was always busy. Lou would be in touch.

I pulled on my boots and thick jacket and went outside.
Even in the short time I'd been here I'd come to love this
early morning stroll to the bottom of the garden. Today, I
could hear rooks cawing in the trees up on the hill, while a
pair of blue-tits flitted about on my apple tree and blackbirds
flew in and out of the hedge. A robin perched on the washing
line and there were squirrels in the silver birch at the bottom
of the garden, playing chase round the trunk.

Puss Hill was veiled in mist but the sun promised to be
strong enough to burn it off later and I could just make out
the hawthorn clump, gnarled and bent against the prevailing
wind. I huddled into my coat then caught a slight movement
out of the corner of my eye. The hare, half way up the hill
this morning – could it be the same one? – was still watching

the house, still watching me. I scarcely dared breathe but suddenly the animal lifted its head, poised for flight.

I'd heard nothing; his footsteps made no noise on the mossy path, but the hare knew he was there. Patrick took my hand and nodded as I whispered, 'Shhhhh, can you see it?'

For what seemed an eternity the hare stayed there, up on its long legs and ready to run but looking at us over its shoulder until it suddenly took flight.

'That was magical,' Patrick breathed, putting his arm round my shoulders. 'I've never seen a hare so close; they're usually disappearing at speed in the opposite direction.'

He smiled warmly at me. 'I like your house, Freya.'

I took a deep breath. 'That's good, I like it too.'

'What's going on over there?' He pointed to the scruffy corner at the far end by the wall. 'What's under the brambles? The remains of an ancestral rockery? The Victorians were very keen on them.'

'Nothing so romantic,' I sighed. 'I suspect it's a derelict privy. It's a long way down on my to-do list so it'll have to wait.' I glanced back up the hill but the hare was long gone, so I headed back up the path.

'Feeling up to tea and toast, Patrick? Come and tell me why you came home so early. Why aren't you hanging out with your old mate Dan in Colorado?'

'I should be,' Patrick lingered for a moment, gazing thoughtfully at the tangle of brambles and thorns that covered the possible privy in the corner, before he caught up with me. 'Except that he collapsed and was rushed into hospital to have his gall bladder whipped out. His wife's message caught up with me when I landed at Denver and obviously she didn't want to be bothered with a visitor, so like I said, I grabbed a taxi to the hotel. I felt awful anyway so it was a huge relief just to lie down and die quietly in a private bathroom!'

I made soothing noises and he laughed. 'After forty-eight hours I felt a bit more human so once I could stand up without my knees giving way, I managed to get a seat on the plane for Heathrow. Trouble was, I couldn't sleep a wink; too wired I suppose but I seem to have made up for it since I've been....'

He broke off his sentence and whistled.

'What the... You've got a church window! You didn't mention *that* in your sparse texts.'

'I know, sorry. I'll show you properly when we do the whole tour but I'm perishing. Let's have a cuppa first.'

I kicked off my boots, wet with the dew, and fussed with the kettle. While we waited for the ancient toaster to finish coughing Patrick looked round at the kitchen, smaller than ever with a tall man looming in the middle.

'What am I doing here, Freya?' He drank some of his tea and grinned at me. 'I'm not complaining, I love this house. When I woke up I thought I'd stepped through the looking-glass and that lovely old wardrobe made me stop and think too. And yes, I did take a look inside but the back wouldn't open. What I don't understand is why you didn't just drop me at home?'

'You were in no state to be left on your own' I gave him a couple of slices of toast and passed him the butter. 'Are you sure you're up to eating? You don't want to overdo it. Of course I couldn't just dump you, we're not that far from Heathrow anyway.'

'It was a kind thought,' he said seriously as he helped himself to marmalade. 'I'm okay, almost back to normal and I'm starving after my enforced fast, thanks. Hey, is this marmalade home-made?'

'It was a present from a small furry pixie. She dropped it in yesterday morning on her way to visit my neighbour, Mrs Penrose.' Yes, and Mary had done that enigmatic thing again when she mentioned her old school-friend Sylvia. I'd floated a couple of leading questions but she'd refused to bite and hurried round to next-door.

I explained about Mary Draper and the way she seemed to have adopted me. 'She was Violet Wellman's closest friend and someday I'm going to sit her down and make her talk to me. There are things here, things I've found out, that I don't...' To my horror I heard my voice crack and the dam broke.

I felt his arms go round me and heard his voice say soothing, calming things, but I couldn't stop crying. 'Just let it go, love,' he murmured and I thought I felt a kiss on the top of my head as he hugged me close.

After a while he tucked me into the curve of one arm while he reached for the kitchen-roll. 'Here, wipe your eyes and blow your nose, Freya, then tell me what's caused all this.'

He got up and made more tea while I obediently blew my nose. While the tea brewed he put more bread in the toaster. 'Blimey,' he snorted as it sparked. 'You take your life in your hands with this thing, it's a death trap. I'll buy you a new one. Here,' he rubbed my shoulder gently as he put the toast in front of me. 'Eat this and stop trying to apologise. You gave me a bucket, for God's sake, best present ever! What's tea and toast compared to what you were prepared to tackle?'

I summoned up a wan smile and sipped my tea.

'That's better. Now, tell me what is it that only your tame Pixie can explain?'

'I don't even know if she can, or will,' I began, and blurted out the whole story. How Violet Wellman had made a will leaving everything to a day-old baby girl. How I'd discovered the antique box in her bedroom and the piece of paper inside it detailing the transaction that sold me to my parents.

'Hold that thought,' Patrick said, getting up again to browse in the cupboard. 'We need more calories to deal with this. Are you saving this fruit cake?' He cut two slices. 'Don't turn your nose up,' he scolded gently as he read the label. 'It's got fruit and nuts, that's some of your five-a-day. And it's from the WI, very wholesome, very good for you.'

Yes it was and it had been a kind thought of Cathy's, but I didn't think I could swallow anything, so I crumbled a bit of cake on the plate and let him talk.

'What's all this about you being *sold* to your parents? From what you've just told me there was no sale. The woman who actually gave birth to you refused payment. To me that says she *gave* you to your mother, as a gift. What could be more generous and loving?'

The tears started again and he heaved a dramatic sigh and fetched the kitchen-roll. 'Here, I'll put it on the table, it'll save me getting up again.'

Outraged at this lack of sympathy I glared at him, only to see his mouth twisted in a crooked smile. 'If you can stave off the waterworks for a while I think we should investigate Pandora's Box. Come on...'

(ii)

I splashed cold water on my face and Patrick looked over my shoulder as I came out of the bathroom.

'If it's okay with you, I'd love to have a bath in here tonight. It's another museum piece and I want to take a closer look at that little old window *and* the big one downstairs.' He smiled reassuringly. 'When we've looked at this mysterious box I'd like a proper tour of your house, Freya.'

I pulled myself together and gave him a watery smile. 'Fair enough. Let's get it over with, then you'll understand why I'm such an emotional wreck. I don't know what it is about this place but that's the second time since I arrived that I've bawled my eyes out.'

He looked concerned, but I led him into Violet's room where he went straight to the window.

'This must have been quite a place,' he whistled. 'When it was all one house and the garden hadn't been chopped about. Even now it's got to be around an acre I should think. She must have been quite a character, your distant cousin Violet.'

I nodded and carefully emptied the Tunbridge-ware box on to the bed. There were the letters, the photographs, a couple of newspaper clippings, and Violet's notes, along with my own birth certificate. I gestured mutely and he came away from the window.

His face was impassive as he quickly scanned the sentences that had changed my life, then he went back to the top and read it again, more slowly.

'Bloody hell! No wonder your foundations have been

rocked, sweetheart. What a thing to turn up in an old box. Let's see what else there is.'

Not a lot, was the answer to that. A photograph showed a middle-aged woman, a younger one and a toddler dressed in a *broderie anglaise* dress and little buttoned boots. I rummaged and found the newspaper article about Dorothy Wellman's retirement.

'I think the younger woman is Dorothy,' I showed the photos to Patrick. 'Look, she's got the same stern gaze and those eyebrows look as though they could frown quite fiercely. Useful for a headmistress. The baby must be Violet and the older woman is Dorothy's mother. I wonder how she took the news of an illegitimate grandchild. Because that's the only inference I can take from the absent father on Violet's birth certificate.'

'She loved the baby,' he said quietly and I stared at him.

'Look,' he said, pointing to the photograph. 'She's holding the little one's hand and smiling at her. It must have been tough for them.'

I peered at the photograph and saw that he was right. 'You really are a very nice man, aren't you?'

'Glad you realise it.' His voice was cocky but his eyes were serious as they met mine. I caught my breath and went back to the scatter of papers on the bed where I found a pencilled note that had been paper-clipped to Violet's note and come adrift. It was a brief explanation that the attempts at pregnancy would take place one at a time.

'I did wonder,' I managed a faint smile as I handed it over. 'They'd have been a bit stumped if all the women ended up with a baby.'

'This one's interesting,' Patrick opened a large manila envelope and extracted a tiny empty bottle of Devon Violets scent and a postcard addressed to Miss Dorothy Wellman. A bunch of pressed violets was carefully wrapped in tissue paper.

The card read, "I'm 'somewhere in France' and the sun is shining as I drink my coffee. There are violets in bloom in the garden next door. Wait for me." It was signed, R.B.

It didn't take a genius to work out who R.B. had been and the tears in my eyes were no longer for myself but for Dorothy and the young man who wrote about violets. Also in the envelope was a yellowed cutting from the Ramalley Gazette, announcing that 2nd Lt Ronald Bracewell, aged 19, only son of Mr & Mrs R. J. Bracewell, proprietors of Ramalley's major emporium, had been killed.

I welled up again and had to blow my nose when we found another more recent photograph of a young man and woman holding hands. On the back, in what I recognised as Violet's writing, was a note: John Brent, died HMS Hood, 1941.

'It must be Violet,' Patrick held it out to me. 'She looks a bit like you, though you can't see her colouring.'

I stared at the woman who had left me her house and she smiled back at me. He was right; even I could see a slight resemblance, in the shape of her face and the light-coloured curls. Poor Violet, to have that radiant happiness destroyed so harshly.

'You see?' Patrick squeezed my hand. 'There are worse things in life than finding you were loved by not just one, but two mothers. Dorothy Wellman had a successful career and so did Violet from what you've told me – as a much-loved midwife. They may not have had it easy but they had their moments. 'Come on, let it all sink in slowly while you show me the rest of the house. I want to see that amazing window. Then you can work out your next step.'

It was oddly comforting to have someone to confide in, because apart from talking to Louise I tend to bottle things up – hiding behind that brave front – and this was Patrick who, it seemed, had come back in from the cold. Even though I had no idea what was going on in his head I felt happier and I could see the sense in what he said about my parents. What *was* my next step? The answer came quickly: I wanted to find her, this stranger who gave birth to me. Was she a local woman? She must have been for Violet to be confident of finding someone to oblige. That being so, had I met her already? I recalled the way Cathy from next-door had watched me when she thought I wasn't aware of it, and how the smart, sophisticated Edwina had quivered with tension when I sat beside her. Perhaps Mary Draper wasn't as elderly as I'd supposed – could she have had a child in her mid-forties? Was it going to be that simple? What if – oh, God – how could I bear it if it was Diane, from the clairvoyant evening?

He was a mind-reader. He said quietly, 'Don't force it, the answer will come when you need it.'

I'd known he'd fall for the long upstairs room and he was full of plans immediately.

'You'll need to find a specialist plasterer,' he enthused. 'The ceiling's been white-washed over centuries and someone took the trouble to cover up the beams, apart from the four main ones. It can't be the original lime plaster but even so you'll need to find an expert. You'd better start haunting auction rooms too. Wouldn't a four-poster look great in here?'

As we made our way downstairs, Patrick paused and sniffed. 'Mmm, it's very early for sweet peas, Freya, where on earth did you get them?' He looked round, puzzled. 'And where have you hidden them?'

'What do you mean?'

'That's odd,' he looked along the hall. 'I swear I can smell sweet peas.'

'What do you know about sweet peas?' I was surprised. 'Have you morphed into Alan Titchmarsh?'

'There's no mistaking them,' he shrugged. 'They're my mum's favourite flower. She grows them every year and fills the house with them.'

'It's odd, you know, Patrick.' My voice was subdued. '*I* keep smelling roses, not sweet peas. I can smell them now.'

We stood like idiots, both sniffing the air.

'I wonder whether anyone else has smelled anything here,' Patrick looked thoughtful. 'Perhaps your house is haunted by the scent of flowers, wouldn't that be something?'

I was startled. 'Mary Draper said she's been coming here for years and has always smelled lavender in the air and she says Violet always swore *she* could smell violets.' I fell silent for a moment. 'It's a bit spooky, isn't it?' I pulled myself together and quickly showed Patrick the dining-room and the parlour, then ushered him into the long downstairs room. Dickon's room. 'Here's the church window.'

'It's stunning,' he said, pulling out his phone and taking photos – of the window, of the panelling, of the stone mantel, one of me – smiling at him. 'It's got to be the real deal. Those fragments of thick, greenish glass all look ancient.' He prowled round the room. 'The size of it,' he marvelled. 'Imagine finding a room like this in a farmhouse.' He came back to the mantelpiece. 'Somebody certainly loved hares, didn't they?'

'The solicitor told me there's a story that if anyone harms a hare at Ladywell it'll do him no good.'

He nodded, admired the hare Louise had given me, and wandered round the room, paying particular attention to where the partition wall had been. 'You'll need a good carpenter,' he pointed out. 'As well as an expert plasterer. This needs to be restored properly.' The built-in bookcase claimed his attention next. 'I bet there was a door here,' he concluded, grinning as I protested. 'Don't worry, I won't start knocking at the back panel. We don't want an irate neighbour turning up but when it was all one house there had to be a way through into each wing. I noticed the other bookcase in the dining-room.'

I watched as he peered at the panelling and stood on a kitchen chair to examine the plasterwork on the ceiling, poking with a disdainful finger at the peeling metal windows.

'It's a crying shame somebody put these in,' he complained. 'Though they'll let in more light than the originals. Thank God they left the big window. There are companies that specialise in double-glazing for historic houses but it won't be cheap.' He caught me watching him. 'What? What's so funny?'

I could hardly tell him I'd been picturing him in this

room, not as a guest but as a man who lived here – with me. I could see him sprawled out on a long sofa in front of a roaring fire, in a beautifully refurbished room, with panelling and plasterwork all immaculate. I could picture him here – in my life.

No, I couldn't tell him that so I checked the time on my phone.

'It's getting on for ten already. We could explore Ramalley if you feel up to it. I haven't been round the Priory yet and there are some decent coffee shops in town.'

'Sounds like a plan,' he agreed. 'I never actually asked if it's okay to stay tonight. I can catch a train in the morning, there are places I have to be later tomorrow. If I'd had any sense I'd have stayed quiet about being back early, but I made the appointment before I left Denver. Still...' He bit his lip. 'I wondered; would it be all right if I came back here sometime Thursday afternoon? This house is wonderful. If it didn't sound ridiculous I'd say it's welcomed me.'

'It's not ridiculous,' I said quietly. 'The house welcomed me too.' I fell silent for a moment. 'I'll just go and find you a proper bath towel. I'd better do it now or you'll find yourself stuck with a skimpy hand towel. There's bed-linen and towels in the chest in your room but I haven't had a proper rummage. It won't take a minute.'

I was wrong about that because I found treasure.

'What are you yelling about?' Patrick found me on my knees before the open bottom drawer.

'Look what I've found!' I gingerly unwrapped the flat parcel that had been tucked under some carefully darned sheets. It was laid flat in tissue paper and held between two large sheets of cardboard, the whole thing slipped into a pillow-case. 'I think it's a sampler.'

We laid it flat on Patrick's bed and removed the protective layers. I was right. An unframed piece of linen revealed a border of green leaves dotted with red berries, beautifully worked in tiny cross-stitch, and I remembered Violet's urgent instruction that I should make a wreath of rowan twigs. Was this a border of leaves from the same rowan tree? How long did they live?

'This must have been hidden away for years,' I said thoughtfully. 'I wonder why Violet tucked it in this drawer and didn't just leave it in its old wrappings?' It occurred to me then that she had probably put it there for me to find and I felt humbled, yet again, by her gift to me.

Within the border were the usual numbers and letters of the alphabet and in the centre of the sampler stood a well, built of neatly stitched grey blocks and topped with a pulley that hung from something like iron poles. On either side of the well stood two small people, one wearing a skirt and the other in breeches.

'They're twins,' I peered at the words. 'Richard Wellman and Anne Wellman, born Twelfth Night in the year 1675.'

Patrick ran his fingers gently down the edge of the linen. 'I don't think it's ever been framed,' he concluded. 'The colours haven't faded. You'll have to see about having it done properly, Freya. It deserves to be on display.'

'There's something at the bottom, "Anne Wellman of Ladywell, aged 10."'

Who was she? I wondered, the Anne Wellman who had sewn so beautifully at such a young age and painstakingly created this lovely piece of work. Why had her sampler never been proudly displayed by her family? I'd never know and I shivered as I realised the most likely explanation was that Anne had died young and her work put away by her grieving relatives.

(iii)

I hate hares.
Her creature stares at me from the field.
I slew it thrice and yet it does not die.
It bides there,
Watching me.
I lit the fire and she died, cursing me.
I am forsaken.
No man will greet me,

None but the hare.
Watching me.
Waiting.

Henrietta could hear the scritch, scratch of the pen as
Gideon stabbed at the paper, ink flying as he wrote the same
words over and over, trying, she supposed, to scratch out the
memory of the screams and wailing of the bystanders as the
flames rose upward and the faggots burned. Trying to scratch
out the uncanny silence at the heart of the fire, even as the
flames licked at her mother-in-law's flesh.

'Why can I find no rest?' he groaned aloud and Henrietta
shivered at the despair in his grating voice. 'No peace, no
sleep, there is no kindness from the Lord, tho' I do his work
with all my heart. Father, why hast thou forsaken me?'

It was blasphemy and she shuddered but dared not speak,
tiptoeing back to the doorway to make a noise, a louder
entrance. She scuttled into the long parlour and put his ale
and bread and cheese on the table beside the strange words
he wrote day by day, always the same, over and over.

'What's this?' He jolted back from wherever he spent his
nightmare days.

She shrank away, her head bent in submission and
whispered, 'You have not eaten, Master Gideon. You need to
keep up your strength.'

Dark eyes burned into her own brown ones and to her
horror he raised a hand, not to strike but worse, infinitely
worse, to stroke her soft, unblemished cheek. She concealed a
shudder and took a step backwards, still submissive, still
meek, but even so – just for a moment – she thought he would
touch her again.

'Get out of my sight.' He flung himself away from her, his
voice rising almost to a scream as he added, 'And keep those
brats away from me, lest I put them to good honest work in
the town.'

Not nine months past, Henrietta's life had been sweet and
merry. Jacob Wellman, her husband, was a good worker,

toiling valiantly about the place, proving a good hand with the beasts. The ten-year old twins, Richard and Little Anne, named for their grandparents, flourished in the prosperous surroundings of Ladywell Farm and she and her mother-in-law, Nan, had many a plan to extend the old house to accommodate the further children that so far eluded her.

The first tragedy was the accident that took Jacob from her in January. The shepherd's boy told how a foolish early lamb had run off towards the river with its mother bleating after it and when Jacob went after the pair he had slipped on the icy mud and into the water. When they pulled him out, he was dead.

After that everything seemed to happen at once. In February of this year of 1685, King Charles took to his death bed, and Henrietta's father-in-law, Dick Wellman, was appalled when the king's brother, Papist James, came to the throne. Memories were long and folk remembered tales their forebears had told. Honest folk, they said, tortured and killed until the Old Queen, Old Bess, put a stop to it. Who was to say the new king wasn't another like Bloody Mary?

The question arose, if not King James, who? And there, living in Holland where plots were being hatched, was James, Duke of Monmouth, eldest son of King Charles. To be sure he was a bastard, but so were the rest of the king's children and Monmouth was at least a Protestant.

Nothing there, you would have thought, to disturb a quiet farmhouse on the outskirts of a snug market town in Hampshire.

Dick Wellman, the farmer, spent his days working and worrying about the cold, dry spring's effect on his harvest. At night he pored over his Bible trying to discover what God wanted from him until suddenly, one day in early summer, he knew.

''The Lord's will be done.' He was eager to make his wife understand. 'I asked for a sign and God has sent the Duke of Monmouth to claim the throne and for godly men to oust the Papist. I aim to join him at Lyme as soon as maybe.'

Nan Wellman argued with him day and night. Still

grieving for young Jacob, her only child, she tried to make Dick change his mind.

'We need you here,' she wept. 'Not running after princes.'

'I'll hear no more, wife,' he told her piously. 'This is God's work.'

She knew that tone of voice so she folded her lips tightly and reflected, not for the first time, that she had never truly loved him. Dick was a hard worker; a good man and a good catch, but never one for jollity, unlike his jovial, open-handed father. Dick Wellman was stiff and shy and awkward, looking askance at his cheerful, laughing wife. Would she have fared better with a gentler man, a man who liked a joke? Or would he, too, have rushed off on this mad undertaking after a dead King's bastard?

All too soon her forebodings were proved right. Slightly wounded in the battle on the 6th of July at Sedgemoor in Somerset, her husband took a long and roundabout route, disguised as a labourer working on other men's farms to allay suspicion. Fate caught up with him thirty miles from home as he made his cautious way through Poole where he was caught up in a brawl and left with a stinking, festering wound to his right arm. In the dead of one muggy night at the very end of August, almost two months after the battle, Dick Wellman stumbled painfully into his own barn.

To find a complete stranger occupying his house.

Gideon Cooper had turned up a couple of weeks after the departure of the farmer who, cursing the sudden rains that broke the long dry spell, had managed to bring in the hay before he left to follow his cause. Nan Wellman was out, but Henrietta sat spinning in the long parlour, soothed by the rhythm of the work. She was flustered to see this short, grey man with a bobbing Adam's apple, standing in the doorway. He smiled thinly as he introduced himself.

'I was the only child of my mother, Mistress Constance Cooper,' he explained, spreading out his papers on the oak table. 'She, when widowed, took a second husband, Farmer Wellman, and moved to Hampshire where she had a son,

132

Dick. I remained in Essex until I had a call to travel the land preaching the Lord's will and I feel a strong desire to make the acquaintance of the only kin I have left. Pray present me to Master Wellman, my dear.'

What to say? How to answer this stranger with the precise speech of a lawyer and the never-ending smile that failed to reach his eyes? His garb was plain and his manner severe, belying his fine words. Henrietta felt a shiver in her bones as she met the visitor's gaze.

'Master Wellman is from home, sir,' she replied. 'He has gone to look at some sheep up Salisbury way. If you give me your direction he will be sure to visit you on his return.'

'I think not.' His calm assurance astonished her. 'No, my dear, I will be very comfortable here in this fine house.' He gave her a level stare as she jerked her head in surprise. 'What? You think I do not know where your father-in-law has gone? I have friends in the town you know. I have a fancy to make a name for myself here so I made sure to linger yonder for a week or so before I came to Ladywell, and a righteous man they soon saw me to be. Oh yes, for a godless place that sent men to fight for the Papist king and hanged true soldiers of the Parliament, Ramalley now has many upstanding folk who see the error of their fathers' ways. I shall soon be a power among them.'

His lips parted in a mirthless smile as she stared in horror. 'I am a powerful preacher, you know. You must not fail to hear my discourse against the sin of disobedience.' Again that cold smile. 'My poor brother, alas, committed an act of treason by taking up arms to fight for Monmouth and I am minded to denounce him. Judge Jeffries, they say, is hot for justice in the King's name.'

'But' she stammered. 'You are surely not for the Papist King?'

He leaned towards her and raised her chin with hard, bony fingers. 'My good woman, I am for whoever will grant me ownership of this plump little holding and all that goes with it. I am the elder son and entitled to claim this farm when Dick Wellman is condemned for treason, alive or dead.

You will do well to remember that.'

'You may be the elder brother.' She was more puzzled than afraid. 'But you have no Wellman blood. It's not your land. Dick's father owned Ladywell and it is for Dick's grandchild to inherit, not you.'

He slapped her hard across the face and as she staggered and cried out, he struck her again.

'That is not the case,' he said calmly. 'You will do well to remember that.'

(iv)

The following weeks were hideous. No word from Dick Wellman and dire tidings of the battle trickling out of the West and the house, so loved, so familiar, was now a place of shadows, of nightmare. Even Dick, serious fellow, used – once in a while – to smile and tap his foot when the women sang, but now they were frozen into silence. Worst of all was the long room, known always as Dickon's Room, though no man knew why, where the family used to gather after the day's work. It was Gideon Cooper's domain now and soured by his presence, as was the best bedchamber above it.

There were other dangers. Huddled in Henrietta's chamber after Nan was ousted from her own fine room, she whispered to her son's widow to keep the twins out of Gideon's sight. The workers at the farm were soon cowed by the man who, slight and insignificant-looking, somehow terrified them into subjection. Threats and blackmail were his weapons and he knew that a son here, a husband there, a brother perhaps, had all made for Lyme when Monmouth landed, and were even now in the West Country with the straggle of rebels in hiding from the King's men.

Gideon had not lied about his new friends in the town and within less than a fortnight he was leader of a group of men who listened agog as he preached burning and beheading against those who committed treason. Back at the farm he spent hours in silence, watching his niece about her daily tasks.

134

'He stares at me, Ma,' Henrietta whispered after the first evening. 'He frightens me.'

'He's dangerous.' The older woman's heart was heavy as she watched her daughter-in-law's face grow pinched and fearful when she had only lately begun to smile again after Jacob's death. 'Never stay in a room alone with him, never let the children near him without you. I do not trust him.'

~

Easier said than done, Henrietta thought now, weeks later, as she escaped from the parlour leaving Gideon scritch-scratching at his words as he sat under the great stone window – the symbol of Popery he had threatened to destroy before the change came upon him. Harvest time now and her world destroyed. Jacob was gone and Dick, his father, had returned on that terrible night when horror overcame them.

~

Near midnight it had been and the air warm and soft, when Nan Wellman laid a hand across Henrietta's mouth lest she cry out on waking.

'Shhh, make no sound. Dick is returned, sorely injured. He's in the hay barn and I'm taking food and drink while I bind his wounds. I've sent his friends on their way for Gideon must not catch them and you must stay in this room, my dear, you and the children. You must not be part of this.'

Henrietta's protests died under the older woman's urgency. 'What you do not know, you cannot tell. Rise as usual in the morning. All will be well, I'm sure, but you must take no risks.'

In the morning all was not well. Henrietta never discovered what had happened to her father-in-law but when she went down to the kitchen Gideon Cooper was already there, a gleam of triumph in his cold, grey eyes.

'The traitor, Richard Wellman, has paid the price,' he said in a conversational tone. 'He was hiding in the hay barn last night and has died of his wounds.'

She turned pale, a hand to her trembling mouth as she ran out to the yard. 'Where is Mistress Wellman?' she demanded when he followed her. 'What have you done with *her?'*

'She too will pay the price,' he shrugged. 'And if you know what is good for you, you will obey me in all things.'

(v)

Nan Wellman was clapped in jail for a week before her travesty of a trial. Gideon Cooper egged on his carefully chosen acquaintances, a justice, a schoolmaster, merchants, men of standing, and put the fear of God in them.

Less than a week earlier, the execution of Dame Alice Lisle in Winchester had been witnessed by one or two of the Ramalley worthies and at Nan's trial Cooper whipped up a frenzy.

'Is it not rumoured that Ladywell folk enjoy better health and longer life than honest men in the town? Does not she, a farmer's wife, have the soft hands of a lady?'

'That comes from handling the greasy fleeces,' pointed out a puzzled bystander.

'Yea!' Gideon Cooper was triumphant. 'She hath a familiar in the form of a sheep. I call her Witch!'

Fuelled by hysteria and liberal draughts of ale spiced with brandy provided by Cooper, Nan Wellman was damned. She was to burn for treason and that right soon. The fearsome Judge Jeffries had sentenced Alice Lisle to death by burning but this had been commuted to beheading. Alice Lisle was a lady but there was no man to speak for a farmer's wife in an obscure market town; nobody to protest that witch burnings were unheard of there.

Henrietta knew nothing could save Nan, but she begged for a last interview on the morning of the execution and made her preparations accordingly. Herbs, were her first frantic thought, but no herb would act instantly; it must be something to end Nan's suffering when the flames blazed. Cooper refused her request but the justices of the town had started to feel uneasy about the burning and declared that a last farewell would do no harm.

''Tis only Christian,' said one and the others nodded

136

sagely.

The two women from Ladywell said little. The condemned woman folded her son's wife in a loving embrace and as their hands clasped, Henrietta slipped a thin, razor-sharp knife into Nan's sleeve.

'All I could find,' the younger woman drooped, almost too ravaged by tears to speak, and Nan answered softly.

'All that I need, my love. Now get you home to Ladywell and look to your babes. I can do what I must, but not if you are here, not if you are watching. It is too hard. You've done your part so go now and remember always the love I bear you all.'

Some of the women of the town came forward and drew the distraught Henrietta out of the market place. One of the men, sickened by the whole thing, put her up behind him on his horse and cantered over to Ladywell, ignoring her wails of anguish.

Nan Wellman approached the pile of faggots and called out to her captors.

'I beg of you leave my hands untied that I may pray to the Lord. You need not fear. I shall not run away.'

They tied her to the stake but out of mercy left her hands free. Gideon Cooper, angry at being once more overruled, lit a torch as he called to his victim, 'Do you have anything to say, foul witch?'

'Yes,' she said in a clear, resolute voice. 'I forgive you, Gideon Cooper. I forgive the foolish folk of this town because they are weak and have followed an evil man. You, I forgive, because the Lord preaches forgiveness but mark this, Gideon. Now, and for your life long, you will find no rest, for your sin will find you out. The Lord will walk with you but you will be bowed down by His sorrow. More, you will feel my eyes watching you. You will look over your shoulder and I will be there, and the weight of your guilt will destroy you.'

Onlookers said that she raised a hand to her breast and seemed to shudder, then to sag against the stake, whereupon Cooper defied the townsfolk who were aghast and fearful now, and thrust the burning brand into the bundles of

137

brushwood.

With a trembling voice, Nan cried out in a foreign tongue – a spell, men said, though none could make out the words and they kept their counsel lest this be witchcraft after all. Then she spoke in God's own English so all men present could understand – but dear Lord, was it a Popish prayer? To the Catholic Mary? 'Lady, save us, Lady, look to your own,' she gasped. The flames beat back the onlookers but those who ventured closer swore that she pressed her hand hard at her breast once more and that death overtook her.

(vii)

Henrietta was left to run the farm alone. Desperate to bring in the harvest, the farmhands rallied round and did her bidding and her two young children helped wherever they could, making sure their mother was never alone with her uncle.

For Gideon had gone mad.

Let the vicar say what he might, that Nan Wellman had died in a state of piety just as she should, Gideon knew that her words of forgiveness were a curse upon him, a curse he could never escape. Why else was he tormented day and night with ungodly dreams, now of the crackling flames and the sickening smell of human flesh and now of himself lying with his nephew's widow? She was a comely wench, but he had suffered no impure thoughts until Nan Wellman began to haunt him.

The hare, he shuddered. He knew, without looking, that it was there again. Bolder than any natural hare, always in the garden, on the wall, or across the stream. The old folks in the cottages gleefully told him how Ladywell was home to many a hare, as if they knew they ran safe about the fields. 'No hare may be killed on this land,' they warned him with toothless glee. 'Lest harm befall he who does the deed.'

Nevertheless he shot the hare but sweat ran into his eyes, despite the chill in his heart, and when he wiped his brow the hare was not to be seen. Day after day he went after the animal, day after day he shot at it and knew he had killed it, but always the next morning it stared at him. Nan Wellman's words rang in his ears like the knell of the passing-bell. In the corner of his eye he would see the hare, yet when he whirled round the creature was gone. In the town when he ventured forth, he would see a flash of brown fur and run after it, shouting, but there was nothing there and people shrank from him, staring.

'Tis a curse on that Gideon,' the old crones nodded, watching to see what he would do next.

He took to writing down the words that came to him in the night whenever he woke from the dreams of forbidden lust. The words frightened him more than he could say for they seemed to come from the mouth of a dying woman, a woman who had cheated him at the doors of death. Always the same words; from a woman who had willed herself to die rather than suffer the agony of burning. Such words had power, words he could never escape, and his eyes burned in his sunken face as he took refuge indoors.

The hare would not die so the hare must be the woman. Therefore, he reasoned, the woman was surely a witch to defy him thus. His eyes turned towards the witch's daughter-in-law and burned anew with the light of madness that merged with desire. Even the house turned against him. The strong, handsome house he had coveted so fiercely at first sight, now frightened him with its dark shadows and brooding, threatening presence. The handsome window that was a papist relic filled him with hatred and dread. If only his limbs were not so heavy, his body so listless, his mind so mazed, he would break the window apart and deface the carved hare – and that other on the mantel. Hares that stared at him in judgement.

People from Ramalley town came across the river and others from the neighbouring villages on the west bank beyond the farm. They came in ones and twos, then in a crowd, anxious to distance themselves from the insanity that had overtaken the god-fearing little town. They brought gifts for Henrietta and the children: wine and food, cloth and spices, a cheese or a pie or a brace of rabbits, anything to wipe away the memories and they sagged with relief when Henrietta thanked them with a wan shadow of her former smile. They would look round anxiously and breathe again when there was no sign of Gideon Cooper. A hardy few would ask after him and Henrietta would murmur that he was not well. They nodded and asked, diffidently, whether she needed help with him, but she always shook her head.

Word soon ran around that the lifelong Puritan, Gideon Cooper, had taken to drink and was to be found late at night by the old well, trying to drown out the memory of the farm-wife's curse.

Henrietta barred her door at night and kept the twins, who hated him, close beside her; they were small for their age and she feared for their safety. She herself continued to behave submissively when the interloper was within the house though after a week with no further outbursts from Gideon, she relaxed her guard slightly and the children were allowed outside, as long as they stayed within earshot. During the day they did their chores about the house and yard and afterwards stayed near the old well, now girded by a low stone wall topped with two tall iron hoops, holding the pulley and chain that hauled the bucket. Little Anne, a tidy child, sat on a log as she sewed diligently at her sampler, never letting a speck of mud near it, while Richard whittled sticks and dug in the kitchen garden nearby.

Ten days after the burning, Charley, the shepherd's twelve-year old boy, knocked on the door in the late evening. 'Mistress,' he whispered, glancing fearfully over his shoulder. 'You must come to the well, there've been an accident.'

'The children?' Her hand flew to her mouth and she breathed again when he shook his head.

'Tis Master Cooper, he's in the well, drownded.' The boy's face was sweaty with the horror of it. 'We all know he's been drinking there of a night, and that shaky on his feet a child could push him over the edge with one finger. He must have fell in, all tipsy like.'

Henrietta prayed never to know another night like that,

worse almost than the blows that had already fallen. Darkness was upon them so she lit a lantern and followed Charley to the well. As she peered down into the depths Gideon Cooper's drowned face stared up at her, making her turn aside as she retched.

'We must get him out, Mistress,' urged Charley. 'You stay here and I'll fetch my dad. Us can't do it on our own.'

The shepherd said little as he took in the situation, but got to work at once. He lowered his skinny son down and bade him attach a rope to Cooper's belt. Together he and the boy, and Henrietta, hauled the body upwards.

'Wh-what shall we do with him?' Henrietta was shaking with cold and fear. 'We'll have to send for the justices and who will believe that I did him no harm? To fall and die so pat upon what happened.' She held her hand to her mouth until the nausea subsided. 'I would not believe it of anyone, myself. What in God's name am I to do?'

'I could bury 'un, Mistress, where he'll not be found,' the shepherd suggested. 'I could dig a grave by the muck heap and shovel more muck on top. Who will look for him there?'

'If they found out, you could be hanged,' she shuddered. 'We would all be hanged, even the boy.'

'Don't talk daft, Mistress,' he said with a bracing nod. 'Nobody won't find out. You think I don't owe my living to Master Wellman? My wife's life to Mistress Nan who saved her when she was like to die birthing the lad? Nor my old father and mother and my grandfer too. Wellmans does well by us and we stand by you and yours. You think up some tale to tell 'em over the river, and me and the boy will start digging.'

While he dug the hole she ran to the house and brought back a bundle. 'Here,' she whispered, holding up a leather bag. 'Bury his Bible with him.' She unrolled a fine-woven woollen cloth. 'Mistress Nan wove this; let it serve as his shroud so he may remember her for all eternity.'

They laid rocks on the makeshift grave and covered it with earth and dung, and Henrietta said,

'I can copy his hand well enough so I'll address a note to

me, from him,' she whispered, shivering despite the warmth of the night. 'It will say he's taking the Lord's word to the Americas. People will recall that he talked often of the land of milk and honey across the sea.'

It was after midnight when Henrietta, afraid of arousing the sleeping household, kept her light low as she tiptoed indoors, where she cleaned her muddy shoes and set them to dry before the kitchen fire. She leaned for a moment against the solid wall, drawing comfort from the strength of the building that had kept the family safe for more than a hundred years.

A fearsome thought struck her. Gideon was not the only man to accuse Nan Wellman of witchcraft. 'Suppose someone decided the witch's kinswoman had the power to curse a man or blight a harvest?'

She ran to the herb cupboard on the wall and checked the neat bags and their contents: lavender for the falling sickness and pains in the head, lady's smock for scurvy and to break up the stone, herbs such as any goodwife kept. She whimpered. God be thanked that Nan's small sharp paring knife was now nothing but ash and melted metal, long swept away from the town square. God's mercy too, that no man knew of the knife's part in Nan's release from the burning.

Her eye lighted on little Anne's sampler that lay on the shelf. The neat stitching of the letters and the border of rowan leaves and berries filled her with pride but her face was sorrowful as she wrapped it carefully in a clean cloth and hid it at the bottom of the carved wooden chest in the hall. Little Anne would be puzzled and upset at its disappearance but Henrietta knew she could not bear to see her children pictured beside the well that was now and forever blighted by Gideon Cooper.

Her thoughts scurried to and fro, casting back to the last time she had seen him. In the kitchen, she thought; he was here, with a pint of ale in his hand when I came indoors at dusk. She shivered, as she imagined a man tormented by nightmares. Had he thrown himself into the well? Had it all become too much to bear?

She made a decision. Better be without a needful remedy than have the townsfolk baying at her door. She tightened her lips and emptied every bag carefully into the fire, which blazed up fiercely, blue and gold and red. Satisfied that all traces were gone she tiptoed up the stairs to her room, exhausted but conscious of a lightening of her burden. The children, who had feared and hated their uncle, could live safe from the shadows.

She gave a tired and tremulous smile at the sight of her little ones curled up together like puppies, and tut-tutted at their clothes scattered on the floor though she had made all tidy at their bedtime.

As she gathered up Anne and Dickon's boots and their clothes, the smile froze on her lips. There were smears of fresh mud on the boots and splashes on the skirt and breeches she clutched. Something, a rag perhaps, had been thrown under the bed in haste. Like an old woman, she bent to draw it out and a spasm of horror shook her. The rag was streaked with fresh mud, still wet from where the boots and small garments had been frantically wiped clean.

In her mind's eye she saw the trampled mud around the Lady's Well and she heard again the shepherd's boy saying, 'A child could push him over the edge with one finger.'

Chapter Ten

(i)

Tuesday, 10th March – mid morning

The sun broke through as I led the way towards Nonie's Café. It was a good place to check emails and the coffee was great. I knew Patrick would like it.

'Good morning,' I greeted the owner cheerfully. 'A small, skinny cappuccino, please, and a black Americano.' I raised an eyebrow at Patrick. 'Large?'

'Are you feeling better?' The owner smiled. 'You were quite shaken up on Friday, weren't you? No,' she said in response to the coins I held out. 'It's on the house. A welcome to Ramalley.'

'That's really kind of you,' I was touched. 'I'm fine now, thanks, it was just so unexpected. Oh, this is my friend Patrick Underwood. Patrick, this is Nonie…' I couldn't remember her surname.

'Anona Radstone,' she supplied, as she handed him his coffee. 'Welcome to Ramalley, Patrick. I hope we'll be seeing more of you?'

'I hope so too.' He thanked her with a lurking twinkle in his eyes.

'What are you grinning at?' We sat in the bay window overlooking the market square. 'What's so funny?'

'Not funny,' he stretched out his long legs and leaned back in his chair. 'It's just that oh, I don't know. It's not just your house, Freya; the whole town has a friendly atmosphere. I really like it here.'

As I hugged this little nugget to myself, he surprised me.

'What was it that upset you on Friday? What happened

144

here that was so unexpected? Are you planning to tell me?'

I met his concerned gaze and spooned froth off my coffee.

'I might as well. You've heard some of it, it's only fair to tell you the rest.'

In as few words as possible I told him about the woman who had accosted me in the square. I described how Alison had taken me to lunch in the pub and how the two women, Cathy and Edwina, had covertly watched me. I finished by giving him a brief description of the evening of clairvoyance and the 'message' I'd received.

He said nothing but he was watching my face and when I leaned back, drained, he reached for my hand.

'You've really had a basinful in the last few days, haven't you? No wonder you're so wound up. Did the woman seem genuine?' He frowned. 'I can't say I believe in messages from beyond the grave though I can see it's comforting. It has to be guesswork, surely? I mean, an elderly woman with a sad face – it's a safe enough bet that she could be a widow, so a few passes might hit the mark.' He shook his head.

'On the other hand, to tell a young woman that her mother didn't actually give birth to her is powerful stuff. When you tie that in with the same young woman discovering that her birth involved a kind of surrogacy, it starts to get very strange.' He squeezed my hand. 'Any chance this woman could know something? Was she was a friend of Violet Wellman's, for instance?'

I shook my head. 'Mary was adamant she'd never seen the woman before, and she seems to know everyone.' I remembered that moment of shared amusement. 'I don't know, Patrick. I read my stars for fun, like most people, and yes, she upset me that first time, but later – I can only tell you I suddenly felt she was genuine.'

I checked my emails via the café's Wi-Fi and found a terse message.

From louise@backofbeyond: '**Am ok, talk soon.**' I answered equally briefly, this was no time to go into detail about Patrick's arrival. We said goodbye to Nonie Radstone

145

and wandered across the square towards the Priory. Patrick suddenly stopped.

'What was that about a man with a funny hat and a necklace?'

He was staring up at the statue of a local bigwig. A portly old gentleman in a long coat over knee-breeches, he wore a tricorne hat at a jaunty angle over his wig, and round his neck hung a chain of office. He had a beaky nose in a round, jolly face and his left eyelid drooped slightly, as though he was about to wink at you.

The plinth bore an inscription.

'*Sir Humphrey Moberley, Alderman of the City of London and latterly resident of*

Ramalley. Greatly esteemed for his good works and generosity of spirit.'

The Alderman, it seemed, had departed this life at the end of a long and philanthropic career at the age of 88 in 1767 and was much missed by his friends in Ramalley.

I walked round the statue staring at the cheerful stone face with its stone hat and necklace.

'Now I *really* feel spooked,' I said with a shiver. 'This just gets weirder and weirder!' I whipped out my phone. 'Here, let's have a selfie in front of him!'

'I thought you didn't do selfies?' he grinned as he put an arm round me.

'I don't. I've made an exception for him, though.'

I made a face at the statue and put my phone away. 'Enough with the supernatural – stone aldermen and ghostly flowers. Let's look round the Priory.'

We followed the brown tourist sign and found ourselves in a maze of narrow streets until we reached the Norman Priory church. Patrick looked back at the old houses.

'Interesting that they're almost all red-brick or rendered,' he said thoughtfully. 'Your house is stone, the first one I've actually spotted. Come to think of it, the grey stone looks remarkably similar to the Priory. I wonder if that's a clue.'

At the far end of the building rose a squat tower and facing the main door was a broad green lawn, in the centre of which was a railing round what looked like the head of a large well. It was the Font that, according to the notice beside it, was the source of the town's original prosperity. It was unusual in that it was about twelve feet across and the same in depth.

Another discreet sign announced that coins thrown into the Font were collected on a regular basis and donated to the Priory Fabric Fund with the proviso that there was "no guarantee" wishes would come true. Patrick fished a couple of pound coins out of his pocket and we threw them in.

'What did you wish for?' I asked, but he shook his head, looking enigmatic. I didn't tell him my wish either.

We sauntered round the adjoining churchyard where no tombstone displayed a date later than the mid-1920s. Completely by chance, in a quiet corner, I recognised a name.

'What is it?' Patrick was wandering among the headstones. I pointed to the simple inscription on an imposing family tomb covered with stern-looking angels.

Sacred to the memory of 2nd Lt. Ronald Bracewell, aged 19

Dearly loved and sorely missed
Born 17th September 1898, killed 27th May 1918
Chemin des Dames, 3rd Battle of the Aisne.
'There is some corner of a foreign field that is forever England'

Patrick opened his mouth to speak but was interrupted by a volunteer gardener who was trimming the hedge nearby.

'It's a funny thing,' she nodded at the grave. 'Until about a year ago there was always a bunch of violets laid there on the 27th May.' She shook her head. 'He'd be buried in France so his family must have added the inscription. I expect whoever brought him flowers has died. Sad,' she added and returned to her pruning.

'You think he was Violet's father?' Patrick squeezed my shoulder as I blew my nose. 'Let me guess. There'll be a bunch of violets here in May.'

I nodded. 'I'll come and hold your hand. I'll bring tissues too,' he added as we headed for the main door to the Priory.

(ii)

The interior of the church had an austere beauty with the light from the windows reflecting off the light grey stone of the walls. An elderly man surged forward armed with leaflets and pointed out the shop with a hopeful smile.

As we walked round Patrick suddenly clutched at my arm. 'Look, Freya, those windows in the side chapel. They're smaller than those in the main part of the church but exactly like the one in your house.' He frowned and took out his phone. 'There's something odd about the proportions of your window though, these are taller. Here, check out the photos.'

I was about to reply when the guide appeared at my elbow.

'You wouldn't be Violet Wellman's heir, by any chance? The girl who inherited her house?'

'How on earth did you know that?' I was astonished. 'I'm Freya Gibson.' I introduced Patrick, and the guide, who said his name was John Fletcher, beamed at us.

'There's only one house in Ramalley that has a stone window like these from the Early Decorated period,' he said with deep satisfaction. 'You're right too,' he nodded to Patrick. 'Your window *was* cut down to fit the room so it looks comparatively squat. You'll also have spotted that someone added a carved hare to the new sill to complement the one on the mantel. If you look closely you'll see where the mason hid the join; it's a brilliant piece of work by a master craftsman. As for the windows here, you'll see flowers and leaves but not a whisker of a hare.'

He twinkled at us. 'I was a friend of Miss Wellman's,' he explained, leading us closer to the windows. 'She was a regular at morning service here but gave it up as her health deteriorated, so I took to dropping in on her.' His smile was nostalgic. 'She was a great one for talking about her house. I suppose you know the stories attached to it?'

'I don't know anything,' I said eagerly. 'The inheritance came out of the blue and I'm desperate to find out whatever I can.'

148

I found myself clutching at Patrick's hand as he asked, 'Can you tell us how a window from this church ended up in Freya's house?'

Mr Fletcher ("Call me John") looked at his watch. 'Time for my lunch break,' he said with an impish grin. 'We're allowed half an hour for good behaviour. It's usually an hour but we're short-staffed today, we're all volunteers. Why don't you join me in the Priory Tea Room? There's stilton-and-broccoli soup today and I'll guarantee it's good. My wife made it.'

We followed our chatty guide to the tea room at the back of the building, Patrick still holding my hand. There was a glimmer of amusement in his grey eyes as he looked down at me so I knew he was happy with the plan. As for me, I was just glad to be with him.

Over Mrs Fletcher's soup, which was as good as her husband claimed, we listened to the history of my stone window.

'According to Violet's grandmother,' John told us, 'who was a great one for family history, the window came from one of the chapels here at the time of the Dissolution. You'll have spotted that the house is built from the same stone as the Priory, and eked out with the local flint. Nobody knows who built your house or how he acquired the stone blocks, let alone how he managed to snaffle a window.'

He warmed to his theme. 'It's an astonishing house, you know. Violet had an architect friend who said that whoever drew up the plans really knew his stuff and had probably lived and worked in London. The detail and standard of design and construction contrasts strongly with the unassuming aspect of the original house, before the wings were added, I mean.'

'This is brilliant stuff.' I was excited. 'I've been so frustrated not knowing any of the history apart from a few notes,' and I explained about Miss Montagu's brief account.

Mr Fletcher finished his soup and crumbled his bread, still talking. 'Records are sketchy but given the style and size of the house it could be that your ancestors once owned the

149

whole area of Ladywell.'

I gasped and he nodded benignly. 'You can't blame the owner for disguising his ambitions; it wasn't safe to attract the attention of anyone who might prove covetous. One thing is certain, a master mason clearly had a hand in it, you can tell by the quality of the carving alone. Some of the side chapels were demolished at that time so that's probably the explanation. Keep it quiet though,' he hissed, glancing round furtively. 'The last thing you need is some busybody deciding the house should be listed. God knows how it's escaped so far, as it is.'

We plied him with questions and he confirmed the solicitor's story about the hares of Puss Hill.

'You won't find any Ramalley local who'd kill a hare,' he said darkly. 'Never mind the stories attached to Ladywell, there's the fact that in Chinese mythology the hare is a symbol of resurrection. Nobody wants to mess with that.' He checked his watch and sighed. 'Back to the grindstone.'

We shook hands. 'Drop in any time. I'm here Monday to Thursday, and I'll be happy to tell you any tales I can. One thing,' he added. 'You do know one of your ancestors was burned as a witch?'

He roared with laughter at my stunned expression and so did Patrick, though I glared at him, which made the pair of them laugh even more.

'I was just surprised,' I said coldly. 'Violet's old teacher, Miss Montagu, wrote some notes on the history of Ladywell Farm and she dismissed any rumours about a witch in the family. Are you telling me there really *was* a witch, Mr Fletcher?'

'Do call me John.' He looked reproachful. 'Oh yes, it was at the time of the Monmouth Rebellion, and technically she was condemned for harbouring a rebel. As the rebel in question was her own husband and he died of his wounds in their barn it was felt locally that the sentence was unjust, but burn she did. The only case ever recorded in Ramalley, in any century.' He nodded, amused. 'Hares and old ladies had much the same protection round here; nobody wanted to tempt fate! They do say...' He looked mysterious. 'They say that as she died she cursed the man who prosecuted her – in a foreign tongue, too – and certainly he left in a hurry soon after and was never seen again. Went to inflict himself on the pilgrims in New England, apparently, and no loss to the town, leaving folk here thoroughly ashamed.'

With that he hurried off, with a friendly wave, leaving Patrick and me to our coffee.

'A witch in the family, eh?' Patrick teased. 'Freya? It was a joke, what's the matter?'

I hunched my shoulders. 'Listen, Patrick. When I arrived that first time, I found a note from Violet.'

I explained how I'd had to pick twigs, leaves and flowers from the garden according to Violet's instructions. 'It was the verse I had to say when I hung the wreath on a nail. It's in Latin and it sounds like a spell. I remember wondering at the time whether Violet could have been a witch. It's in a foreign tongue, like the witch's curse.'

'Do you remember the verse?' He looked keenly interested.

I nodded, and recited it:

'Domina aquarum
Leporumque currentium
Domina custodi nos
Locum benedic.'

'You'll have to translate that,' he shrugged. 'I never did Latin.'

'My school had a campaign to reinstate Latin because of Harry Potter,' I said as I recited the English version:

'Lady of the waters,
Lady of the running hare,
Lady keep us,
Lady bless this place.'

(iii)

On our way out of the Priory, Mr Fletcher hailed us again.

'I forgot to ask,' he said. 'Have you located the holy well, yet? The Lady's Well?'

'What? Sorry, but are you saying there really *is* a well?' I seemed to have done nothing but goggle at him in surprise.

'Oh yes,' he nodded with a sunny smile. 'It ran dry in Victorian times but Miss Wellman always said it was on her conscience so about five years ago she decided to get a man in to put the garden in order and to dig out the well.'

He looked grave. 'Sadly, her sight, which had already begun to fail, deteriorated badly and she had a slight stroke about then, so she reluctantly abandoned the plan. There'd been an old brick outbuilding there for years, and the handyman had made a start by dismantling it. Poor chap, it broke his heart when she made him pile earth on top of the rubble. He'd been all set to dig it out for her and was quite excited. She asked him to plant a rambling Kiftsgate rose on top which would make it less unsightly.'

'Are you saying the old shed is in pieces under that huge prickly patch at the bottom of the garden? And that the well is under the bricks?' I was intrigued now and Patrick's eyes were alight with interest.

'According to Violet,' agreed Mr Fletcher. 'Poor old dear, she was devastated that she didn't have the energy to finish the task. She said her grandmother told her a family tradition maintained that the virtue in the well had somehow been destroyed and that the balance of the place needed to be put right.

'That's fantastic,' Patrick grabbed my hand. 'Let's go home and start digging. Freya?' He turned to look at me. 'What? Something wrong?'

I shook my head, shivering inwardly as I remembered the last line of Violet's note.

'*Restore the balance.*'

Chapter Eleven

(i)

Tuesday, 10th March – afternoon

'I never realised how much tea you drink in a day,' Patrick waved a tea bag at me. 'Okay if I have coffee this time?'

'I drink coffee too,' I shrugged. 'Tea's better.' I reached for my pad and added a coffee maker to my latest list. When I looked up he was grinning at me while the kettle boiled. 'What? What did I say?'

'I remembered how terrifying you were at first,' he said. 'All those lists! Every aspect of my life was documented and mapped out before I knew what hit me.'

'I like to be organised.' I sounded defensive and he patted me on the shoulder as he walked past me to the antique fridge that I'd had no time to replace.

'I'd noticed,' he smirked. 'Here, refresh the little grey cells with your drug of choice and explain all these lists.'

On our way back from town we'd agreed to start exploring Sleeping Beauty's bramble patch but the heavens opened just as we reached home. Mr Fletcher promised to tell me more about the holy well in my garden but he had a party of tourists to take round so he said he'd be in touch. In the meantime I stared out of the kitchen window at the downpour remembering how I'd hidden my lack of confidence under that list-making automaton. I was astonished, and glad, to realise how far I had come. And how much I'd changed in the last few days as though the house had worked its magic on me. Patrick was different too...

'These lists are very important,' I told Patrick, picking one of them up and adding a note to book a chimney sweep.

'I need a new cooker, a fridge-freezer, all kinds of appliances, but before I think about buying anything, I need to design a new kitchen and probably pull this one down. That list is my to-do pile. *This* list is about decorating but first I'll need someone to check out the structural state of the house. I'll need a mortgage if I'm spending money for all this work! I've also begun a list of what furniture to chuck out and what I'd like to buy new, but that'll have to be done room by room. It's endless.' I ran my fingers through my hair and tossed the lists on to the kitchen table.

'Tell you what,' he suggested, leaning against the sink. 'I was all geared up to attack those brambles. Instead, why don't we collect up all the furniture you don't want and break it up? Might be useful for your open fires.'

I jumped up. 'You're on. I'm up for a spot of vandalism. A lot of it's too tatty even to give away.'

It was fun, though we didn't actually break anything up on the spot. Apart from the big sofa, which I liked though it needed recovering, there was little furniture in Dickon's Room. We moved on to the Christmassy front parlour.

'There's nothing good in here,' I sighed, sitting experimentally on the sofa. 'Ouch, that's a spring poking through. It'll have to go.'

The two armchairs were even worse so we piled them on top of the sofa and I peered at the green-patterned carpet. 'At least, I think it must have been green once,' I mourned. 'It's just grunge now, no use to me. Maybe I should hire a skip?'

I found some cardboard boxes and wrapped Violet's bits of china and glass in newspaper. 'I've no idea whether any of this is worth keeping,' I said, 'but I'm not throwing it out, Violet must have loved it. I'll take a closer look later.'

The dining-room was soon dealt with. I'm not a fan of 1930s veneered furniture and this was a shoddy example, so it went on the list. The sideboard contained some cracked china platters and a dingy set of table mats showing a stagecoach and horses, but when I poked inside a cardboard box I discovered more pieces of the violet china: cups, saucers, a sugar bowl and milk jug.

'I bet people gave her things with violets for birthdays and Christmas.' I hesitated. 'I'd have expected more pieces of delicate china when you consider the flowery wallpaper, but it's just occurred to me that it was probably broken. Mary Draper said it took Violet ages to acknowledge her sight was going.'

There was less to throw out than I had assumed, apart from the dining-room furniture which a charity might take. The parlour furniture could go straight to the dump along with some rugs that were beyond redemption, and the downstairs would be clear. I ticked things off my list and we headed upstairs to tackle the bedrooms.

We left the front bedroom alone. The solid Victorian mahogany bed, with a matching wardrobe and chest-of-drawers, was far too good to throw out. Besides, Patrick was using it.

'Like I said this morning, your room is crying out for a four-poster,' he said as he prowled. 'The floorboards are oak and in fantastic condition and once you've had the plasterwork and panelling repaired, the room will be amazing. Pity you don't own the house next-door on this side,' he added, sizing up a cupboard built into the wall. 'You could open this up and make an enormous bathroom, dressing-room and study.'

'I could, *if* I ever actually meet the old lady next door,' I sniffed. 'And *if* she wants to sell her house and *if* I win the lottery. Meanwhile, I'll have to find a wardrobe to match that mythical four-poster, always supposing I find it.'

'Big furniture goes for a song at auction,' Patrick ignored my sarcasm. 'Most people have smaller houses these days but you've got high ceilings and this room is huge. I'd say thirty feet long, and maybe twelve, fourteen feet wide.'

He tapped the flimsy 1970s veneered wardrobe and jumped as it wobbled. 'You're not sentimentally attached to this, are you, Freya?'

I shook my head and stared hopelessly at the bed. 'This will have to go too,' I declared. 'Even if it was genuine Victorian I'm not keen on brass beds.'

Patrick shook the rail at the foot. 'Shall I dismantle it?'

'Don't be silly, I need a bed for tonight.'

'You could share mine,' he said.

There was a taut silence as our eyes met and I held my breath. He took a step towards me and opened his mouth to speak...

A bell rang in the distance. Someone was at the front door.

'I'd better go,' I faltered, and turned towards the stairs.

'Freya...'

The bell rang again, peremptorily this time. The caller was determined to have an answer.

'I... I can't...'

At the foot of the stairs I hesitated and leaned my forehead against the oak-panelled wall. What just happened? What would have happened if...?

Mary Draper was standing outside, looking up at the lowering grey sky.

'There you are, Freya,' she said, stepping briskly over the threshold and putting her umbrella in the big jar by the door. 'I won't keep you but I've a favour to ask.'

She paused as Patrick came downstairs and a smile of approval lit her small, round face. 'I know who *you* are,' she told him, holding out her hand. He looked bemused but it wasn't in him to rebuff anyone, let alone a tiny old woman who was so clearly pleased to see him.

I introduced them and she nodded. 'Yes, dear, I know. I've read all his books and I recognised his picture from the back cover. I get them from the library and very good they are too.'

She turned from him with a smile. 'Now then, Freya, will you be here tomorrow morning?'

I nodded. 'Patrick's catching the nine o'clock train to Waterloo and I'll see him off, but I'll be home by ten at the latest. What can I do for you, Mary?'

She shook her head. 'Can't tell you just yet, dear, it's not my secret, but I'll need your help. Can you have your car ready to go when I say the word? Let's say eleven o'clock.'

I was startled. 'Are you planning a bank heist? Are we kidnapping somebody?'

'In a manner of speaking, dear.' Her eyes sparkled as she picked up her umbrella. 'In a manner of speaking. I'm glad to have met you, Patrick,' she told him, offering another handshake. 'Tell me, do you like Freya's house?'

'I love it,' he said and there was no mistaking the sincerity in his voice.

'I believe you do,' she said thoughtfully, adding, 'Violet would have liked you.' She stood in the open doorway and looked back at me. 'You'd better tell him what you're up to, Freya. About the house, I mean. He has a right to know.'

She stared through the open door of the parlour. 'Are you having a clear out?'

'Uh-huh, tell me, Mary, why did Violet have such horrible furniture?'

'It's no mystery, dear,' she said. 'Violet was paranoid about woodworm. She was terrified it would get into the timbers of the house so the first speck of worm dust under a table, first sight of a hole, out it would go. She'd be in the back garden, chopping it up for firewood.

'I heard there was some good furniture once but Violet's grandmother sold it around the turn of the century. Violet wouldn't have cared anyway, it was the house that she had to keep safe so she'd just buy what she needed, mostly from the second-hand shop near the station. She wasn't hard-up,' Mary added. 'Her mother, Dorothy, was left a tidy sum by her old teacher and there was enough left to keep the wolf from the door. Mind you,' she shrugged. Most of what was left went on the new roof, a few years back.'

'I wondered about that,' put in Patrick. 'It looks sound and the chimneys are good, but these metal windows are all wrong.'

'They *are*,' Mary nodded decidedly. 'Violet was furious. The one time she took herself off for a proper holiday to visit a friend in Scotland, her mother fell victim to a cowboy builder. Told her the old windows were rotten and it would spread to the house if she didn't replace them. Thank God she had the sense to stop him taking out the Priory window and the little ones, or Violet would have killed her! I never saw her so angry, though it blew over. She was adamant that the house must be treated royally, so everything was done as authentically as possible, though as I said, she didn't care about the furnishings.'

'Violet must have taken an interest at some time,' I argued. 'Look at the chintzy curtains and flowery wallpaper. That was all chosen with care.'

'Oh, that wasn't Violet's choice,' Mary shook her head. 'That was her godmother, the retired teacher, who lived with them till she died at ninety. She paid for a lot of repairs in the house and when the war began she insisted on new flowery papers and curtains. Violet said she liked the old lady's taste and as long as the house was in good repair, why bother to change the wallpaper? Mind you, after Johnny Brent went down with HMS Hood in 1941, Violet didn't care about anything, except the house.'

She twinkled up at Patrick as he held the front door open for her. 'You'll be all right with Freya,' she told him, with a wink in my direction. 'Violet always said the women of this house were practical and sensible and could be relied on to do what must be done. I'd say Freya's shaping up to follow the family tradition.'

As the door closed behind her Patrick blinked and raised an eyebrow at me.

'I'm certainly glad to hear that. It was very cryptic though, is everyone round here a witch? Well, go on then,' he invited. 'What is it that I have a right to know?'

I drew a deep breath. 'You're not going to like it,' I began and saw that he was laughing at me. 'What?'

'Shall I put you out of your misery?' He opened the door to Dickon's Room and walked over to the mantelpiece, running his fingers over the carved hare. 'You want to live here, don't you? For ever, not just for weekends and holidays. I can see it in your eyes and the way you walk up and down the garden and stop to touch the plants. You never want to leave, do you, Freya?'

'Is…is it that obvious?' I faltered and he nodded.

'Look,' he said, putting a friendly arm round my shoulders. 'I admit I'd probably have been fed up if you'd sprung it on me, but not now. The house has worked its magic on me too. So, what timetable were you going to put in front of me? Three or four days in London and working from home the rest of the time?'

I nodded, slowly taking in the fact that he was going along with my plan.

'You see, I've had an idea,' he said, with a hopeful expression on his face. 'Your ex-beauty parlour. You said you hoped someone would rent it – how about if that someone happened to be me?'

Before I could say anything he found my coat. 'Here, it's stopped raining, why don't you bring the key? I'd like to look inside anyway. It might make an ideal bolthole.'

'Are you serious about this, Patrick?' I asked as I opened the door to the small building. 'Or is this just a spur of the moment thing?'

'I've been thinking about finding somewhere quiet to write,' he said, wandering round the ground floor. 'Away from London. Initially I thought about Devon, near my family but they're off the beaten track and it's not the easiest journey to London. Hampshire would be a good compromise with its excellent road and rail links. It could work, and this place could work too,' he added.

'All right,' I said slowly. 'You get first refusal but it's not habitable yet. Think it over, there's no hurry.'

He opened his mouth to speak then stopped. 'I think, oh, never mind. Why don't we go and stash the stuff for the dump in the parlour so it'll be easy to get it out of the front door later. The dining-room furniture can stay where it is until we… you…' He stumbled and I felt the tension in the air. 'Until you hire a van or get someone to pick it up. All the tatty wooden bits could go into that rickety shed out the back, to be chopped up for firewood.'

I nodded, half-relieved that, for now, the spark between us could be set aside. I knew I was a coward but there was so much in my life that needed to be resolved before I could consider what this new development meant. I'd told Louise I thought Patrick was simply fond of me, as a friend, a useful assistant, but it was beginning to look as though I'd been wrong about him.

'Let's go and shift furniture,' he said, suddenly energetic. 'Then I'll treat you to dinner in Ramalley, as a thank-you for looking after me. Come on.'

We shied away from what was uppermost in my mind, Patrick's too, I suspected, and kept everything light while shifting furniture and on the drive into town for dinner at the Blue Boar Inn. As we parted on the landing at bedtime Patrick headed towards his room, then suddenly turned back and caught me in his arms. We stood there, not speaking, not breathing until, with a sigh, he bent and kissed me very gently on the lips.

I tensed.

'Don't panic,' he murmured. 'I know you're not ready yet.'

Before I could answer he released me, smiling ruefully. 'I'd better have that bath now. Might even have to make it a cold one so I hope you appreciate all this self-control.'

Later, as I lay awake, I wondered whether he was wrong. Perhaps I was ready after all?

(ii)
Wednesday, 11ᵗʰ March, morning

He said nothing about that late-night moment and greeted me with a groan when he trailed downstairs just before eight on Monday. My natural optimism and bounce had returned in spades so I was singing loudly and cheerfully.

'Is it always like this?' he grumbled. 'I might have to reconsider…' He gave me a mischievous grin and opened the door to Dickon's Room. 'On the other hand, just look at that fabulous window.'

What had he meant? Reconsider what? He smiled but said

nothing as I handed him a mug of tea.

'Plain toast or scrambled eggs on it?' I offered. 'I don't do this every morning but I'm glad to see you looking so much better. You were a sorry spectacle forty-eight hours ago.' I looked out at the sodden garden. 'I'll drive you to the station, it's bucketing down.'

I had just spotted the train in the distance when Patrick took my hand, looking serious.

'Sure it's all right if I come back Thursday afternoon?'

'Of course. I've decided to have a housewarming 'do' on Friday evening. I'll invite everyone I've met so far and you can be barman. It'll be fun.'

I'd started to babble but my voice tailed away when the train pulled in. Patrick put both arms round me.

'We have unfinished business, don't we?' he said quietly and I leaned into him and put my head on his shoulder.

'I know,' I whispered. 'But there are things I have to tell you first.'

'Keep it till Thursday.' He bent his head and kissed me – properly – so that my knees started to buckle and I had to hug him to stay upright.

'And keep *that* till Thursday too,' his eyes gleamed.

I was trembling but I surprised us both by kissing him back, so fiercely it was surprising there weren't clouds of steam encircling us.

'Christ, Freya!' he gulped but the whistle blew and he reluctantly climbed aboard the train. I couldn't help grinning at his expression. I *was* making progress, wasn't I? Louise would be amazed.

Luckily there was very little traffic when I drove home through the drizzling rain because I daydreamed all the way. I did pull in to the bakery by the bridge because today I'd promised to be Mary's accomplice in whatever she was up to. I was sure tea and cake would be welcome, come what may.

Alison was away on her course and there wasn't even the twitch of a net curtain from Cathy, my other neighbour. I supposed she'd be hard at it in the clothing factory on the

161

industrial estate. I sneaked a curious glance at Mary's friend's house but heavy curtains left very little space for snooping from outside.

Oh well, I'd soon find out, so I let myself in to my own house, pausing as always to breathe in the scent of Dad's roses which seemed particularly strong today. Weird that Patrick could only smell sweet peas while Mary insisted that lavender scented the house, but if I had to live in a haunted house I preferred ghostly flowers to clanking chains any day.

It was a worry that I'd heard nothing from Louise since that brief email the day before, which was so unlike her that I took a chance and rang her land-line at home. The answer machine cut in and I took a deep breath as I heard her voice asking me to leave a message.

'Louise? It's me, Freya. Wondering if everything's all right; haven't spoken to you lately. Keep me posted.'

I hastily bashed out some invitations for Friday's housewarming party and at half-past nine I heard a ring at the door. Surely it was too early for Mary to embark on her adventure? A young man with a shaved head greeted me with an ingratiating smile. Parked outside was a long-wheelbase white van

'I'm doing house clearances, love,' he said hopefully. 'Got any old furniture you don't want? Mrs Draper told me you'd just moved in – she's a friend of my Nan's – so I thought I'd drop by on the off-chance.'

'You know what?' He looked engaging and unthreatening. 'You're exactly the man I need to see today. I've got loads of stuff ….'

He was on his own so I gave him a hand and we cleared the parlour first. The saggy sofa and chairs went to the back of the van, followed by all the rugs from downstairs.

'It's Edwardian, love,' he told me when he offered to buy the suite. 'Yes, I know you just want it gone but how about I give you a cut of anything I sell on? I know someone who'll take it off my hands. The rugs are junk, I agree, but they're wool so they can be recycled. What's next?'

'Sorry,' I said as he eyed the huge sofa in Dickon's Room.

'I'm keeping that but you can have all the dining-room furniture.'

Into the van went the horrible mock-Jacobean table and chairs with the matching sideboard, though he protested.

'Why don't you want it? Goes with the house, doesn't it?'

'It's all wrong,' I said. 'Cheap and nasty 1930s stuff. I want solid oak that at least *looks* like the real thing.'

'I'll keep an eye out,' he promised as we moved upstairs. 'And I know people who go crazy over this Thirties furniture.'

'You surely don't want this old rubbish?' I was surprised to see him examine the rickety brass bedstead.

'Everything has a value to someone, love,' he told me. 'I'll take it off your hands and I bet I'll find it a home.'

I raised my eyebrows but he was adamant so I let him dismantle it while I emptied the tatty wardrobe. Luckily I had very little in the way of clothes here so I slung everything on to a chair and helped him lug the lumpy mattress downstairs, along with the wardrobe. His eyes lit up when he poked his head into the front-bedroom and saw the lovely mahogany furniture, but that was staying. Apart from anything else Patrick would be back on Thursday and I realised, with a tingle of excitement, that this was the only double-bed I had left.

White-van-man, who told me his name was Nathan Young, helped me move Violet's single bed into the big bedroom; the mattress was in reasonable shape and would do for now. Downstairs again I gave him tea and a slice of cake and he had me in fits of giggles about things he'd found in house clearances.

'I do odd jobs on the side,' he said, offering me his card. 'Gardening too. I can build sheds, prune trees; weeding, lawns, hedges, the lot. Give me a tinkle when you get yourself sorted.'

On his way out he cast a disdainful look at the front door.

'That's no good,' he said, prodding it. 'Cheap and nasty, wrong for the house. I'll see if I can find something better, all kinds of things get dumped. If I can't, I've got a mate who'll make you a door only an expert could say wasn't the genuine article. He bashes the wood with bike chains to make it look old!'

(iii)

I just had time to tidy myself when I heard the bell again. This time it really was Mary.

'Ready, dear?' Today she had left the fur at home and wore a neat grey coat with a blue hat and matching scarf. 'No, dear, not the mink. It's given good service but it's time to have it put down. This came from the hospice shop in town, best place for a bargain.' She fixed me with a determined eye. 'Thank you for doing this, Freya. There won't be time to explain at first so I'll be grateful if you'll just do as I ask because time is of the essence.'

From across the river we heard the Priory clock strike eleven.

'Now,' Mary issued her instructions. 'You'd better get ready so we can make a quick getaway.' She brushed aside my squeak of surprise. 'Never mind that now, we'll explain later.'

We? I was bemused but nodded obediently.

'Alison from Lamb Cottage is off on her course so she won't get in our way.' Did Mary know everyone in town? She stepped back and peered towards the parking spaces. 'Good girl, you're facing outwards so you can see Sylvia's door at the side. You can't see it from the road here. I'll ring the bell and when That Madam opens it I want you to phone this number.' She handed me a piece of paper and stood over me while I added it to my contacts. She straightened her hat, lifted her chin and peered out at the deserted cul-de-sac.

'Now, take my suitcase with you and get in the car,' she tilted her head towards it. 'Got the number ready? Good. Turn the engine on at once and as soon as That Woman opens the door, you ring the house. Sylvia and I will do the rest. Ah, that's a thought,' she frowned. 'When you see Sylvia come out with a holdall – she daren't pack a case – you'd better

164

drive across and pick her up. She's not as steady on her pins as I am. Once she's in the car, you ring off.'

'Right?' Mary hefted her handbag in a militant way and nodded to me. 'Off you go. Try not to look too obvious when you call the house and once we're both in the car, you must get the hell out of here. It really could be a matter of life and death.'

Startled at Mary's language, I did as I was told, with a slight pang as I wondered whether it might all be some fantasy Mary had cooked up. That perhaps her mind was going. Still...

Her generalship was flawless and I was ashamed of my doubts. It went like clockwork. I had the engine running and tried to look nonchalant as my fingers hovered over the phone. When the housekeeper opened the door Mary slumped and transformed herself into a humble little old woman, holding on to the doorframe. She glanced round and inclined her head slightly so I pressed Call and grasped the steering-wheel ready for my next task.

The housekeeper jerked her head up. She had heard the telephone, so she gave Mary a brusque nod and left her on the doorstep. A moment later another little old lady appeared and I drove swiftly across to pick them both up. They scrambled into the back seat and Mary slammed the door shut as she barked orders at me.

'Hurry, Freya. *Now...*'

I dared not look back, partly for fear that either or both of my passengers might have a heart attack from all the excitement, so I never saw whether the housekeeper ('Warder,' said Mary) recognised their accomplice.

'Which way, Mary?' I asked as I turned right along the river road, then left towards town.

'The Square,' she told me. 'I'll give you directions when we get there.'

I gunned the car at the bridge. 'Did you ever see the film, *The Great Escape*, ladies? We're Steve McQueen and we've just jumped over the wire!'

I nosed the car through an archway I recognised. A familiar, fair-haired, thirty-something man hurried out to help my passengers and I followed meekly in their train as he led us into a large office on the ground-floor overlooking the Square.

'Come and meet Sylvia officially.' Mary was radiant with the success of her master plan and I shook hands with Mrs Penrose who looked frail but happy, then greeted my own solicitor, Harry Makepeace, junior partner in Makepeace & Makepeace, Solicitors-at-Law.

'Now, Mrs Penrose,' he smiled affably at her. 'Everything's ready for you to sign so while we get on with it, perhaps Mrs Draper and Miss Gibson would like coffee.' He gave me a friendly smile as he indicated a cafetière and cups on a side table. 'Settling in okay?' he asked me before making Mrs Penrose comfortable beside his desk.

'I couldn't explain before, dear,' Mary said in a low voice. 'It's all been on a knife edge and I didn't want to jinx it, but everything's fine now.' She leaned over to examine the biscuits on offer and took a shortbread finger.

'Sylvia and I have been friends since Ramalley School where, coincidentally, Violet's mother, Dorothy Wellman, was Head. We've stayed in contact even when Sylvia and her husband lived abroad, so when he died and she came back home to Ramalley, we met up again.'

She sipped her coffee. 'Unfortunately her husband's niece took over. She wouldn't have Sylvia to live with her, which was just as well as Sylvia would have gone kicking and screaming, but she installed That Madam as housekeeper and carer.' Mary snorted. 'Carer! Gaoler's more like it. Poor Sylvia can't even sack her because she's employed by the niece. Everyone's kept at bay and the only reason I'm allowed to visit is because I'm a dear little old lady who wouldn't say boo to a goose.'

She grinned like a shark and I giggled. 'I'd hate to be a goose that came up against you, Mary, but go on. How did you set up this escape bid?'

'We'd been trying out ideas for more than a year but

Violet died just before Christmas and left me that bit of money, at the same time that Sylvia's niece started hinting about her going into a home and selling the house. We didn't know what to do, then at the beginning of January, the housing association that owns my place, gave notice that our block was due for complete refurbishment and all single people would be offered one-bedroomed flats. The larger dwellings, they said, were needed for families.' She snorted again. 'Larger! My second bedroom measures seven foot by six; they'll be lucky.'

'What happened next?' I was agog with curiosity and admiration.

'I suggested to That Madam that Sylvia might like to go to the Ramalley Women's Group with me on a Monday morning. We have coffee and a chat, and sometimes there's a speaker, and a light lunch. She was suspicious at first but when she checked it out she realised she'd get a free day, particularly if we stayed on for a cup of tea at four o'clock.'

Mrs Penrose looked more relaxed as the solicitor plied her with coffee and talked her through whatever she was signing, so Mary carried on with her story.

'We did go to the Women's Group,' she told me. 'The second time, though, we called a taxi and checked out all the sheltered housing around Ramalley. Sylvia had a plan, you see. She was lonely without Frank and when it turned out I was to be re-homed in a rabbit hutch, she suggested we find somewhere together. We'd each have our own room and although she would buy it – Frank left her comfortably off – I'd be able to pay my way, thanks to Violet. I insisted on that,' she added fiercely. 'I'll be popping in to do your housework too, like we agreed, though maybe not next week when we'll be moving in. I'll need something to keep me busy.'

'That's brilliant,' I said. 'Have you found a place yet? I've got plenty of room if you need somewhere meanwhile.' I remembered my orgy of throwing out and hastily added, 'We'd need to get a couple of beds but you could sleep downstairs in the parlour and the dining-room. I'd love to have you.' I pushed the thought of Patrick to the back of my mind but he was far too kind to object to helping a pair of old ladies in distress.

'You're a sweet girl,' Mary smiled at me and patted my arm. 'It won't be necessary though. Harry Makepeace is looking after us. I've known him all his life and he was the very last baby Violet delivered before she retired, so he was special to her. You can trust him, he's a good lad. 'Sylvia's completing today on a ground-floor flat at Groom Hall, not far from the station. The day we visited, one of the buyers had died, poor soul but his misfortune was our blessing. Sylvia put in an offer on the spot, which is why it's all happened so quickly. It's a big old house that's been turned into flats and the manager is a nurse, so it's all geared up for retired people. We'll be comfortable there and the best thing is that Sylvia won't be at the mercy of her niece any more. It's all worked out very well.'

Two women came in from the other office to witness various documents and the business was complete. Harry Makepeace helped Mrs Penrose to her feet.

'It's been a pleasure doing business with you, ladies,' he smiled as he saw us out to the car.

'Where now?' I drove out on to the Square. 'Let me take you to lunch to celebrate.'

'Oh no, dear,' Mrs Penrose was definite. 'Lunch is on me. We couldn't have done this without you. We're booked into a hotel to get our breath back before we move into the flat, so we'll have lunch there.'

I drove them to the 'safe house' in the New Forest and helped them settle in to the rooms Mary had booked the previous day, and we sat down to lunch in the elegant dining-room.

'Champagne, I think,' said Mrs Penrose firmly. 'Here's to freedom and making the most of what life offers.'

I raised my glass and thought of Patrick who had said we had unfinished business. I thought of the past and closed my eyes for a moment until the panic subsided and I surrendered.

'Here's to life,' I echoed. 'And to taking a chance.'

Chapter Twelve

(i)

Wednesday, 11ᵗʰ March, afternoon

I sang all the way back to Ramalley, inspired by those two elderly women's courage. If they could be brave, so could I. Of course, they couldn't have done it without Sylvia's money but Mary had certainly been the driving force.

Before I left them to relax after their strenuous morning I made them promise to come to the party on Friday evening. Mary undertook to organise a taxi and Sylvia told me to look out for Harry Makepeace.

'He was going straight round to the house as soon as we left his office,' she said complacently. 'The plan was that he'd give That Madam an hour to pack up and leave, and you needn't look so concerned, Freya…' she patted my hand. 'I've given her three months' pay in lieu of notice, as well as a bit extra to help while she finds another prisoner to guard. I'm taking no chances though and Harry will get the locks changed once he's sent her off in a taxi to the station.'

'You're enjoying this, aren't you, Mrs Penrose?' I asked.

'You have no idea,' she twinkled. 'The thought of this day has sustained me for a long time. The next thing will be to sell my house, but there's no hurry.'

'What about your niece? Won't she hot-foot it down here?'

'Harry said he'd courier a letter to her, explaining that he's acting for me and that I'm well and happy in my new home – which I will be, shortly. I've settled some money on her which should keep her sweet and Harry's letter will explain that that all correspondence is to go through my solicitor and that she has no further claim on me. Also that she'll get nothing in my will. I was tempted to say it'll go to a cats' home because she loathes cats, but Harry persuaded me to leave it vague.'

Before I left I managed to take Mary aside.

'I really need to talk to you, Mary,' I hesitated. 'About Violet and my father and how I happened to be born.'

'Ah,' she said, looking serious and glancing over her shoulder to where Mrs Penrose snoozed peacefully in the sunny bay window. 'Yes, I've been wondering whether you knew about that.'

'It's not so much what *I* know,' I parried. 'It's what *you* know. And what you're prepared to tell me.'

'I can tell you nearly everything,' she said in a low murmur. 'I knew most of it anyway. Violet and I were very close, and when she knew she only had a month or so left she made me promise to explain it all to you. She'd already written you a letter, years before, so she gave it to me to leave for you. She also said she'd tucked away a brief note for you to find, about the business with your father. I knew you'd come after me, wanting more.'

'I do appreciate this, Mary.' I looked at my watch and noticed that Mary was looking weary after an action-filled morning so I took both her hands in mine and held them for a moment as I kissed her gently on the cheek. 'I'll be in touch.'

(ii)

Back in town I dropped in to the museum and found the same friendly woman at the desk.

'I was wondering whether you have anything about my house?' I explained that Ladywell was very old and that I knew very little about its history.

'I'd like to know, for instance, when the house was extended,' I suggested and showed her a photo on my phone. 'The houses either side are much later; late-Georgian, early Victorian, don't you think? I'd love to know who enlarged the house and when it was divided up.'

She made a note and promised to get in touch. 'I'm a volunteer,' she said with a grin. 'There's only one member of staff here and he'll be too busy, so I'll see what I can dig up. No, it's no trouble. It'll be interesting.' She took another look at the photo. 'I'm sure I've seen something about Ladywell somewhere. You say it was originally a farmhouse? What's it like at the back? Pigsties? A barn?'

'There's what was recently the beauty parlour,' I said excitedly. 'It's at the front, but it could have been a small barn. There's nothing at the back though there's an ancient rockery at the bottom of the garden.' I didn't mention the holy well. 'I suppose the farm buildings were demolished when the side extensions were built; it looks as though the Wellmans were going up in the world. I wonder what happened, because they must have come down with a bump if they had to sell off each end of the house.'

I enquired for Mr Fletcher at the Priory but he was leading a guided tour so I dropped off an invitation for him and his wife and walked back to the shops.

It dawned on me that I'd blithely invited people to a party but had no food to offer them, no plates to put it on, no glasses and no wine either, not to mention anywhere to sit. Luckily, just as I started to panic I found myself looking straight into the window of a delicatessen. Not just any delicatessen, it was 'The Artisan Pantry' and the window was an artistic triumph with quiches and galantines, stuffed this and garnished that, all laid out on rustic pottery. One thing off my list.

Ten minutes later I emerged relieved in mind though considerably poorer in pocket. The competent woman in charge assured me that she would appear at my house at five-thirty promptly on Friday, bearing glasses and wine to spare, as well as trays of canapés and other goodies.

Massively relieved I addressed the next item on my invisible list. Me. I'd packed jeans and jumpers, boots and socks, a thick jacket and a waterproof, not expecting to throw a party. Again, the shops in Ramalley came to my rescue as I

171

stared across the road at a sign that said, 'Our Famous Birthday Sale – Celebrating 32 Years in Business.' The paintwork was grey, the lettering in silver while, displayed beside the birthday cake on a glass stand, was a single dress. It carried no visible price tag so I sighed and was about to pass by when a woman opened the door and beckoned.

'Edwina?' I recognised the brittle brunette from Sunday lunch at the pub.

'Come in,' she urged, smiling as she shooed me in to the elegant sales space. 'I meant to call in before now, but I had the sale to organise. How are you getting on?'

'Fine, thanks.' I wandered round admiring the scarves and costume jewellery on the walls. 'What a pretty shop. Do you have a birthday sale every year?'

'It started on our twenty-fifth anniversary,' she explained. 'It's the shop's birthday, not mine. People were amused and they expect it now. It always goes well.'

'It's nice to be a long-established business,' I observed. 'People appreciate that.'

'Yes, well,' she had a far-away look in her eyes. 'I'd had a rotten year. My husband ran off with my best friend – oldest cliché in the book – and I was in a real state. I had the house and I had some capital saved, but then I had an unexpected windfall and I made a list of things I really wanted to do. You'd call it a bucket list nowadays. Top of the list was to open my own boutique, so here I am.'

I fished in my bag and found the invitations.

'Here,' I said. 'I'm having a small house-warming party on Friday evening. I'd love it if you could come, and bring your friend, of course.'

She looked startled but touched and I added, 'Patrick will be here for it. My boss, Patrick Underwood, the author.'

'I hope you're planning to invite Cathy,' she laughed but I could see she was pleased by the invitation. 'What will you wear?' She gave me an appraising once-over and I clearly didn't pass muster.

'I have no idea,' I sighed and she frowned.

'Skirt or trousers? Dress? Formal?'

'Not formal,' I protested. 'Just a few people for drinks.'

'Here,' she pulled out a fluid jersey skirt and matching top with a draped neck. 'This soft duck-egg suits you and you've got the figure for something a bit clingy. Try it on.'

She was right. We both stared at the vision in the long cheval glass. It was a long way from my usual casual style but I liked it.

'Wow!' I was staggered at how good I looked and she nodded complacently.

'Been a while since you dressed up?' She cracked a smile when I gave a shame-faced shrug.

'I smarten up for work, when I need to,' I said, a bit defensively. 'Mind you, my best friend says I really ought to have a new look to go with my new life. Maybe this is it? I love this draping, it looks Roman.'

I twisted round to look for the ticket but she snipped it off.

'You can afford it,' she said wryly. 'I'll give you a good discount.'

She threw in a string of amber-coloured glass beads. 'House-warming present,' she said, and refused to be thanked. 'You'd better find some shoes to go with the outfit, try the shop on the corner. It's a pity gladiator sandals are out of season if you're going for a Roman look.' She waved the invitation at me. 'I'll look forward to this and I'll bring Graham. See you on Friday.'

(iii)

I tried on half-a-dozen pairs of shoes and decided on bronze leather ballet flats as being the best on offer, then I caught Mary's friend Nonie as she locked up her café. She seemed surprised but delighted to receive an invitation to the party.

'Are you sure?'

'Of course,' I smiled. 'I've been so blessed with my lovely house and I've been welcomed so warmly by everyone in town that I want to give something back. Please come.'

When I reached home I dropped an invitation into Alison's letterbox. My absent neighbour had been so kind but there had been no time to get to know her. Perhaps there'd be a chance to chat at the party. It was getting on for six o'clock by the time I turned the key in my own front-door, just as the phone rang.

'I'm sorry to ring so late,' said a vaguely familiar voice. 'It's Janice from the museum.'

'Of course,' I knew her now. 'How can I help?'

'I've tracked down a snippet about your house and I know how interested you are, so I thought I'd ring straight away.'

'That's so kind of you,' I was touched. 'Are you still slaving over a hot museum at this time of day?'

I heard her laugh. 'No, I brought my notes home. You'll be interested to hear that a Robert Wellman of Ladywell was mayor of Ramalley three times in the eighteenth century.'

'So the family really was prominent?' This was exciting.

'Certainly looks like it,' Janice agreed. 'He had a wife called Katherine and a son – can't find a name for him, but *he* married up, to a granddaughter of old Alderman Moberley who was a great local benefactor.'

My stomach flip-flopped as I remembered the statue in the Square. Here it was again, the Moberley connection. Janice had more to tell,

'It was Robert Wellman who extended the house and just by chance I turned up a throwaway mention in a letter about something else, to the effect that when Master Wellman's newly enlarged house was finished, he set his men to rebuild the barn and other outbuildings some distance away. It would have been over towards where the station is now,' she added. 'Apparently the ancient shepherd at the farm said his old granddad told him it was bad luck to shift the muck heap that had been there since time immemorial!'

'You're kidding! An ancestral muck heap?'

She echoed my laugh and went on, 'Turned out the old man had a point because the workmen discovered a skeleton buried underneath it.'

I gasped and Janice sympathised. 'It's a bit of a shock,

isn't it? The bones were those of a man who'd been bundled into his grave with no coffin and it was reported that buried with him were the remains of something leather that might, just possibly, have been a book. Robert Wellman generously paid for him to be given a Christian burial but there was no indication of his identity, or why – or even when – he'd ended up there.'

'Spooky! I wonder what *did* happen to him?'

'Drop into the museum sometime,' said Janice. 'I'll show you what I've found. Our archive is very varied and we're trying to set up an online resource. Who knows? We might find something else about Robert and his fine house.'

(iv)

After young Tom Wellman died his foreign wife refused to enter the Priory church in Ramalley town. Not one foot would she put across the threshold, not after the first rumours of a battle against Boney over in the Low Countries, nor when the letter came from Tom's colonel. When the last weary straggle of soldiers came home to the garrison in nearby Winchester she still refused to go to church to pray for him.

His colonel called at the house at Ladywell to pay his respects, followed by his sergeant, who cried awkward, angry tears as he told of Tom at Waterloo, at the head of his column of men. He spoke of the shot, of Tom calling out in surprise, clutching his hand to his scarlet coat and falling, falling...

Even then she refused to enter the church, the house of a God who had taken him from her.

'T'aint right,' muttered the local farmers. 'Not with young Master Tom dead at Waterloo.'

'Such unbecoming hysteria,' murmured the townsfolk high and low in the town across the river. 'Of course,' they added in whispered asides. 'She is a French woman. One of the enemy.' They said it very quietly, making sure the dead man's formidable grandmother was not in earshot.

'Give her time,' said old Kate Wellman, blotting her own

tears on a stout linen handkerchief. 'It's natural that it takes you hard when they die, whatever their age, and she so far away from home, poor lass.' She blew her nose angrily, remembering her own enigmatic husband.

Orphaned at seventeen, Kate had heard the whispers that said her father had only been prevented from muddling away his great-grandparents' prosperous farm by his timely death. Ladywell, it was said, was a place of women; that no man prospered there and that the house itself was hostile to the menfolk, so it became a settled fact in the minds of the townspeople that only an exceptional man would marry happily into the house at Ladywell. That it took an exceptional woman to seize disaster and wallop it into success by sheer force of will was overlooked, but young Kate Wellman was such a woman.

The husband she chose for herself was a handsome young stranger who applied for work at the farm a month after her father's death. Not a word of his past life did he vouchsafe and he agreed without question when, after another month during which she had observed his hard work and noted that he was educated above the usual, Kate proposed marriage to him on condition he took the Wellman name.

To everyone's astonishment – and to none more than Kate herself – Rob Wellman proved an exemplary farmer, three times mayor, a fond husband and a firm but affectionate father to their only son. He died too young, with his lips still sealed about his past.

He was a good man, Kate Wellman sighed, as she patted the foreign bride's shoulder and wiped away her own tears. Their son had married into the Moberly family and life had been good until first Rob died, and then, in an accident, their son. Two years ago tragedy struck again when cholera ravaged the town: her elder grandson Rick dead all in an instant, and his mother, the alderman's granddaughter too.

And now the hardest blow. Her darling, her younger grandson Tom, dead by a Frenchman's bullet. Gone, all of them gone, unless...

(v)

After he died, Marie-Simone believed she would die too and every morning she wept anew as life persisted in denying her fervent prayers.

'What was it all for?' she would cry aloud to Tom's grandmother who held her hand in wordless sympathy. 'He saved me after the battle of Orthez last year when my father was killed. I was the daughter of his enemy, but he saved me. He even shot the man who tried to rape me. Why did he save me?' Her tears fell unchecked. 'If I had died then, I would never have known such happiness. If I had died then, I would never have known this grief.'

The farmhands and the townsfolk alike watched in united disapproval as every Sunday the two women would walk in silence over the bridge to the Priory, even in wet weather when they carried umbrellas. Every Sunday, as they approached the west door, the younger Mrs Wellman would drop a slight curtsey to the elder. She would then retire to a seat in the churchyard, or the porch, and remain there during the service, weeping quietly throughout.

'T'aint right,' insisted the farmhands. 'T'aint decent and worse now we all knows Master Tom left her in the family...' They would shake their heads.

'My dear, how excessive,' murmured the better folk of the town, studiously averting their eyes. 'Of course, it was all very sad, but really, foreigners! Such a display, particularly in her condition...'

Marie-Simone and Tom's grandmother lived in sad but companionable isolation at the old house at Ladywell, making preparations for what was to come. The young widow's body thickened and grew cumbersome as frost silvered the autumn leaves and holly berries hung like jewels in the dark trees, but still she refused to set foot in the church.

One day early in the New Year the two women walked over the bridge to take tea at the doctor's house. While the doctor's old mother, who kept house for him, and the grandmother from Ladywell, nodded over half-remembered *scandals and grew sleepy beside the roaring fire, Marie-Simone, half-asleep herself, struggled suddenly awake. She lifted her head. Had she heard a whisper? A voice? His voice, calling her?*

The old ladies slumbered on but though she strained her ears she heard only the crackle of the flames and the soprano and contralto snores beside the fire. Nonetheless, she slipped out through the side door and stumbled the hundred yards past the ancient yews and the toppled headstones to the Priory church.

As the door creaked open she stepped inside without a thought for the recent months of denial, barely recoiling as the chilly darkness enveloped her. She sat in a pew halfway down the aisle and held her breath.

There was only silence. In an agony of disappointment and grief she wept with quiet desperation. 'Tom, oh Tom, where are you? What was it all for?'

At first there was nothing, not a whisper, not a voice. Not his voice. But suddenly she was almost overcome by the scent of flowers; flowers that were not to be seen in this church with the chill of ages, or in this wintry land. As she sat quietly, intoxicated by the perfume, she knew what he wanted her to do.

The doctor's mother and Tom's grandmother roused themselves in amazement when she rushed into the house with her bonnet askew.

'We must go home at once, Grandmère. I went into the church and Tom was there. He told me to hurry home.'

The two old ladies stared in amazement as she stood before them, clutching her belly. Light dawned. 'Is it time, do you think?' Tom's grandmother looked in trepidation at her friend.

'It's time,' agreed the doctor's mother, with a decisive nod.

She scurried to the study to rouse her sleeping son while Kate Wellman struggled to contain her anxiety. In the slender body of the young French girl lay the last hope of the Wellman family and Kate was consumed with fear.

Somewhere, from the depths of memory, she heard her spinster great-aunt, Anne Wellman's voice, shaky with age, telling her about the Lady who watched over the people of the well; fragments of legend and with it a protection spell. I must write down the words, she thought even as she repeated the charm in her head. When all is safely over I must tell Marie-Simone and make sure she passes on the knowledge. Her mind closed firmly against the possibility that the French girl might not survive the birth, that there might be no living child.

The doctor summoned the musty closed carriage his mother used, rather than his own gig, and they reached Ladywell in good time just as snow began to fall. To their horror Marie-Simone insisted on stumbling out to the garden.

'I must,' she said, brushing aside their protests but at that moment her waters broke and she wailed as they hustled her up to bed. 'Tom said the rowan would help me,' she sobbed. 'The water, as well.'

The midwife had joined the doctor and the pair stared at her. 'She's rambling,' said the doctor, shaking his head. 'That's not a good sign, not good at all.'

Kate Wellman rose to her feet, ignoring the protest of her aching hip as she took the girl's writhing hands in her own strong grasp. 'Rest easy, child,' she said quietly. 'I'll fetch a branch of the rowan and bring you water from the well. I promise the Lady will understand.'

The doctor and midwife looked aghast but she left them abruptly. Ten minutes later she re-entered the long bedchamber where a fire now roared. Brushing the snow from her shoulders she took off her cape and carried a leafless branch from the rowan tree to the labouring girl. From the bottle in her other hand she poured water into a glass and bade the girl drink.

All through that long, hard night the French bride was aware of sunlight, of summer heat that made a mockery of the northern weather she had struggled to endure. Bathed in a warm golden glow she kept her eyes shut and even at the worst of the pain she managed an occasional faltering smile as she felt the comfort of Tom's presence. As her daughter was born, yelling furiously, and the pangs began to subside, Marie-Simone let out a cry of delight. She lay in wonder as she breathed in the scent of flowers, of flowers from the southern lands where they had met and where Tom had first loved her.

'He was here, Grandmère,' she said, raising her sweat-bathed face to Kate Wellman. 'He brought me flowers, lavender and lilies, roses and jasmine. You can smell their perfume still, can you not?'

Little Catherine Wellman grew strong and loving, the darling of them all at Ladywell, servants and farmworkers alike, and every year they celebrated her January birthday with a service in the Priory church, followed by a party at the old family house.

On her fourth birthday the usual doting crowd, bearing little gifts and nodding and smiling, gathered in the long panelled room with the handsome carved fireplace. When Kate entered bearing a leafless branch from some tree or other, she and Marie-Simone began to weep as the child lifted her voice in wonder.

'Why, Maman,' she exclaimed. 'I can smell flowers.'

Chapter Thirteen

(i)

Wednesday, 11th March – evening

I was thrilled at Janice's call and hastily made a note of what she'd told me but I would have to contain my excitement. Tomorrow, Thursday, was her day off from the museum. The phone rang again.

'Hi, Freya.' Patrick.

I gulped at the sound of his voice, light and amused and warm. Oh yes, there was certainly a great deal of warmth in his voice, but my wretched insecurity made me wonder whether I was wrong. Was friendship all he had in mind? I remembered that moment at the station and smiled; there'd been other moments, other clues so I stopped fretting and listened.

'Hang on,' he said, distracted. 'I automatically called you on your mobile. How come I got through? I thought the signal was dodgy?'

'It is, very dodgy, but I'm upstairs at the moment and the signal's better. It's not perfect but it works sometimes. I've taken to lugging both phones everywhere I go in the house and it's a pain. Violet's old walkabout one weighs a ton, but it won't be forever.'

'I'm calling because I'll be tied up this evening,' he said regretfully. 'I can't explain now but I've been invited to dinner to discuss a proposition that's too hush-hush to discuss in a public place, even with you.' He broke off for a minute as someone spoke to him. An American voice, was that a clue? 'Sorry, Freya, I'll tell you all about it when I see you tomorrow but I wanted to tell you an idea I had on the train

181

this morning.'

'What kind of idea?'

'This surrogacy thing, your parents and the unknown woman – or women.' He hesitated. 'I wanted to say, you've assumed it meant your father had an affair with one or more women, haven't you?'

'I can't see any other way,' I frowned. 'What's this about, Patrick?'

'Just this,' his voice was eager. 'You haven't said so but I could tell it made you think less of him. Anyway, it occurred to me that by 1982 when you were conceived, IVF was a reality, though in its early stages, but the idea of surrogacy was already afloat, particularly in the States. I looked it up. The first publicised case was in the mid-seventies, using artificial insemination.'

'I'm not sure where this is going,' I said slowly and he hurried to explain.

'What I'm saying is that your father need not actually have had sex with any of these women. He might not even have met them; it could all have been stage-managed by Violet Wellman, armed with a turkey baster!'

I choked as I pictured my quiet, gentle father under orders from Violet and egged on by my mother – oh yes, I could easily imagine Mum issuing orders. I started to laugh.

'Freya?'

'I'm sorry, Patrick,' I managed to halt the giggles and wiped my eyes. 'I think it was either laugh or cry. The thing is it makes perfect sense to me. Mum wore the trousers in the family and I know she always wanted a big family. She did tell me once that she'd almost despaired until I came along. Oh, yes, I can picture it.'

I swallowed and he rushed in, 'God, I didn't mean to upset you. I thought you'd feel better about your dad. Sorry, I seem to have cocked it up.'

'You haven't,' I reassured him. 'It hadn't occurred to me, but it could easily have happened that way.'

He had to go then so I couldn't tell him about my upwardly mobile ancestor, Robert, but I had something more important to think about. As I made tea I thought about what he'd said. Yes, in many ways I could believe my parents would have gone along with the idea, but I wondered. Memories crowded in, of my mother laying down the law on everything, not brooking dissent, and of Dad, who liked a quiet life, saying, 'Yes, dear,' and letting her get on with it.

The trouble with Patrick's theory was that I could easily believe my masterful mother giving Dad permission – orders, really – to have sex with another woman if it meant she could fulfil what she saw as her God-given purpose. Had that quiet life of Dad's contained secrets? I had a sneaking suspicion that with or without permission from his wife, an affair with another woman would not have been a novelty.

I'd forgotten to check the land-line. Finally there was a message from Louise.

'Hi, Freya, sorry not to be in touch, Andrew's confiscated my iPad and phone, supposedly to keep me calm. It's not working! I'm in the Infirmary at the moment but don't panic. I had a bit of a bleed and as my blood's Rhesus Negative and Andrew's is Rhesus Positive they're taking extra care. My BP is up too. I'll get Andrew to call you if anything happens but I'm not in pain, just bored stiff. I've been here two days already! Love you.'

I made myself calm down. I don't deal with illness very well, not in people I love because I had such a small family. Louise is very special to me. I know I coped with Patrick but he wasn't seriously ill. Clinging to Lou's reassurance – how well she knows me – I forced myself to eat something, just a sandwich because lunch had been lavish, and went upstairs to read in bed. I was absorbed in one of Violet's novels, awash with huge Victorian families and struggles where decency triumphs over wickedness, when my mobile bleeped a text, proving my theory about the reception upstairs.

'Pee-break. Meeting going well. Checked 1982 cash values against today. £5k then equals £20k now. She must have been comfortably off to refuse it or maybe too proud. £500 then equals £2k now – a useful windfall. If anyone was paid off, how did she spend it? All my love,

Patrick.'

I dropped my book and sat up. He was right. Twenty thousand pounds in today's money was a hell of a lot to turn down. Scenarios skittered through my mind, how could she afford to do that? I felt an unexpected glow that my birth mother might have refused to sell me, but that did rather point to Patrick's suggestion that she hadn't needed the money. I tested the idea and came to the conclusion that while I might have felt the same, in not wanting to turn it into a transaction, I was probably too practical to pass up on a chance to change my life. Not that giving away a baby hadn't already changed her life for ever.

My mouth twisted in a wry smile at the thought as I considered what she might be feeling now, that unknown woman. Was my instinct right, that Violet had chosen local women for her experiment? Anyway, even if she had, there was no reason to assume all or any of those women still lived in Ramalley. No reason apart from this unfounded gut feeling that was probably wishful thinking. *Was* she unknown? Might I have met her already? And if so, what did she think of me?

I turned out the light and was almost asleep when I heard another bleep. Yawning, I reached for the phone.

'Last, late thought, sorry. Date on Violet's note was early Sept '82, right? 7 months before you were born so your birth mother was already pregnant. How does that fit with Violet's plan? P xx'

'Oh, my God!' He was right. I ran downstairs to Dickon's Room. I had put the antique inlaid box on the small table in there when Nathan and I carried the unwanted furniture out to his van. I fumbled with the catch and drew out Violet's note.

There it was, signed by Marion and Stephen Gibson and Violet Wellman, dated 7th September 1982. It recorded their agreement that, as soon as possible, Violet would seek out a suitable woman who would agree to bear a child for them. I read the words again, *'as soon as possible'* and heaved a shuddering sigh. So much for Patrick's suggestion that the whole transaction had been a clinical exercise not involving sex, or indeed, any contact at all between my father and my birth mother. On this showing it seemed only too evident that there *had* been some kind of sexual encounter; whether a one-night stand or a full-blown affair.

I trailed back to bed, worn out by all this emotion on top of the day's excitement, but as I drowsed on the edge of sleep something in one of Patrick's texts niggled at me. It came to me at four o'clock the next morning: a windfall. Patrick had pointed out that the £500 pay-off for the unsuccessful candidate (or candidates) would have provided a useful windfall. Once again I heard Edwina Malcolm talking about her shop's thirty-second birthday celebrations and how she had come into a windfall that enabled her to start her business. Five thousand pounds would have been even more useful.

I would be thirty-two in less than a fortnight. Thirty-two years ago was nearly seven months after the strange agreement recorded in Violet's neat handwriting. Edwina Malcolm was in possession of a windfall around that time. I had no idea about rents or retail prices back then but she'd told me that the windfall, on top of her own savings, had been the clincher.

How was I going to get through the party with Edwina there? I needed a serious talk with her but it would be a very delicate subject to broach.

(ii)

Thursday, 12ᵗʰ – early morning

I dozed off again and it was nearly half-past seven when I struggled out of a puzzling dream. A low rumbling filled the air and oddly, even as I struggled awake, the rumbling persisted and I felt something touch my face.

'What the...' My heart was pounding and my eyes snapped open in fear. There, sitting on my chest, was the ugliest, skinniest cat I'd ever seen. It had a snowy white body, sleekly healthy but snakily thin, and a pointed face topped off by a large black patch like an ill-fitting toupée. It had yellow eyes and its imperious stare was fixed on my face.

'Where on earth did you come from?' My heart rate went back to normal and as I put out a hand the cat craned its neck to take a sniff, then sat back on its haunches and began to stare me out. It didn't take a detective to work out how the cat had managed to appear on my bed, daring me to kick it off. There was that cat-flap in the backdoor, that I had assumed belonged to long-gone pets. Was this self-assured interloper a stray? It seemed very much at home so I stroked it, feeling for lumps and bumps, but it seemed to be in peak condition. It was just naturally thin and it had to be somebody's pet as it was well-fed, though it was trying to hypnotise me into getting up. I gently tipped it off my lap.

'All right,' I sighed. 'I'll be five minutes.'

The cat was waiting at the top of the stairs.

'Do you like ham?' I asked as the cat set off downstairs with its tail up and me following meekly in its wake. 'Because if you don't, tough.'

It seemed that ham would do, so I made tea and toast for myself. The ham disappeared, as did the milk I offered, and to my surprise the cat jumped up on my lap, head-butted me – without losing a shred of its haughty dignity – and curled up for a nap. As the kitchen reverberated to the sound of loud purring, the land-line rang: Violet's brick of a phone that, as I'd told Patrick, I took everywhere.

'Miss Gibson, of Ladywell? Joyce Johnson, of the Ramalley Cattery. I wonder if by any chance Mrs Simpson has turned up at your house?'

'Mrs Simpson?' The cat opened one yellow eye and looked shifty. 'Is Mrs Simpson long, white and skinny, looks like a ferret in a black wig?'

'Oh, thank heavens.' Her sigh of relief was audible even to the cat who sneered and went back to sleep. 'I really don't know how she escaped, I take such careful precautions but she has a will of her own. Oh well, no harm done. Mrs

Draper said you'd be picking the cat up soon anyway.'

She explained that the cattery bill was paid up-to-date and rang off, leaving me staring at my new house-mate.

'Well?' I addressed the cat severely, not that she took a blind bit of notice. 'What have you got to say for yourself, Mrs Simpson? I'm surprised that psychic woman didn't warn me, I'd have bought some cat food. However, there *is* somebody who could have told me.'

I waited until nine o'clock in case the previous day's excitement had exhausted the intrepid old ladies.

'Tell me about Mrs Simpson, Mary,' I demanded when I got through to her at the hotel. 'She turned up on my bed this morning, then some woman from a cattery rang and said you knew all about it.'

'Ah!' I detected a touch of guilt in Mary's voice. 'I was going to tell you, Freya, but not just yet. Violet said I should wait till you'd been in the house a month before I sprang the cat on you. She left some money with me for Mrs Simpson, you see,' she explained earnestly. 'Besides what she left me in her will, I mean. It was when she knew she was going into the hospice. She knew as well as I did that she wouldn't be coming out so she asked me to make arrangements for the cat. The cattery's been paid handsomely, don't you worry. Fancy Mrs Simpson turning up out of the blue like that. She's very attached to her home, so you won't have to worry about her roaming, but she always was a stubborn little devil.'

'She scared the hell out of me.' I tried to sound stern but Mary heard the laughter in my voice.

'Get on with you! She's well-trained and a cat is good company. You're not allergic, are you? Besides, in an old house a good mouser can always make herself useful.'

'It's okay,' I conceded, 'but tell me, Mary. Why Mrs Simpson? It's not a usual cat name. And how old is she?'

'She turned seven last November,' Mary explained. 'She's named after the Duchess of Windsor. You know? The one who said, "You can never be too rich or too thin". I don't know about rich, but it'd be difficult to be thinner than that cat, Violet used to say. She walks with a kind of elegant strut, too, full of herself she is, so you don't notice she was behind the door when looks were handed out. Violet didn't approve of Mrs Simpson, the Duchess, that is, but she used to say you had to admire her tenacity and that the cat was probably a reincarnation.'

As soon as I put down the phone I cursed. With the business of the new arrival I had completely forgotten to remind Mary that I wanted to quiz her about the vexed question of my parentage. It could wait. I surveyed my lodger and had to agree with Mary and Violet. The cat was thin enough to be considered emaciated if you ignored the glistening fur and the rippling strength of the muscles under the skin, and while the pointed face was definitely not pretty, it was certainly arresting. Her serene self-confidence did have a touch of the Duchess about her and when I stopped stroking her she twisted her head to glare at me.

'Sorry, Mrs S,' I apologised. 'It looks as though we're stuck together, so I hope you'll find me an attentive host. As long as you're a considerate guest.'

The cat confounded me then. Still wearing that snooty expression she rose and stretched, then lifted her head towards me. Again she did the head-butting thing, this time accompanied by a little 'Prwl?' sound, and settled down again on my lap.

I was touched by the contrast. All that independence and a brief moment of affection. 'Friends? All I ask is that you don't do anything antisocial, otherwise you can just be ornamental, a lily of the field. I'll go and buy some food.'

Mrs Simpson strolled over to the huge shabby sofa in Dickon's Room. Judging by the way she settled down immediately it was a favourite haunt and she was soon fast asleep. I washed up my breakfast things and stood irresolute, wondering what to do next, so I consulted my lists.

On the practical side, I needed to find those experts Patrick had suggested: a plasterer who could cope with a Tudor ceiling, if that was what it still was, and a carpenter skilled enough to repair my panelling. More immediately I had to check I had enough chairs to seat the people coming to my house-warming party, though the delicatessen would take care of crockery and cutlery. What had possessed me to chuck out the dining-suite?

It was trickier trying to sort out the unknowns. When I thought about Patrick my stomach turned somersaults and I clung to that sudden shared moment of passion at the station. I hardly dared let myself think I might be on the brink of happiness; my time with my ex, Ben, made even my innate optimism waver. Much easier to remember that Patrick would be back at Ladywell later today and that whatever might happen, we'd still need to eat.

I made a note to buy salmon, his favourite, but other thoughts crowded in and this time I had to act on them.

'Listen, Mrs Simpson,' I addressed the cat who opened one golden eye. 'I'm going out to buy you some food, I hope that's acceptable? I'll be back by lunch-time so you're in charge.' As an afterthought I remembered Mary's comment and added, 'I'd rather not have any little creatures as presents, if it's all the same to you. If you absolutely must catch anything, kindly leave it outside.'

I was amused to find myself talking to the cat because a pet was a novelty. My mother disliked animals and Ben, of course, would never have tolerated a rival to my affections. However this particular cat seemed happy with the conversation and I shivered suddenly. Somebody walking over my grave.

'Did Violet tell you about me?' I asked the cat. 'No, don't bother to sneer, you wouldn't tell me, even if you could.'

I squared my shoulders and made a decision. 'There's someone who *does* know all about it and it's high time she gave me some answers.'

Chapter Fourteen

(i)

Thursday, 12th March

The hotel receptionist indicated the lounge where I found Mary quite at home in a chintzy armchair, reading *Country Life*.

'I need some answers, Mary,' I said quietly but firmly and she nodded.

'You do,' she agreed, 'but we'll have to be quick. Sylvia's just gone upstairs to put her hat and coat on and a taxi will be here soon to take us to inspect the new flat. The things we wanted from our own houses have been delivered already and the new furniture will arrive from John Lewis soon. What is it you want to know?'

'You know about the agreement they made, don't you? My parents and Violet? It was signed 7th September 1982, but I was born seven months after that, which means Violet had nothing to do with finding a surrogate. I was already on the way by then.' I hesitated. 'Who was she, Mary?'

'I can't tell you that, dear,' Mary was very firm. 'I haven't had a chance to discuss it with her and until she agrees, I'm not able to tell you. What I will tell you is how it came about.'

She settled herself more comfortably, holding my breathless attention. 'I don't want to say anything unkind about Marion, but she was a very dominant character, while your father was sweet-natured but weak, bless him; always took the easy way. Most of the time it suited them both; she pushed him in his accountancy job until he was far more successful than anyone would have believed. He was always

190

delightful with her but it wasn't hard to guess he'd slip away if he needed a break.' She paused. 'I got all this from Violet, of course. I didn't know either of them that well. Anyway, it was unbearable for Marion when she was finally told she could never conceive a child so she and Violet cooked up the surrogacy idea between them.'

Mary grinned. 'Peas in a pod they were, those two women. Poor Stephen didn't stand a chance, what with Marion being fierce in Guildford and Violet even fiercer in Ramalley, so he agreed in principle. What neither of them realised was that he was in the throes of an affair at the time. It wasn't the first and I doubt it was the last, but Marion – if she'd had suspicions in the past – ignored it. All her energies were poured into her obsession so they made him sign up to the plan, only to have it made redundant when Stephen's lady friend, who lived in London at the time, found she was pregnant.'

I started to well up but motioned Mary to go on.

'She was married but her husband was... well, let's say he wasn't a nice character. He'd had lots of affairs himself. This, with your father, was *her* first – and only. It wasn't to pay her husband back, she really fell for Steve and while I'm sure he loved her in his own way, it was much more serious for her.

'You know what happened, of course. Stephen had to confess to Marion and it was Violet who insisted it changed nothing. She'd already approached two local girls but would pay them off, and the plan could go ahead. And that's what happened. A couple of months before you were born your birth mother came down to Ladywell. Her family was local and she didn't want them to know so she stayed with Violet.' Mary looked thoughtful. 'She fell in love with Ladywell. Said the house comforted her at a dark time. Maybe that has something to do with the way you fell for it at first sight? That and your Wellman blood.'

She shook her head. 'Violet was cracked about the house. Now, where was I? Oh yes, when the labour started, Violet rang Stephen and Marion at midnight and they drove straight

191

down here; the minute you were born you were put into Marion's arms. Violet told me years later that she'd never seen Marion cry before.'

'But what about *her*?' I asked in a tremulous whisper. 'How did she feel about handing over her baby?'

'She bore up well in public,' Mary sighed. 'Violet told me though that she broke her heart when they were alone. Her husband, you see, had got on his high horse and said he'd forgive her but he wouldn't take on another man's child. Forgive her! She only gave in because her father was dying and her mother frail, and she was afraid the shock and shame would kill them.' She shrugged. 'Pity really. Within six months of your birth they were both dead and a couple of years later she'd had enough and left her husband anyway.'

'She didn't take the money.'

Mary nodded. 'No, she refused it. Said she wasn't selling her baby but giving her to a loving home. Like I said, it broke her heart but she felt it was right for you and that got her through.'

'Marion made sure Stephen cut off all contact with Violet, you know,' Mary sighed. 'Apart from Christmas cards and that dwindled away in the end. It was hurtful but Violet always knew why she did it, and she couldn't blame her. Guildford's not far enough from Ramalley, you see, and Violet knew too much. Marion couldn't keep up the pretence that she'd given birth to you herself, because Violet delivered you. It was an obsession. She'd even padded herself out and told her friends she was pregnant so you can see why she didn't want Violet around.'

I was close to tears but I had one more question. 'Mary, why did Violet write it all down?'

'Insurance,' said Mary. I stared at her. 'No, that's not the right word. She wanted a record of it because she thought you should know. Not as a child, it was Marion's right to play it her way and Violet went along with it, but she insisted that you should know the truth.'

I nodded. 'She was right. It's been a shock, but it's better to know.'

'Violet told me the bare outline,' Mary explained. 'When Marion died, Stephen might have told you, but I was her extra insurance, if you like. There was always the chance her note might be overlooked.'

I digested it all but before I could say anything else, Mrs Penrose appeared. She gave me a kiss and enquired whether I was going with them to inspect the new flat. I shook my head but walked with them to the waiting taxi. As the driver settled Mrs Penrose, I took Mary's hand.

'I appreciate you telling me, Mary,' I sighed. 'I understand how it happened. It won't be easy to be patient till you can tell me the rest, but I'll try.'

'Don't you worry, my dear,' she nudged me, smiling. 'Patrick will take your mind off it.'

(ii)

Patrick texted as I drove back to Ramalley – **'Back later than planned, stuck in all-day meeting, x'**. I was disappointed but excited too, as well as restless and frustrated by Mary's story. She had satisfied some of my longing but I was impatient to hear the rest and as I'd seen Cathy set out for work at half-past eight, I sucked up my courage and decided to see if Edwina would be receptive.

More frustration awaited me at the shop. It was the last day of the sale and when I looked in the window I could see several women perched on spindly chairs, each holding a glass of something while Edwina held court. It would be tactless to barge in and ask if she just happened to have mislaid a daughter!

I thought I'd better let it all simmer and I headed for the museum to drop in an invitation for nice, helpful Janice. I briefly considered her as a candidate for my missing mother but although she was about the right age, surely she would have shown a flicker of emotion when I introduced myself and told her about Ladywell? No, it wouldn't do, though I really liked her. I bought cat food then made my way to the Priory and had lunch in the refectory but John Fletcher was busy with tourists so I abandoned my research. After a brief visit to the grave of Dorothy Wellman's young lover – would Mary know if we were right about him? – I trailed back to Waitrose and remembered to buy cat food.

The landline rang as I was eating yoghurt, with the cat keeping a close watch on me from her perch on the draining board. Andrew Barton, Louise's husband.

'It's a boy!' He was almost incoherent but calmed down enough to supply some details. 'James Andrew, born at 10.15 this morning, weight 6lb 8oz.'

I burst in with anxious questions and he reassured me. 'No, no, they weren't worried that he was three weeks early, dates are never written in stone. It was only this Rhesus Negative and Positive thing, because Lou's been bleeding. They just wanted to be sure. She's fine, they both are, and Lou sends you tons of love.'

I flopped down on a handy chair as exhausted as though I had run a marathon because the worry about my dearest friend had been underlying all the rest. I had a moment's panic because I couldn't Google a florist then remembered there was a phone directory somewhere so I mopped up a couple of thankful tears and rang the florist in town.

(iii)

I answered a ring at the door just before three and found Nathan, the friendly white-van man, with a pleased, not to say smug, grin on his face.

'I've got something you'll really like,' he announced and at that moment Patrick walked round from the parking space at the side of the house.

'That was going to be *my* line. Hello, Freya,' he said, kissing me lightly on the lips.

'So,' Nathan looked him up and down, initially with a slight frown which vanished as they appraised each other. 'You and Freya, eh? Great girl you've got there.'

'I think so too.' There was a twinkle in Patrick's eyes as

194

he looked at me before introducing himself. 'Who are you then?'

'Oh, sorry, mate,' Nathan pulled out a business card. 'Here you go. I took a load of old stuff off her hands the other day.' He turned to me, looking pleased with himself. 'I've found a table and chairs exactly like you said: old repro oak refectory table with eight chairs and two carvers. It's too big for most houses but it would fit your big room lovely.' He nodded at Patrick. 'To be honest, Pat,' he shrugged. 'I couldn't see what she meant about the old chairs she chucked out but when I saw this set – well, there's no comparison. I just knew she'd want them.'

'That's very kind,' I said faintly, feeling shaky at how glad I was to see Patrick and light-headed at the conversation going on about me. I'd had no chance yet to ask if they thought I was invisible and I didn't get one now.

'The thing is, Freya,' Nathan looked at his watch. 'The old lady who owns it wants to sell and she's got some cowboy turning up around six. If you can get there before he arrives she'll give you first refusal, but we'll need to be quick.' He looked from Patrick to me and urged, 'Go and get your cheque book, love, just in case you like the stuff. You two can come in the front with me. Leave your car, Pat, it's only a fifteen-minute drive but we need to get a move on.'

He headed towards his van. 'Come on,' he wheedled. 'If you don't like it there's no harm done, is there?'

I surrendered and ran to check on Mrs Simpson who stared defiantly at me from the middle of Patrick's bed. I shrugged; he liked cats anyway, so I locked the back door and picked up my bag while Patrick dropped his things inside the hall.

'It'll be fun,' he murmured as I caught up with him. 'You can sit on my lap if you like.'

I knew I was blushing and I had no idea how I was going to sit so close to him and not give myself away. He reached for my hand and smiled, his eyes dancing, and I knew it was already too late. I'd given myself away long ago.

Trembling with excitement and something like terror I

clambered into the van and sat primly in the middle, tucked in between the two men. Patrick slid an arm round my shoulders and gave me a comforting squeeze.

'It'll be all right, I promise,' he said quietly.

'Course it will,' Nathan chimed in staunchly. 'I know you've got a lot of work to do in the house before you think about furniture, but my motto is – take a chance. This old lady's got a lot of other furniture you might like.'

'Really?' Patrick leaned forward. 'Has she got a four-poster bed, do you know?'

'Might have, I didn't go upstairs. I was only there on the look-out for Victorian garden furniture for a client when I spotted the dining set. She's got one of them big sofas you like, Freya, with the drop-ends. Some nice rugs, too.'

It was all getting out of hand, as was Patrick who, though saying nothing, was actually kissing my ear. I shivered but it seemed churlish to tell him to stop so I spent the rest of the journey in a charmed state, a bit like Sleeping Beauty stirring at the end of her hundred-year sleep. Had she dreamed, I wondered, that the Prince was already at the door? I must have shivered again because when Nathan was concentrating as he drove through the gates of a large Victorian villa, Patrick took advantage of his distraction and pulled me towards him.

'Now,' he said, and kissed me so thoroughly that neither of us noticed Nathan park the van and turn off the ignition. Nor were we aware when he climbed down from the driver's seat.

'Er, 'scuse me,' he coughed, appearing at the passenger side. 'I don't like to interrupt, but the lady of the house will be here in a minute and if you can tear yourselves apart it's time to think about furniture.'

The only thing to do was laugh so, sheepishly, we did as we were told and followed him hand-in-hand to the door where a large, elderly woman was watching with interest.

'Mrs Ormsby, this is the young lady I told you about.' Nathan did the honours and we trailed along in her wake to the dining-room.

'Wow!' Patrick said it for me. The refectory table and chairs looked almost as old as the house at Ladywell though I knew it was repro. I was hooked. I'd expected black oak but the table matched the panelling at Ladywell, a darkish golden brown.

'It was made for my husband's grandparents around 1896,' Mrs Ormsby explained. 'I've never liked it. Mahogany would have suited this house better, but he was attached to it.' She glanced at Patrick, then at me and her smile broadened. 'What we put up with in our husbands, eh?'

'Oh, but we're not…' I began and she put a hand on my arm.

'Why not?' She fixed Patrick with a stern stare. 'It's as clear as day that you're in love, the pair of you. If there's nothing in the way, no impediment as they say, why on earth don't you get married?'

Startled at such bluntness I opened my mouth but Patrick got there first.

'You're quite right, Mrs Ormsby,' he said. 'I was just thinking that.'

'Get on with it then.' She beckoned to Nathan. 'You, come upstairs and see what you think. As for you two,' she wagged a finger at us, laughing loudly. 'I won't sell you my dining-room table unless you're getting married!'

'Freya,' he took my hand and as far as I was concerned Nathan and the old lady simply vanished. 'I really *was* going to ask you today. Will you?'

'Well,' I stroked my chin thoughtfully. 'If it means getting hold of that table…'

'Look, Romeo and Juliet,' Nathan had a huge grin on his face. 'You can do all that later. Meantime, Mrs Ormsby's got some more furniture to sell. Mind you,' –he looked over his shoulder but the old lady was still upstairs – 'let me do the negotiating. The way you two are you'd hand over a million quid without noticing. I can see little bluebirds chirruping round your heads. Come on, she says there's something in the spare room that you'll like.'

Mrs Ormsby was right. We did like it.

'It's quite old, in places,' she explained. 'The posts are believed to be eighteenth century but the bed itself was another thing my husband's grandfather commissioned. He was an enormous man and his wife wasn't much smaller, so he insisted on having a six-foot wide bed, most unusual in those days. I bought a new mattress a few years ago and it's hardly been used because I've given up having visitors. They're such a nuisance.'

Mrs Ormsby insisted on sealing the bargain with glasses of sherry so dry it took the enamel off your teeth and it was later, just as Patrick and Nathan were loading the van, that she buttonholed me.

'Hmm,' she said, appraising me. 'I thought so earlier, but now you're standing in the light I can see I was right.'

'I'm sorry?' She had left me behind.

'Tell me, my dear, exactly which branch of the Moberley family tree do you perch on? I can't figure it out.'

I frowned at the mention of the old alderman's name, remembering how the psychic woman had told me he was the key to everything. 'I don't understand. My name is Gibson.'

'That's as may be,' she sounded irritable. 'Nevertheless, you're clearly a Moberley.'

'I don't think so,' I said politely and she shook her head.

'Nonsense, of course you're one of them,' she barked. 'You can't mistake the Moberley beak.'

With that she stomped back into the house leaving me stunned until Nathan called me.

As far as I could see, what she had said could only mean one thing. The eighteenth century Wellman who had married into the Moberley family had surely not passed down a characteristic nose? Wasn't it more likely that if I did perch somewhere on the Moberley family tree it was through my mother, that shadowy, unknown woman who had borne me.

Twenty minutes later we were home, the van stacked high with the old lady's furniture. Besides the dining-table and chairs we had squeezed in some lovely old rugs and two high-backed, carved chairs that Mrs Ormsby vaguely thought might date from Charles II "or perhaps Cromwell."

'You bring the chairs, Freya,' instructed Nathan. 'We'll fetch the table.' He checked his phone. 'When we've done that, you'd better come back with me for the rest, Pat. I'll ring my brother to meet us there with his pick-up for the old lady's garden chairs.'

The men set up the table under the Priory window in Dickon's Room, where it looked perfectly at home while I scuttled in and out carrying chairs. They dumped a couple of Mrs Ormsby's rugs on the floor and while Nathan was fetching what their former owner had called hall chairs, the two very old, carved ones, I met Patrick on the stairs.

'Did you know there's a cat on my bed?' he asked and without waiting for an answer he grabbed me, his eyes gleaming with amusement.

'Was I hallucinating?' he asked, kissing me. 'Did we actually get engaged just now?'

I was about to answer when Nathan looked in through the front-door and rolled his eyes.

'Oy, you two, save it for later,' he scolded. 'First things first. We've gotta get back before that cowboy turns up, he only offered her a hundred quid for the lot, and I wouldn't put it past her to forget you've already paid good money for that bed and the rest.' Nathan had given me an idea of a fair price so I'd written a scarily large cheque and Patrick helped out with another, saying, 'Don't fuss, we'll sort it out later.'

'Get a move on, Pat,' Nathan called out. 'You don't want to lose that four-poster, not now you're engaged. You'll need it! Follow me in your car then you can take the old dear to get those cheques safely deposited.'

Patrick grinned at me and followed Nathan obediently out to the van once more. I grabbed his arm as he opened the passenger door.

'See if you can find out what she meant, Patrick. About the Moberley family. I know she clammed up but she might open up to you if you unleash the full charm offensive.'

It was nearly six when Nathan let Patrick off the hook and announced that there was nothing left at Mrs Ormsby's that I would want. Between them they humped the four-poster upstairs; luckily it came apart and I was summoned to the long bedroom to admire it.

I was hugely impressed. 'It looks wonderful set up like that and I can't wait to go shopping to dress it up.' I calmed down. 'Not yet, though, all the other work must come first: the plasterwork and the panelling and all the structural stuff. Tempting though it is, I can't think about textiles for ages.'

Patrick had his arm round my shoulders. 'The old lady refused to talk about your delightful beak, which, by the way,' he said, 'makes you look like a particularly beautiful hawk.' I laughed at that but then I sighed, not surprised she wouldn't talk.

'The bed looks good, doesn't it? It'll need a better mattress,' he said, changing the subject. 'Nathan and I tested it when the old lady wasn't looking. It feels as if it's made of solid concrete.'

'I hope she didn't catch the pair of you,' I snorted. 'Still, if that's the lot, let's all go downstairs and have a drink to celebrate.'

To my amusement the cat followed us and inspected the two men. Nathan was soon dismissed.

'She'll be able to smell my dog,' he said, crestfallen, but Patrick, it seemed, passed the test. She allowed him to pick her up and stroke her while I explained how she had taken me by surprise in the small hours. I left them to it and disappeared into the kitchen, reappearing with a bottle of Laphroaig, a jug of water, and three glasses.

'Sorry, we don't have any champagne,' I said. 'I've only got half a bottle of Merlot but Patrick brought this with him. I do think we should toast Nathan's keen eye for a bargain.'

He blushed at that, clearly pleased. As he drank he prowled round the room. 'I never took a proper look the other day,' he remarked. 'It's incredible, isn't it, the window and the fireplace and all the carving. You were saying you'd need some experts, well, I can't help you there but...' He looked suddenly shy. 'Like I told Freya, Pat, I'm a good worker and I can help you sort out the garden. That rickety old shed out the back wants knocking down for firewood and I could easily put you up a good solid one. Last you for years, that would.'

He confided that he and his brother hoped to set up an architectural salvage operation and spent their spare time looking into suitable sites. So we toasted that dream too.

When he tore himself away, with an apology for having stayed so long, I gave him an invitation to the housewarming party.

'I'll bring my girlfriend,' he said. 'She'd better not get any ideas about living in a house like this. It'll be a studio flat to start.'

(v)

'We'd better eat,' I suggested as the door closed behind Nathan. 'Before we have any more visitors.'

'Too late,' Patrick raised his head as the bell pealed. 'I'll go.'

I put aside all idea of food when I heard sounds of distress. Patrick brought Cathy into Dickon's Room and sat her down on Mrs Ormsby's sofa.

'She's had bad news,' he whispered as he headed to the kitchen and reappeared with another glass in his hand. I sat down beside her and put an arm round her shaking shoulders.

'Whatever's the matter, Cathy?' I asked, waving at Patrick to bring the kitchen roll.

'I've been made redundant,' she sobbed, scrubbing at her eyes and trying to sit up straight. 'Oh, goodness,' she gulped. 'I'm terribly sorry, I don't know what I was thinking, but all of a sudden I needed someone to talk to. I don't want to interrupt, not when you've got a visitor.'

At that moment she registered the identity of the visitor and was covered with confusion.

'It's all right, honestly,' I insisted. 'Patrick's lovely…' I saw him grin appreciatively at that. 'He wants to help.' I took the whisky from him. 'Here, drink up, Cathy. It's all right, you're not driving anywhere tonight. Tell us…'

She fluttered apologetically. 'I've been made redundant,' she repeated with a hiccup. 'Nobody said anything but we've all known there've been secret meetings. We hoped it would be all right but at five o'clock the Managing Director called us in and said the company's been sold and our jobs are going. He said we were lucky to get a redundancy package at all and it was no use making a fuss, we were all in it together, even him. Then he told us to vacate the premises immediately.'

Patrick eyed her empty glass. 'Have you eaten anything since you left work, Cathy?'

When she shook her head he cocked an eyebrow at me and reached for his jacket. 'I'll get fish and chips,' he said, his keys jangling. 'We could all do with a hot meal, it's getting cold out there and I'm hungry. It's over the bridge, isn't it, Freya?'

I nodded and he set off while I devoted myself to Cathy. She finally stopped crying and I took her upstairs to the bathroom for a wash. Before we went downstairs again I showed her the four-poster and explained about our adventure with Nathan and Mrs Ormsby.

'I feel a bit guilty, chucking out Violet's furniture,' I told her. 'But it was poor quality and the house didn't like it.'

'You sound just like her,' was Cathy's surprising comment. 'She was passionate about the house though I don't remember her ever talking about furniture. It was as if the house was her baby.'

'That's what Mary Draper says,' I said. 'Do you know her?'

'Of course I do, she's a fixture in town. Her husband had the butcher's shop in the Square for years. He was such a nice man.'

'She never grumbles.' I thought of Mary who looked sad at moments but was mostly cheerful. Pity she's too old to have given birth to me, I'd have liked that.

As though she had been listening to my thoughts, Cathy stirred.

'Has Mrs Draper told you anything about... um... well, about anything to do with your parents?'

I stared at her. Was this it? Could she be my birth mother? My heart sank slightly; she was a nice woman but I felt no kinship with her. I brushed that aside and drew a deep breath.

'Did Violet Wellman ask you if you'd be willing to have a baby for my parents?' I asked bluntly and began to tremble when she nodded.

'And... did you?' It was a whisper.

'No,' she shook her head and I felt a ridiculous surge of relief, though she was perfectly pleasant. 'She did suggest it and I agreed but in the end nothing happened.' The colour came back to her cheeks. 'You have to understand what my parents were like,' she urged. 'My brothers both died before I was born, one in a cycling accident and the other from polio. I was a surprise baby long after they'd given up all hope and I was born into a house of perpetual mourning. They were terrified I'd be taken from them so I was wrapped in cotton wool and kept from all harm. They could hardly bear to let me go to school.'

She was well away with her story and I listened eagerly, aware of parallels with my own upbringing.

'My mother was brilliant at sewing and she taught me everything she knew and when I left school they got me a job with an elderly French woman. She'd been the best dressmaker in town since long before the war, when all the local posh people would go to her for their clothes. By the time I was apprenticed to her most of the posh people bought their clothes from Bracewell's, the department store, or went to London, but I did get a thorough training.' She managed a watery smile. 'I could make you a bespoke tailored suit, if you like, even a winter coat. I can do it all. When my old lady died I escaped to Brighton, where I went into another very upmarket dressmaker's establishment, but I had to come home. My father was dying and my mother was in a state.'

203

She sighed. 'Am I boring you?'

'Goodness, no. Go on, what happened?'

'Miss Wellman caught me in the garden one day and put it to me, this idea that I could have a baby for her cousin. I was pretty shocked, of course but she told me to sleep on it and gradually I could see advantages in it for me. I didn't want...' She blushed and ducked her head to one side. 'I've never hankered after marriage or children, but Miss Wellman dangled the money in front of me and it was a huge amount.'

'The equivalent of twenty thousand pounds today,' I nodded. 'Must have been tempting.'

'Oh, you've no idea.' Her face glowed. 'With that much money I thought I would go to America, to Gracelands, and see where Elvis is buried. I've always loved him. Edwina was taking the mickey, the other day, but she was right. I was almost twenty-eight and I'd hardly had a life so I thought I'd be able to get a job there; a good needlewoman is always useful. It was no good, though.'

Her voice tailed away and I held her hand. I'd left the door on the latch and plates warming in the antique oven so when I heard Patrick arrive I knew he would organise the meal.

'I'd hardly had time to get excited about it when Miss Wellman caught me again and told me it was all off. There was already a baby on the way, but not to worry, I would certainly be paid £500. It was very generous, I hadn't done anything.'

She looked up as Patrick came into the room but he just smiled at her and carried on setting the new table. I'd thrown out the old mats so he spread a towel to stop the hot plates marking the wood and I smiled mistily at him before tuning in again to Cathy.

'There's not a lot more to tell,' she said sadly. 'I was disappointed in a way, but actually it was a huge relief. I'd had time to worry, you see, about the actual birth. The five hundred pounds would still be enough to get me to America but then my father died and after the funeral my mother cried herself into hysterics. She'd been buying things from mail-order catalogues and got herself into awful debt. The infuriating thing was that she just bought anything that took her fancy, not things she needed. She was like a magpie, but the debts had to be paid and of course I had the money.'

Patrick carried in the fish and chips and a bottle of wine he must have had in the car. He summoned us to the table as Cathy gave me a despairing look.

'Since then I've festered away in that house. My supposedly frail mother lived until she was well into her nineties, she only died ten years ago. That's when I found the job on the industrial estate. My attic is full of the stuff she bought, still in its wrappings. I put it up there when I paid off her debts and I've never been able to face it.'

Patrick was very good with her, encouraging her to eat, and he talked to her gently on every topic under the sun. As she relaxed he moved on to her current problem.

'You know, it might sound insensitive of me to say this, Cathy,' he began. 'But I think you should look at this whole situation from the opposite perspective. I know you haven't had time to digest it, and it's only just landed on you, but suppose you see it as an amazing opportunity instead?'

She stared at him and I made approving noises. I could tell we'd both had the same idea.

'Yes,' he said. 'Why don't you use the redundancy money to fund the trip of a lifetime? There are package holidays to the States that take in Gracelands, you know. Why not sign up for one? Everything would be organised for you and your fellow travellers would all be Elvis fans so you'd have heaps in common.'

Cathy's eyes brightened and Patrick pressed home the idea. 'I don't know how you're placed financially,' he said tentatively. 'If you sold your house you could buy a small flat in Ramalley, so you'd still have friends locally, but you could travel *and* have a home to come back to.'

'I... I'd need some kind of job,' she said thoughtfully. 'I won't get my pension for a few years. I'll have to do something.'

I chipped in. 'Why not set up as a dressmaker in your own right? You could do alterations too, hardly anyone can sew these days and dry-cleaners offer alterations as a service. You could ask around. I'll tell you what.' I had a sudden brainwave. 'You could make party dresses. I've heard mums moan about how sixteen year-olds all go to school proms at the end of the summer term and want fiendishly expensive dresses. You could specialise in that, there are loads of schools in the area. Alison from Lamb Cottage would know about that. And who knows?' I added. 'The stuff in your attic might be worth something.'

Chapter Fifteen

(i)

Thursday, 12th March - evening

I cleared away the supper things while Patrick took Cathy home. He was longer than I expected.

'She showed me round her house,' he said, looking smug as he came into the room.

'Why?'

'I asked her. I was curious about how it could be reintegrated back as part of this house,' he said. 'It would be easy enough.'

'That was a bit insensitive, wasn't it?' I was still feeling sorry for my neighbour and her blighted, unfulfilled life.

'Of course it wasn't,' he protested. 'She asked for my autograph, she's got all my books, in hardback too. I just suggested that if she did ever think about downsizing to a flat she should give us first refusal.'

Before I could say anything else he moved swiftly across the room and took me in his arms. 'Never mind all that,' he murmured. 'We've wasted enough time and somebody's sure to knock on the door any minute, so come here. You do know that I love you, love you, *love* you?'

'Are you sure?' I held back as all the doubts rose up again.

'Of *course* I'm sure, what on earth do you mean?'

I bit my lip and looked at him. 'I didn't *know* how you felt, not for certain. And you've been so irritable lately I thought you wanted to get rid of me.'

'Seriously?' Patrick stared at me. 'I've been treading on bloody eggshells round you for months, trying not to frighten you off. I'm sorry if I've been difficult – it's not easy being around you when I want you so much and it was driving me nuts not being able to say or do anything. Why do you think I raced back to you from Colorado? I could have been ill in comfort in Denver! Surely you realised I loved you?'

'You didn't say anything,' I faltered. 'We were good friends but I didn't *know* if you...'

'For God's sake, Freya,' he rolled his eyes then pulled me towards him. 'Enough. What about that unfinished business?'

'No, no, Patrick,' I wriggled out of his arms and went to stand by the mantelpiece. 'You have to hear me out … I need to tell you about Ben. It's not that I… I just need to draw a line under him, and everything that happened. Until I've done that I can't…'

His expression was very serious but he sat down on one of the big sofas whereupon Mrs Simpson curled up on his lap.

'You're not trying to tell me you don't love me, are you?' he asked. 'Because I won't believe you.'

'Of course I love you,' I shook my head and leaned against the stone mantel. 'It's just that… Oh well, I'd better start at the beginning.'

'Go on then,' he said, with a slight smile and I nodded, feeling a bit stronger.

'Until I met Ben Chambers,' I began, 'I was a normal, cheerful, twenty-something leading a nice ordinary life with the usual worries and hassles but nothing major. I enjoyed my job at a charity's head office and I shared a flat in Battersea with Louise. You met her; she's been my best friend since we were five years old. I had lots of other friends, boyfriends too, but none of them serious. Life was fun.'

I paused, marshalling my thoughts. 'I was twenty-six when my mother, Marion, was diagnosed with cancer. I was devastated but she was defiant and refused to be beaten. They lived in Surrey so I could easily go home for visits and she seemed to be doing well. What she didn't tell me, and wouldn't let Dad tell me either, was that it was terminal. It was a terrible shock when she went downhill and died after a year.'

He half rose and the cat grumbled, but I shook my head. 'I'm okay, honestly. Dad insisted he'd be fine on his own and he'd been offered some consultancy work, including a couple of stints abroad, which kept him busy. I thought I was all right too, and a year after Mum's death Ben Chambers swept me off my feet. Literally. He was running for a train at Waterloo and didn't see me. Luckily he grabbed me before I hit the ground and dusted me down while apologising profusely. He'd missed his train by then so he insisted on buying me a drink to make up for the shock. That was it, really.'

'Love at first sight?' Patrick's mouth twisted. 'Been there, done that. Poor Freya. Go on.'

'He was stunningly good-looking,' I said, picturing Ben. 'I'm not just saying it, he had that effect on everyone. He was an economist, divorced with two teenage sons. Did I say he was older than I was? He'd just been offered a prestigious job at this university in America. Within a week of our meeting I handed in my notice and flew to the States with him.'

I waved to Patrick to stay where he was. 'I need a drink, what about you?' I'd tidied up after Cathy left so I found clean glasses and poured us both another single malt.

'Here…' I splashed water in his glass and sat down at the other end of the enormous sofa. 'We'll be drunk. Anyway, there I was, madly in love and far from home. I couldn't work because I only had a tourist visa so I volunteered at a couple of charities. I hoped to get a green card through Ben but he said there was no hurry.'

I shook my head at that poor, silly girl. 'I should have known better. Ben became the darling of the campus and I had no status at all, which was how he liked it. A little wifey to come home to, except that I wasn't a wife, and to call him an alley cat is an insult to cats all over the world.'

I knocked back a swig of whisky and spluttered. I'd forgotten to add any water.

'I tried, I really did, but gradually I felt as though I was behind a sheet of glass. Ben barely spoke to me and my visa was going to expire. I was never going to get that green card and I knew I had to get myself home but my brain was in a fog. Less than six months! That's all it took for me to fall apart. In that short time I practically turned into a Stepford Wife except that Stepford Wives are happy in their gilded cages.

'You see,' I shivered – somebody walking over my grave. 'What I didn't realise was that I wasn't fine at all about Mum's death and that running off with Ben wasn't a romantic adventure. I was escaping from *me.* It all caught up with me when I got to Colorado. I was going through the motions but nothing felt real. I'm normally upbeat and resilient but after the first glow of excitement of being in love and in a new country, the grief and everything that came with it caught up with me, pole-axed me. I didn't know who I was, my foundations had vanished and all I could do was watch endless, mindless TV soaps and cry till I was empty, day after day.

'Ben being very possessive just made it more difficult. He never wanted to share me so he'd made me put Dad off when he got in touch to suggest a visit or that I should go home for a holiday. But then my dad arrived out of the blue. "I don't want to be a nuisance," he said. "I'll book into a hotel in town, but there's something you need to know." I think it must have been this surrogate stuff but I had no chance to find out.

'When Dad did arrive, Ben was as nice as pie, though he was careful to keep us apart. He didn't want me by then and I overheard him say, man-to-man, that I'd been suffering from depression since shortly after my arrival and that he'd had a hell of a time with me. He was sure Dad's visit would do me good – and here was a great idea – we, Ben and I, were off that very evening for a weekend to Santa Fé. Why shouldn't Dad go with me instead? No, it was no trouble at all. He'd arrange everything and drive us to the airport. Right away.'

I blew my nose, took another gulp of whisky and told it baldly. 'I hadn't thought I might be depressed and now I think that Ben only said it to make himself look good. It was the first I'd heard of a trip too, but off we went an hour or two later. Ten minutes away from the airport Ben suddenly made this weird noise and slumped forward, except he was held up by the seat belt. The car slewed across the freeway and smashed into a concrete pillar under the railway bridge and when I woke up I had a broken arm, slight concussion, no father, and no boyfriend. It was an aneurysm they said and Ben would have been dead before the crash. Dad was killed instantly.'

Without saying a word Patrick put the cat gently down on a cushion and came to rest beside me. I put out a hand to push him away but he ignored it and put his arm round me.

'I'm not done yet,' I whispered. 'When they finished patching me up I was taken back to the apartment only to discover that besides his casual encounters, Ben had been having an affair with the Dean of Women's Studies. Not a single acquaintance had thought it necessary to tell me. He'd grown tired of me anyway and I don't really blame him, looking back. I was hard work, not the fun girl he'd met in London.'

I sat up straight. 'His wife flew out the next day. His not-in-the-least *ex*-wife, his very much *present* wife who, beside her two teenage sons, was three months pregnant. They'd been separated, not divorced, and on his first trip home they'd started to talk – and more than talk. I'd been so understanding about those frequent trips to London. After all, he had to keep in touch with his boys. I'd even bought presents for him to give them, and all the time...

Patrick hugged me close. 'The stupid thing is, like I said just now, that when Ben told Dad I was depressed, he was spot on. Louise was supply teaching in Australia while I was with Ben and when she planned a visit, he said we'd be away. She rang Dad in the end and insisted he must go at once, something was badly wrong. When she heard the news she dropped everything and flew over. I owe her everything.

'Lou brought me home and my own GP put me on Prozac and sent me to bereavement counselling because it was clear

211

to everyone but me, that I hadn't come to terms with Mum's death. And now I'd lost Dad as well, I really needed help. To put it bluntly, I was a mess.'

I felt warm and safe with his arm round me but I needed to make it clear, once and for all. 'I said it was less than six months, but of course it wasn't, it was much longer, with Mum's illness and the time before I met Ben. I had a couple of happy months in the sunshine and then everything dumped on me.'

I wiped my eyes. 'I was all screwed up, too lost to help myself but ashamed of what I'd become. I've no idea what would have happened to me if the accident…

'Still, that's all in the past.' I smiled tiredly. 'Lou rescued me and I had counselling and gradually got back to some kind of normal. My self-confidence had oozed away into a puddle so I temped for a while until I felt strong enough to look for a proper job. And that was when I found you.'

He said nothing but kissed me very gently and I closed my eyes. 'I'm fine now, Patrick, honestly. I've put myself back together. Louise helped, but it wasn't just grief. Ben was controlling, yes, but so was my mother. She loved me but her love was so intense I could hardly breathe. I think I fell into Ben's arms because I felt so guilty after Mum's death; because I felt free. Another reason why I never managed the grieving thing properly.'

I leaned my head on his shoulder and he stroked my hair.

'Ben alternated between enjoying keeping me under his thumb and being disgusted at what I'd become: increasingly reluctant to leave the apartment or to do anything at all. We were both tired of the whole thing but I was a skinny wraith, sunk in grief and apathy and I suspect he didn't want to look bad by dumping a woman who was clearly ill. Dad's arrival must have offered Ben the chance to make himself look noble by sacrificing his own feelings for the good of my health. Oh, yes,' I saw Patrick's expression. 'That's how he'd have played it.'

'I needed to tell you this,' I reached up and touched his cheek. 'You see, it wasn't all Ben's fault – well, apart from the lies and being a total arsehole. He'd fallen for a cheerful, bouncy English girl and that's what I am really, but because of what had happened he found himself stuck with a woman who could barely get out of bed. He *was* possessive though.' I heaved a sigh of relief. 'There, I've let it go...'

'I'm not the possessive kind,' he said, pausing to kiss me again. 'I certainly don't want a clinging vine but I don't want a woman so ambitious she has no time for a family.' I could tell he was reliving unhappy memories of his own. 'I did something similar, you know. I let myself be turned into a City type, though I knew it was wrong for me. I need a wife who thinks for herself and loves me enough to argue her case and occasionally let me get a word in edgeways. I love the way you've reassembled yourself and I love Louise for helping. You both did a great job.'

'I may not be done yet, Patrick,' I warned him, as a glow I identified as happiness filled me. More than that, for the first time in years, I had real faith in the future. 'It's mostly you but it's also this house. I can feel myself shape-shifting here and I love it. I'm home.'

He raised his glass in a toast. 'I'd like an equal partner, will that do?'

'That will be quite satisfactory,' I said primly, knowing it would make him laugh. It did, but the laughter was stilled as he reached for me.

(ii)

Friday, 13th March – early morning

Grey light filtered through the faded curtains of the front bedroom and Patrick leaned on his elbow, peering down at me.

I stirred as he murmured something.

'What did you say?'

'You might at least pay attention when I'm trying to propose. Didn't count when we were buying furniture.'

'How was I to know? I was asleep and anyway, you're not down on one knee...'

He kissed me to stop me talking. 'I'm not going down on one knee when I'm stark naked, it's bloody cold. Anyway, it's a wooden floor, I might get splinters. Will you marry me or not?'

'Oh, all right,' I caught his eye and we both burst out laughing, tremulously in my case. 'If it means so much to you.'

The laughter died away and he pulled me close. 'Oh, it does, Freya. You have no idea how much it means to me.'

'Show me.'

After he'd shown me, he rolled over and kissed the tip of my nose.

'Let's get married as soon as possible. I'm sure Miss Violet Wellman would give us her blessing.'

Long after Patrick had dozed off I drowsed, thinking about my cousin Violet and her legacy to me. Happy and hopeful in his arms I felt sad that she had lost her sweetheart and sadder still when I remembered that long ago card from wartime France, and the newspaper clipping that ended her mother's romance. It seemed pretty certain that Ronald Bracewell, the boy whose parents owned the local department store, *was* Violet's father. I finally dropped off to sleep, thinking how tough life must have been for an unmarried mother in that day and age. Poor Dorothy.

(iii)

Dorothy was only at the Vicarage bazaar on sufferance because her friend's mother, the Vicar's wife, thought she would be useful, and so she had been, roaming the woods to pick dozens of early violets. On another day the invitation would not have been forthcoming, not for the little Wellman girl.

'A pleasant girl but of course, she comes from over the bridge and really, you know…' said the Vicar's lady to a friend. 'The mother is very hard-working – takes in lodgers, old ladies. I'm sure she's very worthy but…not quite…'

Dorothy was certainly in demand. While her friend was

constantly summoned to her mother's side to be introduced to this worthy or that, Dorothy helped to pour tea, serve sandwiches and cakes, and carry parcels and flowers.

One of the ladies said, 'Go and restock the flower stall, dear, their table looks frightfully bare.' So she refilled a basket with more of the violets she had painstakingly tied into bunches. Stopping to pick off a dead leaf, she bumped into a young man; literally bumped into him, scattering the flowers and leaving her winded.

He reached out to steady her and something happened. At his touch, electricity sparked between them and they stared at each other, startled, smiling. She saw a stocky, brown-haired boy of nineteen, in uniform and with a nice, ordinary face and a nice, ordinary smile, and she could scarcely breathe.

He blinked as he saw a slim girl of eighteen, with light brown eyes and a mass of shining sandy curls, tied back with a velvet bow. She had a round face, pretty but not remarkable apart from a deep, unexpected dimple when she smiled.

They picked up the scattered bunches of violets and shivered when their hands touched in passing, and they walked together in a dream to the flower stall. For the rest of the afternoon they saw nothing, heard nothing, only each other.

Everyone else saw two helpful young people.

'How charming, that nice Bracewell boy is giving a hand to that pretty little girl. The dear vicar's daughter, I believe. Not? From Ladywell, you say? Oh, I see. Oh my dear, I do see....'

For Dorothy and the Bracewell boy time stood still.

They had a week; seven days to last for ever. His embarkation leave lasted until Friday so Dorothy skipped school, pleading a sick headache to her busy mother, and they took secret walks along the river or picnics among the sheep on the Ladywell hills. The weather was kind, unseasonably warm with not a drop of rain.

All the time they talked and laughed and marvelled at this miracle, this meeting of like with like, this wonderful, *comforting togetherness. The first time they kissed they were so dazzled by love they could hardly breathe, and the radiant happiness they felt was so tangible they could scarcely contain themselves. Dorothy wondered that nobody seemed to notice.*

'You have a nice colour, dear,' was all anyone said.

Kissing was all they did, despite feelings that took them by storm, so intense that they were shocked and delighted. 'When I'm next on leave...' he said, looking sidelong at her while she lowered her eyes, suddenly shy.

Though she prayed for a delay, something, anything – he could break a leg, or the war might end – still the last day arrived. The afternoon was all they would have because his family insisted on that evening. 'I've cried off so many things,' he said. 'Mother will be dreadfully hurt if I'm not at home tonight.'

They were up on the hill above Ladywell with their arms tightly round each other, watching a hare lollop by, when she reached out a shy hand to touch his cheek.

An urgent, pitiful voice in her head said, 'Don't let him go without something to treasure for the worst of times.' So they made love in the shadow of a clump of hawthorns.

Very early next morning she ran to the station. He was alone, eager but slightly forlorn, his gear already aboard the waiting train. He heard her pattering footsteps and turned, a smile lighting his solemn young face.

The whistle blew and there was no time for words. Only a convulsive hug, a last passionate kiss, a last, 'I love you' and he was gone.

After that, a postcard. "I'm 'somewhere in France' and the sun is shining as I drink my coffee. There are violets in bloom in the garden next door. Wait for me."

Three weeks after the postcard Dorothy heard one of her classmates sobbing. His sister. At morning assembly the headmistress sadly informed the school that a stray shell had taken him, and Dorothy, as one of the prefects, had to stand on the platform and give out the number for the next hymn.

216

She held up all through that day until she managed to burrow into her own bed. Days later a small packet arrived from France. A tiny bottle of violet scent, with a note. "I saw this in a shop today and thought of you. R."

'Are you feeling quite well, Dorothy?' Her mother put the question regularly over the next few months, too busy with her elderly lodgers to do more than accept the reassurances about the regular sick headaches. Dorothy managed to conceal her condition at school, excusing herself from the gymnasium and from tennis and cricket by forging notes from her mother.

By early July she could no longer deceive Mrs Wellman who was seriously concerned about the bouts of sickness and threatened a visit to the doctor. A brief, tearful explanation sufficed; her mother, a practical woman, concocted a plan to salvage her daughter's future.

'I wish it hadn't happened, Dorothy,' she said calmly after a day spent in profound consideration. 'That goes without saying, but now we need clear heads to deal with it.'

As though in answer to a prayer, a letter arrived, to say that Dorothy had won a scholarship to the teacher training college in Salisbury.

'The very thing.' Mrs Wellman sighed with relief as she scanned the letter. 'Here's what we'll do.'

Dorothy finished her examinations and left school at the end of term, two weeks' later. Meanwhile, Mrs Wellman wrote to the principal of the teaching college, explaining that Dorothy must postpone taking up her scholarship, due to sickness in the family. All being well, she would be ready to resume her education in September of the following year. Mrs Wellman understood that this was not ideal but was sure that, in the circumstances, the principal would be kind enough to understand.

Ladywell was a house of elderly lady lodgers, four of whom had poor sight, poor hearing and only a tenuous grasp on reality at best. The fifth, a retired governess, could see only too well what was amiss and sought out her landlady in the kitchen one day in September.

'I have no wish to pry, Mrs Wellman, but I believe I can be of assistance in your daughter's dilemma.'

There was a moment's icy silence followed by a terse, offended protest but Miss Montagu brushed it aside. 'Pray do not think I condemn Dorothy. My own sister found herself in a similar situation and to my lifelong sorrow drowned herself when her baby was taken from her at birth.'

Mrs Wellman was startled and Miss Montagu explained.

'Dorothy has an excellent brain and I am fond of her. I will not stand by while another girl ruins her life, so I propose that once we reach mid-December I and my four fellow guests will travel to stay at my brother's house near Winchester. I have an open invitation to visit and to take a guest but I have rarely taken him up on it. I shall invite myself and the other ladies for December and January. There we will remain until all is safely over. He will be startled but there will be no difficulty as his wife, a woman for whom I had the utmost contempt, mercifully died last year, and my brother is a placid, sociable man.'

Miss Montagu's plan was simple. Even the muddled old ladies could hardly fail to notice the coming and going attendant on something as momentous as the birth of a baby, so Mrs Wellman was to send a coded message when all was safely over. Miss Montagu and her entourage would return to Ramalley and the baby would be presented as a fait accompli.

'I propose to give Dorothy lessons in preparation for her teaching course,' said the old lady. 'It will stand her in good stead and will give her confidence.'

'That's too good of you,' Mrs Wellman was stiff and embarrassed and Miss Montagu shook her head.

'It will give me great pleasure to use my brain in a good cause,' she said, surprising her hostess. 'Dorothy has a thirst for knowledge and will easily fit lessons with her household duties and caring for her baby.' She pursed her lips as she stared out of the parlour window. 'Did I understand you to say that the lease on your little barn will not be renewed by your tenant?'

Mrs Wellman stared. 'Why yes, the publican at The Fleece used the old place as a store but he no longer requires it. It's more a cottage than a barn, really. I'll have to look for a new tenant.'

'Look no further,' said Miss Montagu. 'I propose to make it habitable, and no, my dear, do not protest. I am quite comfortably off.' Her expression softened. 'I could afford a grander lodging but I doubt I should find such comfort and kindness elsewhere.'

The old governess added, 'There's something about this house, you know. It seems to me that it always smells of the Christmases I loved as a child.' She shook her head. 'Sentimental nonsense! About the cottage, Mrs Wellman. I persuaded the publican to let me look round. The room upstairs will do for Dorothy and the baby and the downstairs can be arranged for my own use. I'll continue to eat here with the other ladies.'

She became brisk. 'It is, of course, imperative that the training college must not hear about the baby; one word and she'll be out on her ear. We must announce that we have adopted a fatherless war baby. Dorothy will stay in Salisbury during term-time and the increased rent that I pay for the cottage will amply cover the hire of someone to look after the baby.'

Astonishingly, it all went according to plan. Miss Montagu's tuition was invaluable in teaching Dorothy how to manage a class of children. Mrs Wellman hired a young girl as nursery-maid and general help, and Dorothy gave birth to her daughter with an ease and speed that was, as Miss Montagu tartly informed her on hearing of it, shockingly unladylike.

'What name do you propose to give this child?' asked the redoubtable old lady.

'Her name is Violet.'

Chapter Sixteen

(i)

Friday, 13th March – morning

A guilty conscience made me wriggle out of bed just before eight and the cat made quite sure I knew I was in disgrace. She sat with her back to me, turning up her nose up at the food I apologetically put in her bowl.

'Look,' I told her. 'I know it's out of order and it won't happen again, but today is really, really special. You don't get engaged every day, you know, so go on, eat it.' As an added sweetener I cut a bit off the salmon in the fridge. 'Here, don't tell Patrick.'

'Don't tell me what?' He wrapped his arms round me. 'I saw that. Come here, puss.'

To my indignation the haughty Mrs Simpson deigned to let him scratch the top of her head.

'Flirt!' I sniffed. 'She'll have you at her beck and call if you're not careful.'

'Are you jealous of the cat?' He scratched the top of my head too. 'That better? Come back to bed, the cat's fine.'

One thing led to another but eventually I remembered we had a party to prepare so I wriggled out of Patrick's arms ready to tackle the coming day.

While the kettle boiled, the cat and I took a leisurely stroll down the garden to look over the wall. Mrs Simpson lost interest but to my delight the hare was there, almost as though it was expecting me. I'd done some research using the library's Wi-Fi and there were dozens of legends about hares, including my favourite – the hare that carried a goddess into the sky on its back. I liked, too, the note by old Miss

Montagu that suggested that the two Ladies, one of the old religion and the other of the new, had become one and the same.

Today, the hare pricked up its ears and I knew Patrick was there. He hugged me; the morning was bright but chilly.

'Where's Violet buried, by the way? You never said.'

'She isn't.' I was startled. 'The solicitor said she was cremated and wanted her ashes scattered on Puss Hill. What made you think of that?'

'Mr Fletcher at the Priory said hares were a symbol of reincarnation,' he said thoughtfully.

'It's a Chinese belief. What's that got to do with Violet?'

'Just wondering... Could be your cousin Violet over there, keeping an eye on how you're looking after your inheritance,' he suggested with a laugh.

I stared across the ditch that had once been a stream, not laughing at all, as I wondered whether he was right.

After breakfast I checked my lists. I'd invited extra people and I needed to contact the caterer.

'Simple,' Patrick took the list out of my hand. 'We'll go into town and order more food. We need a cake and champagne anyway, now it's an engagement party. There's your friend Louise's baby too, we should wet his head. Besides,' – he shooed me out to the car – 'we need to look for an engagement ring.'

Just over a week ago I'd worried that Patrick might sack me and here we were shopping for a ring. I had to force myself to relax and let happiness flow over me.

He knew what I was thinking. 'That's right,' he said as he drove to the car park in Bridge Street. 'Believe it... I'm not Ben and you're not that girl now; you're my lovely shape-shifter. The sun's shining and Spring's round the corner. Let me share the load, Freya.'

We looked in jewellers' windows and I began to despair. Nothing appealed until I was overwhelmed at the sight of a dozen beautiful antique rings laid out in shabby velvet boxes.

'Are you sure about this?' Patrick took my hand and

examined the Edwardian ring, a square yellow stone surrounded by brilliants.

'I love it, I'd never even heard of a yellow diamond.'

I flaunted my ring in all the other shops we visited but sadly nobody remarked on it so we called in at the patisserie and found the owner fuming over a large iced sponge.

'The wretched woman's just this minute cancelled,' she grumbled but she was wreathed in smiles when Patrick offered to buy it. 'I'll throw in some decorations.' She waved a hand at the shelves.

'Are those crystallised violets?' I peered at the display. 'We have to have those.'

With the cake box carefully under Patrick's arm we called in at the delicatessen and ordered more canapés on our way to the car park.

The pretty village of Bychurch, a mile or so along the river, had a well-known pub so we had lunch there, talking and planning and occasionally falling silent.

'It'll be all right, Freya,' Patrick said, reaching for my hand across the table. 'I promise.'

'Did I look worried? I don't mean to,' I said apologetically. 'It's just…I'm not used to the idea of happiness like this.'

He leaned across and kissed me, much to the amusement of two elderly couples at the next table. Blushing, I took out my notepad.

He groaned. 'Not another list?'

'Wedding guests, or would you rather we just go off and do it and have a party later?'

'Oh my God!'

I jumped out of my skin as he clapped a hand to his forehead and stared at me.

'No need to react like that,' I mocked. 'I don't have a shotgun pointed at you.'

'I completely forgot my news. How did that happen?' He grinned. 'Oh, all right, I can see why it receded to the back of my mind, but listen. How do you feel about a honeymoon in Hollywood? Starting the week after next?'

The hush-hush meetings in London during the past couple of days had been about an offer from a streaming company with an increasingly high profile. Amid great secrecy Patrick had been wined and dined, to discuss a series based on his first three novels, more if all went well. It was huge news and unlike a couple of earlier offers, this looked as though it would take off.

'They want me over there but it's only for a couple of weeks,' he urged. 'To tie up loose ends. I won't be writing the screenplay so we could turn it into a honeymoon. What do you say?'

'I say yes,' I said happily. 'You don't want a Las Vegas wedding, do you? I'd like to get married quietly in the Priory. I don't have any family, so let's see... Your parents and brother and his family and on my side there's only Andrew and Louise, if she'll be up to travelling with such a new baby. Oh, and Mary and Mrs Penrose, I'd like them there.'

(ii)

The sun kept on shining and the light that filtered through the Priory window made wavering greenish patterns on the oak floorboards. With the dining-chairs and carvers, plus the other two I'd bought from Nathan's old lady, the rear end of Dickon's Room was ready for serious eaters, while the two huge sofas provided comfortable seating.

Kick-off was timed for six o'clock but Cathy dropped in not long after five-thirty, followed by the woman from the delicatessen who took over the kitchen.

'I wondered if you'd need a hand,' Cathy asked diffidently. 'I could wash up or make tea. Anything really.'

She looked so prepared for a rebuff that I was touched.

'How nice of you, Cathy. I'm going to meet and greet but Patrick's in charge of the bar, why don't you help him?'

Patrick beamed at Cathy and took her to the bar we'd set up by the kitchen door. They were soon deep in conversation and although I had no time to eavesdrop I did notice Cathy light up with excitement.

I let out a shriek when I saw the time and hurried upstairs. Mrs Simpson was on my bed and she raised her head to watch me dress, yawned, and went back to sleep, quite unmoved by my sudden attack of nerves. What if nobody came? I took a deep breath and mentally slapped myself.

The soft blue of the outfit Edwina had selected for me looked great and as I twisted my hair up into a clip I stared at my shining goldy-brown eyes in the mirror. Wasn't it Mary who'd said the Wellman family could be recognised by their amber eyes? I wondered whether any of the guests would have the aquiline Moberley nose.

John Fletcher bounded in, followed by his placid, pleasant wife. He kissed me on both cheeks and shook hands with Patrick.

'I know who you are, now,' he announced. 'We're great fans, aren't we, dear?'

She smiled kindly then moved across to talk to Cathy, a fellow church-goer, while John handed me a gift-wrapped parcel.

'This was intended as a house-warming gift,' he twinkled. 'However, it seems to have turned into an engagement present. Congratulations, both of you.'

I thanked him and unwrapped an oak-framed, antique print. 'Goodness,' I exclaimed when I realised what it was. 'Patrick? Come and see what John's given us. It's an illustrated map of Ladywell.'

'It's only a copy, I'm afraid,' John looked downcast though he cheered up when I gave him a tearful hug. 'The original is in the town archives but when I explained who it was for they let me photocopy it on watercolour paper because it gives a nicer finish. It's a mid-eighteenth century engraving.'

The house looked much as it must have done when it was built, without the two later wings. There was much more land and the front of the house looked out on a wide green area with a sandy track along the river and a sign to a tannery which was out of sight. What made me gasp was an area marked 'Supposed site of Roman villa' (where the station is now) away down to the left as you looked at Puss Hill. This was also named and illustrated with cheerful-looking hares and lots of woolly sheep. To the right of the property was another 'supposed site', this time of a mediaeval house and in the centre, where the modern boundary now met the wall at the bottom of my garden, was the well, and beside it the legend, 'Supposed site of monk's chapel'.

Janice from the museum brought her husband and she was thrilled when I invited her to prowl round the house. 'Are you sure? I love nosing round houses and this one's very special,' she smiled.

Hot on her heels was my elusive neighbour from Lamb Cottage over the road.

'Alison.' I was so pleased to see her. 'I'm glad you made it. Here, have a drink and meet Patrick.'

'My,' she laughed, surveying the room full of people. 'You've had a busy week! Congratulations, it's great news.'

We never did manage to sit down to chat but there would be plenty of time in future. I rushed around talking, being hugged, checking people were happy, and at seven o'clock I met Patrick in Dickon's Room. I dashed in with plates as we were about to cut the cake and he made sure everyone had a glass ready. Cathy was in her element, beaming with pleasure as she dispensed drinks, and Mary and Mrs Penrose were parked on one of the big sofas. Mrs Simpson sat between them, graciously accepting admiration.

'Hello, you,' Patrick smiled at me. 'You look like a Roman goddess in that outfit. Enjoying your party?'

'Hello yourself, and yes, I'm having a lovely time.'

He kissed me and a loud cheer went up. Nathan was standing by the fireplace with a broad grin on his face as I blushed. Luckily, very little puts Patrick off his stride and he took over.

'Thanks, Nathan, and thank you all. Has everyone got a glass? My charming assistant Cathy will make sure everyone has some champagne while my beautiful bride-to-be and I cut the cake.' He gave a theatrical bow and pushed me gently towards the table.

'I claim the right to toast the happy couple.' To my surprise it was the solicitor, Harry Makepeace, who'd called in on his way home from the office. 'I was the first person in Ramalley to meet Freya and welcome her to her new home. Ladies and gentlemen, please raise your glasses and drink to a long and happy married life for Freya and Patrick.'

I wasn't the only person to well up. Mary and Sylvia wiped their eyes and Cathy was frankly crying, but with a smile on her face. Edwina's usually brittle expression softened as she nestled close to her friend Graham, while John Fletcher's wife blew her nose and Nonie Radstone took off her glasses to polish them.

(iii)

Gradually everyone went away, with hugs and kisses and promises to be in touch, until only Mary and Mrs Penrose were left. The woman from the delicatessen had taken all her own equipment away with her and Mary insisted on helping with the rest of the tidying up.

I fed Mrs Simpson some leftover prawns then, while Patrick helped Mrs Penrose with her coat, I buttonholed Mary with my suspicions.

'Look, Mary,' I urged. 'I know you said you can't tell me yet but will you listen to my ideas?'

'I might,' she said guardedly. 'Not saying I'll answer, that last bit of the jigsaw isn't my secret and until I've had a chance to discuss it with... er... with the person concerned, I'm not spilling any beans.' She patted my hand. 'Don't worry, dear,' her smile was kind. 'It'll turn out well, you'll see.'

'Right.' I took a deep breath. 'I've talked to Cathy and she admits Violet approached her about the... surrogacy thing, and that she agreed in principle. I was already on the way, so it never happened.'

I narrowed my eyes but Mary stayed silent. 'I suspect, though I haven't tackled her, that Edwina was in the same boat. She told me 1982 was a rotten year: her husband did a bunk and around that time she had a windfall that enabled her to open her boutique.'

I glanced across the room and saw that Patrick and Mrs Penrose were deep in conversation but Patrick looked up just then and smiled. He evidently guessed I was pumping Mary.

'I have no logical reason for believing my birth mother was a local woman,' I told her. 'And still less reason for suspecting that I've actually met her since I came to Ramalley, but it's in my head and it won't shift. Besides,' I managed a wavering smile, 'that psychic woman as good as told me I'd meet her.

'The thing is, Mary, I've met several women in the last week including you and Mrs Penrose but you're the wrong generation. The psychic woman's about the right age but you said you'd never seen her before and I think I can discount Mr Fletcher's wife. I can't imagine my dad having an affair with Cathy who's explained her part anyway, and while I can easily picture him fancying Edwina, I know for a fact that she opened her shop about two weeks before I was born. She'd have been hard pushed to start a new business and give birth at the same time.

'It seems to me,' I cleared my throat, 'that there's only one candidate left if she's someone I've already met. One of those women had her glasses on each time I've seen her but tonight,' – I tried to make a joke of it – 'I got a good look at her close up, and I believe she does have the infamous Moberley aquiline nose.'

I whispered a name to Mary, who nodded.

'Her maiden name was Moberley, dear. Not many of the old Alderman's descendants left now.'

I bit my lip and heard my voice tremble as I said, 'I didn't have the nerve to speak to her this evening, not with so many people around. What shall I do, Mary?'

'I think…' Mary sighed, then nodded. 'Look, here's her number, ring her up, then. Yes, do. She'll be home by now.' She gave me a comforting hug. 'Go on, Freya, get it over with. She knows you'll work it out and she won't bite.'

227

When the taxi had taken away the two old ladies Patrick handed me a cup of tea.

'I was going to make it champagne,' he grinned, 'but I guessed Mary was spilling the beans and you always crave tea at moments of high drama! Are you going to tell me?'

I told him and shed a few tears till he tilted my chin. 'Before you get on the phone I have a spot of news for you. Mrs Penrose just offered to sell us her house and I accepted on the spot. Hope that's okay?'

Afterwards he tactfully left me on my own so, standing by the great stone mantelpiece with my fingers tracing the carved hare, I made a call.

A voice answered. 'Anona Radstone.'

In a half-whisper I said, 'This is Freya. I think we need to talk.'

Epilogue
'The Balance Restored'

(i)

Sunday, 29ᵗʰ May 2016

The star of the show was fast asleep in her pram under the shade of the rowan tree, worn out after her christening in the Priory. Curled up in his car seat beside her was Louise's toddler, James, with Patrick's fifteen-year old nephew Felix in charge. Skinny Mrs Simpson dozed under the pram and as I approached Felix put his finger to his lips.

'Shh. Violet woke up for a minute but they're both asleep now.' I obediently tiptoed away to where Patrick was watching the scene.

'Been told off?' He smiled and indicated his other nephew, thirteen-year old Theo, who was sitting between Mary Draper and Mrs Penrose. 'Have you seen that? He's doing a history project about World War II and they're his primary sources. Hope he doesn't bore them to death.'

'No fear of that.' I waved to Mary who looked happy with her company. 'They'll do the tiring out; they love to talk about the old days.'

Patrick put an arm round me.

'It's looking great, isn't it? My cunning plan worked perfectly.'

His cunning plan had been to persuade both neighbours to sell us their houses but in truth no persuasion had been necessary. Mrs Penrose had made her offer after the party, and the next day Cathy called in.

'Did you mean it, Patrick, about buying my house?' she'd asked anxiously. 'Because I've been awake all night thinking about what you said and I'm going to do it.'

She did, too and bought a flat near the Priory before jetting off on a package tour to the States that culminated in a visit to Gracelands. One or two of her fellow Elvis fans on the trip lived not too far from Ramalley so she had new friends and was now happier, she insisted, than she had ever been in her life. I'd offered her the Beauty Parlour as her showroom but she decided she needed to be right in town, so that renovation project was on hold.

'I'll make all your curtains for you,' Cathy promised and she had, beautifully, so we were happy to recommend her to everyone we knew.

My idea of specialising in teenage ball dresses had been too late to take off the previous year but Cathy was already snowed under with orders for the coming school prom season. With curtains, alterations and other commissions she was making a small but comfortable living and was embarrassingly grateful to Patrick who, she insisted, had inspired her. Naturally he lapped up this adulation, pointing out that his wife and daughter had much to learn when it came to appreciating him.

Alison from over the road was sitting beside Nonie Radstone, eagerly discussing gardening with Patrick's father while his mother and Mr Fletcher inspected the well. Nonie must have felt my eyes on her because she looked up and smiled.

We both cried when we met up the day after the party and although we were cautious at first our friendship was now firmly established. I never asked about her relationship with my father, it felt too much of a betrayal of Marion, my mother, but I gradually began to understand her. She had no wish for any official status but it was known to a few people and she adored being an unofficial grandmother to Violet Louise Underwood who had arrived at the end of March.

'I see you've changed Violet out of that gorgeous christening gown,' Patrick's sister-in-law came to stand beside me. 'Just as well, you don't want baby sick all over it. Is it a family heirloom?'

'In a way,' I told her. 'It's Edwardian and real silk. Nonie offered it and I was terrified it would be spoiled.'

'Two little ginger nuts,' Patrick arrived, pointing at the sleeping babies.

Louise was indignant. 'James isn't ginger. He has his father's chestnut hair...'

'Yes, and I want it back,' interrupted her husband, running a hand through his thinning locks. 'I can't afford to lose any more.'

'Violet isn't ginger either,' I put in, amid the general laughter, thinking of the soft sandy fuzz on my daughter's head.

(ii)

'Show me round again.' Louise was at my side. 'It was a rush before and I didn't take it all in.' We entered the back of the house via double glass doors where the old lean-to kitchen once stood. On our right was Dickon's Room, its plasterwork and panelling restored to their former glory and a door where the bookcase had been. We were very proud of that; someone had recommended a craftsman who specialised in doors made to look like bookshelves and it seemed appropriate, though it cost an arm and a leg.

The big room looked as splendid as I'd always known it would and on one wall Anne Wellman's sampler, beautifully framed, hung beside the antique map of Ramalley. I laughed as I drew Louise's attention to the exquisite needlework. 'I've been thinking I'd like to have a go at making a sampler, but when I look at this I doubt I'd ever measure up to it. I've got this idea that I ought to learn a craft of some kind, something to connect me to the history of Ladywell, which was a sheep farm, after all. I can't see me spinning or weaving but I want to try something. Mary tried to teach me to knit but it was a complete dog's breakfast.'

I took Lou into what had been Mrs Penrose's house and which was now Patrick's domain with a study, cloakroom and reception room for business visitors. The outer door at the side remained but the staircase had gone, while upstairs a palatial bathroom and dressing-room led off from the long bedroom where Patrick and I now slept.

'We'll divide this off when we can afford more building work,' I said when we went upstairs. 'Nobody needs a dressing-room this big. It'll probably be my study.'

'Good idea,' Louise nodded. 'What are your plans, Freya? I know this year's been action-packed, what with getting married, having a baby and acting as site manager for a major refurbishment, but what's next? Will you go on working as Patrick's assistant?'

I shook my head. 'I'll help out with research where I can but he has someone starting next month; the work's piling up. As for me,' I wandered over to look out at everyone in the garden. 'I don't yet have a coherent plan, which is unlike me. One idea is to help get the museum archive online. A friend volunteers there and I can do that from home. Otherwise, I'm not sure, but I know one thing. I love Mary and Sylvia. I didn't have any grandparents, as you know, and I'm going to consult them about how I can help other women to fill in forms, ask questions on their behalf. That kind of thing and maybe some other kind of business, along with lots of other ideas I haven't yet had!

'It's all very vague so far but there's fund-raising too. Mary reminded me that lots of women love poking around old houses and she reckons people would pay decent money to come to a coffee morning or tea party at Ladywell and meet Patrick.' I grinned. 'I haven't suggested it to him yet, I'm waiting for the right moment.'

Violet Wellman's namesake would one day sleep in her old room, and the large front bedroom was a little smaller now that a passage had been made through to Cathy's house. There were two more bedrooms over there, and a bathroom.

'We've left the staircase there,' I explained. 'It leads down to the new kitchen and family room that we've made from the ground floor of Cathy's house and into Violet's old dining-room.

'It's fabulous,' Louise approved. 'I love the kitchen, it's big but friendly and oh, my God! I'm *really* jealous of that huge walk-in larder. So, you've finished this phase of the alterations?'

'Patrick completed on his sale the day I found out I was pregnant. Such a relief or we'd have had to hold fire on the building project. I was terrified how much money we were spending! It made sense to sell Patrick's place. He had a house and my flat is small but handy for Waterloo. It meant we could spend more on Ladywell.'

'You're besotted with your house.' Louise's laugh was affectionate.

'I am,' I admitted. 'Right from the moment I first set eyes on it.'

Louise paused in the hall. 'I can smell freesias again,' she said. 'I did the first time I came here.'

I hesitated. 'It's different for everyone: Patrick with his mum's sweet peas, me with Dad's roses. I know it sounds mad,' I faltered, 'but it's always something special to each individual.'

She didn't laugh. 'My grandmother loved freesias,' she said.

I thought of the final note in Miss Montagu's sketchy history of Ladywell. 'My dear friend Mrs Wellman told me, in strict confidence and a little shame-facedly, of a belief that the original Lady of the well holds the women of the family in her heart. From my own observation I can certainly say that most women, but few men, are conscious of the scent of flowers in this house. Who is to say that this is not the legacy of a benign spirit?'

For once Violet had nothing to say – and neither did I.

(iii)

Outside we bumped into Nathan, fresh from showing his girlfriend the garden. 'You wouldn't believe how good the old well looks, would you?' he said, with a friendly nudge

'I still can't,' I said frankly. 'So many people helped us; the dowser Mr Fletcher found, and all the hard work you and your brother put in, clearing it out and rebuilding the wall. And don't forget our front door,' I grinned at him and turned to Louise. 'Nathan was all set to get his mate to make us an 'authentic' front door, complete with scars and bruises from being walloped with bicycle chains.'

'Honestly?'

'Uh-huh,' I nodded. 'By a stroke of luck though, he picked up an old door at a farm sale. It's about a hundred years old and his friend cut it to size, but it was Nathan who spotted the potential.' He blushed as I added, 'Did I tell you, Lou, that he knows *everybody*? He built the stone wall and even introduced us to a blacksmith who made us two elongated iron hoops, crossed over each other with a fixing to hold the pulley and chain for the bucket as well as the grille on top to stop people falling in. We had to copy the picture on the sampler to give us an idea how it looked because there's no written description, although it's on record that it was about four feet across, not as wide as the Font by the Priory.

'Your housewarming hare looks just right, Lou, standing guard by the Lady's Well; Mr Fletcher says that was the original name. And there's water in the well. After they built the station in the eighteen hundreds, the well dried up; it happens sometimes. Now there are new houses on the old railway sidings, they've done something... Don't ask, I've no idea of the mechanics but if you have a week to spare Patrick will bore for England on the subject! Anyway, it's a miracle because the well and the stream both have water again.'

When the visitors had gone, apart from Patrick's family and Louise's, I strapped my sleepy daughter in her sling on my chest and wandered down to the bottom of the garden. Across the stream, as I'd scarcely dared hope, was the large brown hare staring at me from bright amber eyes. I remembered Patrick's half-serious suggestion that Violet might be watching over us and I hoped she was happy with what she saw. We communed for a moment until the hare whisked away and I took the baby to inspect the well. Louise's carved hare, beside the well but poised for flight, already had a shiny head where people automatically touched it – for luck, I thought. I stroked it now and then had to stroke the cat as she twined herself round my legs before skittering across the garden.

The blacksmith's sturdy wrought-iron grille was padlocked firmly in place and the two tall crossed hoops were topped with a finial in the shape, naturally, of a hare. Underneath hung the pulley and chain so the bucket could be drawn up when we wanted to water the garden but just hauling water for a drink would be a palaver with the grille in place. Nathan had made a niche in which sat a metal beaker and it was this that I took now, dipping it through the grid to reach the bucket drawn up to the top.

Not long ago my solicitor, Harry Makepeace, had dropped in to see Patrick. They were good friends now and Harry was highly flattered to be asked about some legal details for the new book. I showed him all the alterations and on the spur of the moment asked, 'Does the house still feel sad to you?'

He was taken aback but smiled. 'You know what? It doesn't feel sad at all now.'

The cheerful bustle of Violet's christening party was

over and Patrick was pouring drinks for the remaining visitors so, in the sudden hush that seemed to encircle us, I poured a drop of water from the Lady's Well on to my daughter's forehead.

She opened her eyes at that and gazed seriously at me, with not even a squeak, so I blessed her with the charm that the elder Violet had bequeathed to me, along with her house.

'*Domina aquarum*
Leporumque currentium
Domina custodi nos
Locum benedic.

'Lady of the waters,
Lady of the running hare,
Lady keep us.
Lady bless this place.'

'*The Balance Restored.*'

Timeline & The Wellman Family

4th century AD ~ *The Roman Girl*

Aula	the farmer's daughter
Flavia Petronilla	her grandmother
Marius	the renamed runaway
Acilius & Livia	the farmer and his new wife
Gaius Neronis Tallum	a distinguished but unwelcome visitor

I have 'borrowed' the tenuous suggestion that Venta Belgarum (present-day Winchester) had an Imperial Fulling Mill that supplied the Roman Army with cloth.

Late 10th century ~ *The Dog Boy*

Wat	the dog boy
The master and mistress	the farmer and his wife
Mistress Osburga	the farmer's daughter
Brother Aelfric	the monk
The Prior	

Late Saxon burials (Chapter 5) have been found in Hampshire. This story was inspired by a fascinating talk I attended by Dr Annia Cherryson, an archaeologist with the Winchester Museum Service. Any errors are mine.

Mid 14th century ~ *The Heiress*

Philippa	the heiress
The young man	the visitor
Cicely	the grandmother

My fictional town of Ramalley is loosely based on Romsey, where it was said that half the town's population died during the Black Death.

1539 ~ *The Tudor Nun*

Katherine	the nun returned from her convent
Dickon Wellman	the farmer, ready to build himself a house
Brother Ambrosius	the Infirmarian, ready to build a new life

Three ancient monks from the chapel

Again I've borrowed from Romsey's history. The secret Dickon Wellman confides is based on a rumour that Richard III sent his nephews, Edward V and Richard, Duke of York, to safety in Sherriff Hutton in Yorkshire before the Battle of Bosworth.

1685 ~ *The Witch*

Anne Wellman	the accused
Henrietta Wellman	her daughter-in-law
Gideon Cooper	the usurper
Little Anne and Richard	the twins

The Monmouth Rebellion was largely as described in Chapter 9 though there are no reports of witch burning at any time in Hampshire.

1815 Peninsular War ~ *The Foreign Bride*

Kate Wellman	the old widow
Marie-Simone Wellman	the young widow

Battle of Orthez 27ᵗʰ February 2014.
Battle of Waterloo 18th June 1815

1918 World War I ~ *The Schoolgirl*

Dorothy Wellman	still at school
Ronald Bracewell	off to the war

Mrs Wellman   an overworked mother
Sarah Montagu   a retired governess
*Chemin des Dames Ridge, 3rd Battle of the Aisne 27 May
– 6 June 1918*

Fantastic Books
Great Authors

CROOKED
CAT

Meet our authors and discover
our exciting range:

- Gripping Thrillers
- Cosy Mysteries
- Romantic Chick-Lit
- Fascinating Historicals
- Exciting Fantasy
- Young Adult and Children's
  Adventures

Visit us at:
www.crookedcatbooks.com

Join us on facebook:
www.facebook.com/crookedcatbooks

31202300R00148

Printed in Poland
by Amazon Fulfillment
Poland Sp. z o.o., Wrocław